THE COLLAR

Stories of Irish Priests

FRANK O'CONNOR

THE
BLACKSTAFF
PRESS

BELFAST

6751

First published in 1993 by
The Blackstaff Press Limited
3 Galway Park, Dundonald, Belfast BT16 0AN, Northern Ireland
with the assistance of
The Arts Council of Northern Ireland

© Selection and Introduction, Harriet O'Donovan Sheehy, 1993
All rights reserved
The acknowledgements on page 216 constitute
an extension of this copyright page

Typeset by Paragon Typesetters, Queensferry, Clwyd

Printed by The Guernsey Press Company Limited

A catalogue record for this book
is available from the British Library

ISBN 0-85640-502-7

Contents

THE COLLAR

I STRUCK the board, and cry'd, No more.
     I will abroad.
  What? shall I ever sigh and pine?
My lines and life are free; free as the road,
  Loose as the winde, as large as store.
     Shall I be still in suit?
  Have I no harvest but a thorn
  To let me blood, and not restore
What I have lost with cordiall fruit?
       Sure there was wine
   Before my sighs did drie it: there was corn
   Before my tears did drown it.
  Is the yeare onely lost to me?
    Have I no bayes to crown it?
No flowers, no garlands gay? all blasted?
      All wasted?
  Not so, my heart: but there is fruit,
     And thou hast hands.
    Recover all thy sigh-blown age
On double pleasures: leave thy cold dispute
Of what is fit, and not; forsake thy cage,
     Thy rope of sands,
Which pettie thoughts have made, and made to thee
   Good cable, to enforce and draw,
      And be thy law,
  While thou didst wink and wouldst not see.
     Away; take heed:
     I will abroad.
Call in thy deaths head there: tie up thy fears.
    He that forbears
  To suit and serve his need,
    Deserves his load.
But as I rav'd and grew more fierce and wilde
    At every word,
  Me thought I heard one calling, *Childe:*
    And I reply'd, *My Lord.*

        GEORGE HERBERT
         (1593–1633)

INTRODUCTION

FRANK O'CONNOR WAS OFTEN ACCUSED of being iconoclastic – of being in a perpetual state of annoyance with the Catholic Church. It was even written that 'the sight of the collar was enough to make his hair stand on end'. It is true that he had little time for the institutional Church's pedantic and legalistic moralising, and even less for its Byzantine secrecy and triumphalist and authoritarian voice. But towards the actual men set apart by the collar – those called 'father' by people who are not their children – he had an attitude compounded of amusement, respect, curiosity and, above all, compassion.

Unikely as it may seem, he felt a certain kinship with them. In a review of J.F. Powers's book *The Presence of Grace* he wrote:

> The attraction of the religious life for the story teller is over-powering. It is the attraction of a sort of life lived, or seeking to be lived, by standards other than those of this world, one which, in fact, resembles that of the artist. The good priest, like the good artist, needs human rewards, but no human reward can ever satisfy him.

Perhaps this explains the large number of stories about priests in his work – the first written when he was in his thirties, the last, unfinished and untitled, the year he died. Taken as a whole, they not only seem a salute from one maverick to others, but also show an interesting development in his understanding of the difficulties of the job. Some of the stories are funny – sly, wry evocations of the antics, foibles and vulnerability of cranky celibates. Others, however, look with respect at the difficulties inherent in the vocation, and the misunderstandings, failures and disappointments incurred in trying to live it. But perhaps the best of them attempt to look behind the collar at the loneliness of those 'trying to live by standards other than those of this world' and to show the struggles this can involve – the fight to overcome vanity and arrogance and quick-temperedness, the desire for a different, more ordinary life, the boredom, the longing for a woman's tenderness, the fierce urge towards self-justification and dogmatism.

Perhaps, too, the stories reflect the ambiguity in O'Connor's own attitude, torn between empathy with the men and antipathy towards the institution. Because of this they have been interpreted in very different ways. Take, for example, 'News for the Church'. When it was first published in the *New Yorker* magazine, the editors received a lengthy telegram from the pastor and congregation of a Catholic church in Brooklyn stating that they were cancelling their subscriptions because of the 'blasphemous attack on the sacrament of penance' in O'Connor's story. Three weeks later the same editors received a letter asking them to thank Frank O'Connor for his story because it had reminded the writer – a lapsed Catholic – of the healing power of the sacrament of penance, as a result of which he had gone to Confession for the first time in twelve years. And a feminist friend of mine heartily dislikes the story because she feels that O'Connor sympathises with what she sees as the priest's 'cruel and bullying behavior'.

'An Act of Charity', one of O'Connor's last stories, shows where his sympathy lay when it came to a conflict between an individual priest and the Church. A friend had told him about a priest's suicide and he wanted to write the story, but found it difficult to imagine what had driven the man to reject the Divine Mercy he'd dedicated his life to serving. Since O'Connor never wrote about something he couldn't understand, he continued to mull it over, until one day he said: 'You know, the worst of it is that the poor man's final protest, whatever it was about, was never *heard*, because the Church covered it up to avoid giving scandal.' He could appreciate the Church's attitude, like Father Fogarty, who at one point says: 'Believe me, it's the best way for everybody in the long run.' But ultimately, O'Connor wasn't at all sure that it was the best way. Nor, in the story, is Father Fogarty. There is a great deal of Frank O'Connor in Father Fogarty – an emotional, compassionate man with a profound sense of his own frailty and inadequacy, who needed human rewards but was never totally satisfied by them.

But, of course, there were also actual priests, friends, whose stories O'Connor made his own and whose characteristics are blended to create a Father Jackson or a Father Devine. Perhaps his best friend was Father Tim Traynor, whom Father Fogarty most closely resembles. I'd like, therefore, to dedicate this book to the memory of Father Traynor, about whom O'Connor once wrote: 'He gave me an understanding of and sympathy with the Irish priesthood which even the antics of its silliest members have not been able to affect.'

HARRIET O'DONOVAN SHEEHY
MAY 1993

UPROOTED

1

SPRING HAD ONLY COME and already he was tired. He was tired of the city, tired of his job, tired of himself. He had come up from the country intending to become a great man, but he was as far as ever from that. Lucky if he could carry on with his teaching, be at school each morning at half nine and satisfy his halfwitted principal.

He lived in a small house in Rathmines. His window looked down on a little oblong of garden. The trams clanged up and down outside it. The house was kept by a middle-aged brother and sister who had been left a bit of money and decided to end their days enjoying themselves in the city. They did not enjoy themselves and regretted having sold their little farm in Kerry. Sometimes about midnight Finegan woke up to the fact that another day was passing, and sat at the piano and played through Moore's *Irish Melodies* with one finger. Miss Finegan did not even play. 'Ah, Mr Keating,' she said with a sad smile, 'you will always be happy. You have your dreams.'

Keating felt that now he had little else. He was a slow, cumbrous young man with dark eyes and a lock of dark hair which kept tumbling into them. When he spoke he stammered and kept running his big hand slowly through his hair. He had always been dreamy and serious. Farming had meant nothing to him. Sometimes on market day he could be seen for hours in Nolan's little shop among the bags of meal, stepping from one foot to another as he turned over the pages of a book. After his elder brother Tom had decided to enter the Church there had been a fight between himself and his father about the teaching. His father had not helped him. Nor even his mother, who felt that in some way he intended it as a slight on Tom. And Tom himself, no book-lover, joined in the conspiracy. With an obstinate, almost despairing determination he had fought his way through the training college to the city, and the city had failed him. In the evening he might still be seen before the bookstalls on the quays, drooped, powerfully built, shambling; obviously a country lad, but no longer seeking a certain path to glory.

It had all seemed so clear! But he had not counted on his own temper. He was popular enough, but popular because of how many concessions to others, from the children up! He was hesitant, gentle, slow to see round a thing and slow to contradict. He felt that he was constantly underestimating his own powers, but he could not straighten out his confused and passionate thoughts.

And ideals! He had enough to set up a federation of states but they were all at war with his slow, cautious, country wits. Gentle, submissive, suspecting everyone, he was glad if he could create a momentary good impression, no matter what it might cost afterwards in loss of self-esteem. He did not drink, smoked little and saw dangers and losses everywhere. He accused himself of avarice and cowardice. His favourite story was of the country man and the pillar-box. 'What a fool I am! Put me letther in a pump!'

He had only one real friend, a nurse in Vincent's Hospital, a bright, flighty, vivacious girl. He was fond of her, but something – shyness or caution – kept him from going farther. Sometimes he planned excursions beside the usual evening walk, but they never came off.

He no longer knew what had brought him to the city but it was not the prospect of his solitary bed-sitting room in Rathmines, the shelf of books beside the window or the occasional visit to the pictures with Nora Delea; the long evenings of rain, the solitary musings. To live, that wasn't enough. He would have liked to leave it all and go off to Glasgow or New York as a labourer, and it was not the romantic quality of the gesture which appealed to him; it was the feeling that only when he had not a roof to his head, only when he had to cadge a bite to eat, would he see what all his ideals and emotions meant and where he could fit them in. When he thought of this he looked at his hands. They were huge, powerful hands, which could pull a heavy boat or hold a plough in the straight.

But no sooner did he set out for school next morning than the fancy took flight. He wouldn't do it. Put his letter in a pump, indeed! He would continue to be submissive and count his salary and wonder how much he could save. And his nature would continue to contract about him till in ten years' time it would tie him hand and foot.

2

Tom wrote, suggesting that they should go home together for the long weekend, and he agreed. Tom was a curate in a small country parish.

He arrived on Friday night and on Saturday morning they set off in his old Ford. It was Easter weather, pearly and cold. Tom stopped at several hotels on the way and called for whiskeys in which Ned, in an expansive mood, joined him. He had never quite grown used to his brother, partly because of old days when he felt Tom was getting the education he should have got, partly because he was a priest. Tom's ordination seemed in some strange way to have shut him off from the rest of the family; even his parents, who liked him far better than Ned, found themselves ill at ease with him.

He was very different from Ned, lighter in colour of hair and skin, fat, fresh-complexioned, autocratic, a great hand with girls or a gun, an irascible, humorous, energetic man, well liked by his flock who knew him for a zealous priest and a good friend in time of trouble. Listening to his breezy, worldly talk, watching his way with men in garages and maids in hotels, Ned envied him. He was lavish and frank with some, pugnacious and exacting with others, differentiating as if by instinct between those who were honest and those who tried to cheat.

It was nightfall when they reached home. Their father was at the gate to greet them, and immediately their mother came rushing out. The lamp was standing in the window. Brigid, the little girl who helped their mother, stood by the door, looking up every few minutes, and when her eye caught theirs, instantly looking down again.

Nothing was changed in the tall bare kitchen. The harness hung still in the same place, the rosary on the same nail within the fireplace, by the stool where their mother sat; table under the window, churn against the back door, stair mounting straight without banisters to the attic door that yawned in the wall; all seemed as unchanging as the sea outside. Their mother was back on to the creepy, her coloured shawl tied about her head, tall, thin and wasted. Their father, stocky and broken-bottomed, stood with one hand on the dresser, looking out the door, while Brigid bustled round him, preparing the tea.

'I said ye'd be late,' he exclaimed. 'Didn't I, Brigid? Didn't I keep on saying they'd be late?'

'You did so.'

'I did indeed. I knew ye'd be making halts on the road. But damn me, if I didn't run out to meet Thady Lahy's car going east the road!'

'Was that Thady Lahy's car?' asked his wife with interest.

''Twas. He must have gone into town without our knowing it.'

'There now, didn't I tell you?' said Brigid.

'I thought 'twas the Master's by the shape of it,' said their mother wonderingly, pulling at the tassels of her shawl.

'I'd know the rattle of Thady Lahy's car a mile off,' said Brigid.

It seemed to Ned that he was interrupting a conversation which had been going on ever since his last visit.

'Wisha, I never asked ye if ye'd take a drop!' said old Tomas with sudden vexation. Ned knew to his sorrow that his father could be prudent, silent and calculating; he knew too well the sudden cock of the head, the narrowing of the eyes. But as well as that he loved an innocent excitement. He revelled in scenes of passion about nothing.

'Is it whiskey?' asked Tom with the roguish twinkle of his father.

'There's whiskey there as well.'

'I'll have it.'

'The whiskey is it?'

''Tis not.'

Tomas chuckled and rubbed his hands.

'Ah, you're not as big a fool as you look! There's fine heating in it.'

'Who made it?'

'Coleen Jameseen.'   .

'Coleen is it? Didn't they catch that string of misery yet?'

'Yerra, what catch! There's nothing on legs would catch

Coleen without you cut off his own. But, listen here to me!
The priest preached a terrible sermon against him!'

'Is old Fahy on the warpath still?'

'Oh, my sorrow!' Their father threw his hands to heaven
and strode to and fro, his bucket-bottom wagging. 'Such a flak-
ing and scouring was never heard! Never heard! Never heard!
How Coleen was able to raise his head after it! And where
that man got all the words from! Tom, my son, my treasure,
you'll never have the like of them.'

'I'd spare my breath to cool my porridge. I dare say you
gave up your own still so?'

'My still, is it? Musha, the drop that I make, 'twouldn't harm
a Christian. Only a drop at Christmas and Easter.'

The lamp was back in its old place on the rere wall and
made a circle of brightness on the fresh whitewash. Their
mother was leaning forward over the fire with joined hands.
The front door was still open, and their father walked to and
from it, each time warming his broken seat at the fire. Someone passed up the road. Ned covered his eyes with his hands
and felt that everything was still as it had been years before.
When he closed his eyes he could hear the noise on the strand
as a sort of background to the voices.

'God be with you, Tomas,' said the passer-by.

'God and Mary be with you, Taige,' shouted Tomas. 'What
way are you?'

'Well, honour and praise be to God. 'Tis a fine night.'

''Tis, 'tis so, thank God, a grand night.'

'Musha, who is it?' asked their mother looking up.

''Tis young Taige.'

'Shamus's young Taige, is it?'

''Tis, of course.'

'Where would he be going at this hour?'

'Up to the uncle's, I suppose.'

'Is it Ned Willie?'

'He's sleeping at Ned Willie's,' said Brigid in her high timid voice. ''Tis since the young teacher came.'

Between his hands Ned smiled. The only unfamiliar voice, Brigid's, seemed the most familiar of all.

3

Tom said first Mass next morning and the whole household, excepting Brigid, went. The chapel was a good distance away. They drove, and Tomas, sitting in front with his son, shouted greetings to all they met. Many of the neighbours were there to greet Tom in the sacristy. The chapel was perched high up from the road. Outside the morning was grey; beyond the windy edge of the hill was the bay. The wind blew straight in, setting petticoats and cloaks flying.

After dinner Ned and he went for a walk into the village. Tom halted to speak to everyone he met. They were late in coming back for tea. Tomas had come out to meet them. He was very pleased about something.

'Well,' he said when they were seated, 'I arranged a grand little outing for ye, thanks be to God.'

To mark the source of the inspiration he searched at the back of his neck for the peak of his cap and raised it solemnly.

'Musha, what outing are you talking about?' asked their mother angrily. Clearly, she and Tomas had had words about it.

'I arranged for us to go over the bay to the O'Donnells.'

'Can't you leave the poor boys alone?' bawled Maura. 'Haven't they only the one day? Isn't it for the rest they came?'

'Even so, even so, even so,' said Tomas with mounting passion. 'Aren't their own cousins to be left put an eye on them?'

'I was there last summer,' said Tom.

'Yes, but Ned wasn't, and I wasn't.'

"Tisn't us you're thinking of at all,' said Tom. 'Over for a good drinking bout you're going.'

'Oh – ' Tomas fished for the peak of his cap once more, 'that I might be struck dead – !'

'Be quiet, you heathen!' crowed Maura. 'That's the truth of it, Tom, my pulse. Plenty of poteen is what he wants, where he wouldn't be under my eye. Leave ye stop at home.'

'I can't stop at home, woman,' shouted Tomas. 'Why do you be always picking at me? Don't you know well I must go?'

'Why must you?'

'Because I warned Red Patrick and Dempsey. And the woman from the island is coming as well. And what's more I borrowed Cassidy's boat, and he lent it at great inconvenience to himself, and it would be very bad manners in me now to turn his kindness back on him.'

'Oh, we'll go, we'll go,' said Tom.

It blew hard all night, and Tomas was out at the break of day, all anxiety, watching the white tops on the water. While they were breakfasting he came in and, leaning upon the table, announced that it was a beautiful day, thank God, a perfect day with a moist gentle little bit of a breezheen blowing, but Maura nagged and scolded so much that he stamped out again in fury, and sat on the wall chewing his pipe. He had dressed in his best clothes, that is to say, he had turned his cap almost right way around so that the peak covered his right ear; he wore a respectable blue coat cut very long and with the suspicion of a tail and pale grey trousers with but one patch on it.

He was all over the boat like a boy. Dempsey took the helm, a haggard, melancholy man with a soprano voice of astounding penetration, and Red Patrick took charge of the sail. Then Tomas clambered into the bows and stood there, leaning forward with one foot raised. The island woman was perched upon the ballast with her Rosary in her hands and her shawl drawn over her eyes to avoid the sight of the waves.

The cumbrous old boat took the sail lightly enough.

'She's laughing,' said their father delightedly when her bows ran white.

'Whose boat is that, Dempsey?' he asked as another brown sail tilted ahead of them.

''Tis the island boat,' shrieked Dempsey.

''Tis not, Dempsey, 'tis not, my love. That's not the island boat.'

'Whose boat is it then?'

''Tis some boat from Carriganassa.'

''Tis the island boat I tell you.'

'Ah, why will you be contradicting me, Dempsey, my treasure? It is not the island boat. The island boat has a dark brown sail; 'tis only a month or so since 'twas tarred, and that's an old tarred sail, and what's more, Dempsey, and what proves it out and out, the island boat sail has a patch in the corner.'

Tomas was leaning well out over the bow, elbow resting on his knee, looking back at them, his brown face lashed with the spray and shining with the accumulated flickerings of the water. Ned half closed his eyes and watched sky and sea mount and subside behind the red-brown sail and the poised and eager figure.

'Tom!' shouted the voice from the bow, and the battered old face peered at them from under the sail.

'Well?'

'You were right last night, Tom, my boy. My treasure, my son, you were right. 'Twas for the sake of the drink I came.'

'I know damn well it was.'

''Twas for the sake of the drink. 'Twas so, my darling. They were always decent people, your mother's people, and 'tis her knowing the decency of her own family that makes her so suspicious. She's a good woman, a fine woman, your poor mother, may the Almighty God bless her and keep her and watch over her.'

'Amen, O Lord!' chorused Tom ironically as his father shook his headgear piously towards the spring sky.

'But Tom! Are you listening to me, Tom?'

'Well? What is it now?'

'I had another reason too.'

'Had you now?'

''Twas taking pride out of the pair of ye,' shrieked Dempsey from the helm, the wind whipping the shrill notes from his lips and scattering them like scraps of paper.

''Twas so, Dempsey, 'twas so. You're right, man. You're always right. God's blessing on you, Dempsey, for you always had the true word.' Tomas's leprechaun countenance gleamed under the bellying chocolate-coloured sail, fierce and wild and full of humour, and his powerful voice beat Dempsey's down. 'And would you blame me?'

'The O'Donnells haven't the beating of them in their own flock.'

'Thanks be to the Almighty God for all his goodness and mercy,' shouted the old man, raising his cap once more. 'They have not. They have not so, Dempsey. The O'Donnells are a good family and an old family and a kind family, but they haven't the like of my two clever sons.'

'And they were stiff enough to you when you came for their daughter.'

'They were. They were, Dempsey. They were stiff. They were so. You wouldn't blame them, Dempsey. They were an old family. I was nothing but a landless man and like a landless man they treated me.' The old man dragged his cap still farther over his ear, gave his moustache a tug and leaned

at a still more precarious angle over the bows, his blue eyes
dancing with triumph. 'But I had the gumption, Dempsey.
I had the gumption, my love.'

The bare mountainsides drew closer, the islands slipped past,
the gulf of water narrowed and grew calmer, and white cottages could be seen scattered about under the tall ungainly
church which seemed identical with what they had left behind.
It was a wild and rugged coast; the tide was only just beginning to fall, and they had to pull in as best they could among
the rocks. Red Patrick leaped lightly on shore and drew them
in. The others stepped after him into five or six inches of water,
and Red Patrick, himself precariously poised, held them from
slipping. Rather shamefastly Tom and Ned began to unlace
their shoes.

'Don't do that!' shrieked their father. 'We'll carry you up!
Ah, your poor feet! Your poor feet!'

'Shut your clob!' said Tom angrily, as he took Red Patrick's
hand, and clambered up the slimy rocks. Then the whole party
set out across the fields. As they entered a little winding lane
they were met by the Caheraghs, who insisted on their coming
in for a few minutes. Old Caheragh had a red beard and a
pleasant, smiling face. His daughter was tall and good-looking.
After they had given their customary greetings and promises
to return they resumed their way up the hill to the O'Donnells.

The O'Donnells had two houses, separated only by a yard.
In one lived their Uncle Maurice and his family, in the other
Maurice's married son. While their father went across the way
Ned and Tom stayed with Sean and his wife. Sean was a grim,
silent fellow, but Tom and he were old friends. When he spoke
he rarely looked at the priest, merely gave his a sidelong glance
which barely reached to his chin, and then dropped his eyes
with a peculiar, timid smile. His wife had once been a beauty.
She was a tall, matronly, nervous woman who clung to her

visitors' hands with a feverish clutch as though she could not bear to let them go, at the same time uttering ejaculations of tenderness, delight, surprise, pity and admiration. Her speech was full of diminutives, 'childeen', 'handeen', 'boateen'. Three young children scrambled and crawled and howled about the floor with a preoccupation scarcely once broken by the strangers, and she picked her way through them, hastening to fill the kettle, and then, as though fearing she was neglecting her guests, interrupting this to take up their hands again. When she spoke her whole body swayed towards them, and her feverish concentration gave the impression that by its very intensity it bewildered her and made it impossible for her to understand a word they said.

Tom and Sean went outside the door. They talked in low voices. Ned could not catch what they were saying. Then young Niall O'Donnell came in with his girl, one of the Deignans from up the hill. The Deignan girl was plump and pert; she had been in service in town. Niall was a well-built boy with a soft, wild-eyed, sensuous face, and a deep mellow voice of great power.

Barbara laid the meal for Ned and his brother in the sitting room. She was very proud of her parlour. It was a long, bare room with a table and three broken-backed, upholstered chairs. Two or three small family photographs had been placed at a height of eight feet so that the details of them were invisible.

'Oh, my treasure, isn't it the pity I didn't know ye were coming and I'd have had something better than this for ye,' Barbara complained. With joined hands she stood before Ned and surveyed him with adoring eyes.

'It is so,' said Tom with pretended indignation.

'Ah, Father Tom, you were always a great joker.'

Sean leaned against the wall, cap over his eyes and hands behind his back, and whenever he looked at Ned he smiled the same mysterious smile and dropped his eyes. Through the back window they could see Niall and Delia Deignan standing on the high ground. He was asking her something but she, more interested in watching the sitting-room window, only shook her head.

After the two young men had had their meal all of them went across the yard to the other house.

'You only just missed your father,' said their Uncle Maurice, shaking a hand of each.

'How so?' asked Tom.

'He went off to Ownie Pat's only a couple of minutes ago.'

'The divil he did,' said Tom. 'I knew damn well he was out to dodge me.'

They had their dinner with Maurice and his family. Tom took the place of honour. He was clearly the favourite. He remembered everyone, and every detail of the days he had spent there in boyhood, fishing and shooting with Sean. Through the doorway into the bedroom could be seen a big, old-fashioned bed and on the whiteness of a raised pillow a white, skeleton face surrounded by a halo of smoke-blue hair and surmounted in a distinctly odd way by a mauve tea-cosy. Sometimes the white face would begin to stir and everyone fell silent while Niall translated the scarcely audible whisper for the priest. Sometimes Niall would go in and repeat one of Tom's jokes for the old man in his drawling powerful bass. The hens stepped daintily about the feet of the diners, poking officious heads between them, and rushing out the door with a flutter and shriek whenever they were hooshed at.

'Listen here to me,' said Tom, with a look of mock concern at Niall. 'Is that young fellow courting Delia Deignan?'

'Was he with Delia again?' asked Maurice.

'He was. Is any of them married yet?'

'The Deignans? No.'

'Because I want to make a match for Ned with one of them. He's not safe up there in Dublin by himself. Now, seriously, seriously, which of them will I make the match with?'

'Cait! Cait! Cait!' shouted half a dozen voices, the deep voice of young Niall loudest of all.

'Well, now, Delia looks a smart little piece.'

'No, Cait! Cait! Delia isn't the same since she went to a situation. Let him marry Cait!'

'Is she a quiet sort of girl?'

'She is, she is, she's a grand girl!'

Suddenly Sean rose and walked to the door with a grin.

'Damn well he knows she's a quiet girl. No one else would have put up with him, the way he used to maul her.'

Tom sat stiff with mock indignation while the whole gathering rocked. Niall rose and repeated the joke to the old man in the bed. The mauve tea-cosy shook; it was the only indication of the ancient's amusement.

4

Before returning to the Caheraghs they decided to call at the Deignans 'to choose a wife for Ned', as Tom proclaimed. The purpose of the visit excited so much amusement and Tom was such a favourite that they had a following. Sean and two of the O'Donnell girls came as well. Niall preferred to remain at home.

The Deignans' house was on top of a hill over the road and commanded a view of the countryside for more than a mile on every side. They went to it up a winding muddy boreen whose walls of unmortared stone rose here and there against the sky like lacework. On their way they met another procession coming from a house some distance from the

Deignans'. It was headed by the father and the island woman, arm in arm, and it numbered two locals as well as Dempsey and Red Patrick. Their father was already drunk. That was plain when he rushed forward to shake them both by the hand and ask how they were. In answer to Tom's good-humoured queries he said that devil such honourable and kindly people as the people of Carriganassa were to be found in the whole created world, and that the O'Donnells were kings and sons of kings and you could see that same at a glance. He promised to be at the boat within twenty minutes. He had only one more call to make.

They looked in over the Deignans' half door. The kitchen was empty. It was a beautiful room, the woodwork and furniture painted a bright red-brown and the dresser shining with pretty ware. Over the fireplace was a row of caps and hats of different colours and sizes. They entered and began to look about them. Nothing was to be heard but the ticking of the cheap alarm clock over the fireplace. One of the O'Donnell girls began to giggle. Sean raised his voice.

'Is there anyone in?'

There was silence for a moment. Then a quick step resounded upstairs and a girl descended at a run, drawing a knitted black shawl more tightly about her shoulders. She was perhaps twenty-eight or thirty with a narrow face and blue, nervous eyes. She stepped across the kitchen in an awkward manner, sideways, giving the customary greetings but without once raising her eyes.

'A hundred welcomes before you! . . . How are you? . . . 'Tis a fine day.'

The same girl who had laughed first made herself objectionable again. Nora Deignan looked at her in surprise, nervously biting the tassel of her shawl.

'What is it?'

'Musha, stop your old antics and tell us where's Cait from you,' said Tom.

'Cait!' called Nora in a low voice, clearly glad to share such an embarrassing position. There was the same quick step upstairs and another girl came down. It was only afterwards that it struck Ned that he had never seen a more lovely creature. She had the same narrow face as her sister, the same slight features sharpened by an animal delicacy, the same blue eyes with the startled brightness, but her complexion was as fresh as morning and the blush that covered it made it seem fresher still. She entered the kitchen in the same embarrassed, hostile way.

'Have you nothing to say to me, Cait?' asked the priest with a grin.

'Oh, a hundred welcomes before you.' Her blue eyes rested on him for a moment with a fierce candour and penetration and then wandered past him to the open door. The rain was beginning to fall outside.

'Is that all?'

'How are you?'

'The politeness is suffocating you. Where's Delia?'

'Here I am,' said a low voice, and Delia was observed standing in the doorway, immediately behind him. It was so unexpected that everyone began to laugh. And then the silence fell again.

'The reason we called,' said Tom, clearing his throat, 'was this young brother of mine looking for a wife, and I told him I'd show him the three prettiest girls in Carriganassa.'

'Leave him take me,' said Delia.

'Why? Aren't there your two sisters before you?'

'Even so, I want to get up to Dublin... Would you treat me to lemonade, mister?' she asked Ned. 'This is a rotten hole. I'd go to America if I could.'

'You don't have to make up your mind, Ned,' said the priest.

'Write and tell them. I have to be rushing not to keep my father waiting.'

'We'll go with you,' said Nora unexpectedly.

The three girls took down three black shawls from inside the door.

'I'll go under the shawl with you, Cait,' said Tom.

'You will not,' she said, starting back.

'She'd rather the young man,' said Delia.

'She had enough of the other,' said Sean.

Cait looked at them both angrily and then began to laugh. She stretched out her shawl for Ned. Outside it was raining, a mild, persistent drizzle, and a strong wind was blowing. Everything had darkened and grown lonely about them, and under the blinding shawl Ned felt he had dropped out of Time's pocket.

They sat waiting in the Caheraghs' kitchen. The old man sat in one chimney corner and the little boy in the other. The dim blue light poured down the chimney upon their heads with the delicacy of light on old china, and between them the fire burned a bright orange in the great white hearth and the rain fell softly, almost soundlessly outside the half door. The twenty minutes had already strung themselves out to an hour. Tom was again the life and soul of the company, but even he was clearly beginning to be anxious. Two of the little boys were sent off to search for Tomas. All the while Ned could scarcely take his eyes off Cait Deignan who with her elder sister occupied the form against the rere wall, the black shawl drawn across her chin, the white wall behind. Sometimes she caught his eye and laughed softly; then she sank back again into pensiveness. Pensiveness or utter vacancy? He found it hard to say, but while he looked at her narrow face with the animal instinctiveness of its over-delicate features he was seeing, as if painted, the half door, the rain falling, the rocks and hills and angry sea – all that had given it birth.

The first to arrive was Red Patrick. After him came the island woman. Each of these had apparently last seen Tomas in different places. Then came Dempsey. Dempsey was glad the rain was falling. It would quiet the bay. The only question was, would Tomas be in a state to take a boat anywhere? Opinions varied. The Deignans said it made no difference. They would make room for Ned. Cait laughed and looked away. Tom began to grow angry. And then Tomas appeared.

He entered like a seawind, scattering all before him. He rushed to Tom and shook him heartily by the hand, asking him passionately if he were well. He did the same by Ned who only laughed. 'In God's name,' he shouted, waving his arms, 'let us be going now before the night comes.'

The rain was still falling. The tide had dropped. Tomas grabbed an oar and pushed the boat on to a rock. Then he raised the sail, let it fall again and had to be extricated from its folds. They shouted their goodbyes to the little group of figures revealed upon the naked rock against a grey background of drifting rain. For a long time Ned continued to wave back at Cait Deignan. A strange feeling of exaltation and loss descended upon him. Huddled up in his overcoat he sat at the stern with Dempsey, not speaking.

'It was a great day,' Tomas declared, swinging himself to and fro, tugging at his moustache, dragging the peak of his cap farther down over his ear. His gestures betrayed a certain lack of rhythmical cohesion, they began and finished abruptly. 'Dempsey, my darling, wasn't it a grand day?'

'It was a grand day for you,' shrieked Dempsey as though his throat would burst.

'It was, my treasure, it was, a grand day for me. I got an honourable reception and my sons got an honourable reception.' Flat on his belly, one leg on the edge of the boat he

stretched a hot hand to Tom and then to Ned. 'I got porter
and I got whiskey and I got poteen. I did so, Tom, my calf.
Ned, my brightness, I went to seven houses, and in every house
I got seven drinks, and with every drink I got seven welcomes.
And the O'Donnells are honourable people. It was no slight
they put on me at all, even if I was nothing but a landless man.
No slight, Tom, my treasure, no slight at all.'

Darkness had fallen, the rain had calmed the sea, and nothing
was to be heard in all the waste of water but the splush, splash
of the boat's sides, and Tomas's voice raised in song.

5

Ned was the first to wake. He struck a match and lit the candle.
It was time to rise. It was just after dawn and at half past nine
he would be in his old place in the schoolroom. He lit a
cigarette and closed his eyes. The lurch of the boat was still
in his blood and the face of Cait Deignan refused to be put
out of mind.

He heard his brother mumble something and nudged him.
Tom moaned and was still. He looked fat and big and helpless
with his fair head rolled sideways and his open mouth dribbling
onto his shirtsleeve. Ned slipped out of bed quietly, put on
his trousers and went to the window. He drew aside the
curtains and let the cold, thin daylight enter. The bay was just
visible and seemed perfectly still. Tom began to mumble again,
crying moodily and whining. Ned shook him. He started up
with an exclamation of fright. He looked first at Ned, then
at the candle and drowsily brushed his eyes.

'Is it time to be going?' he asked in alarm.

'No hurry. It's only that you were whining about
something.'

'What the hell? Did you hear me say anything?'

'Not a word.'

'Are you sure?' the priest asked suspiciously.

'Certain,' said Ned with his soft laugh. 'The secret is safe. Were you dreaming?'

'Oh, God!' Tom shivered and stretched out his arm for a cigarette. He lit it at the candle flame, his drowsy face puckered and distraught. 'I slept rotten.'

'Did you?'

'I didn't sleep properly for months.'

'Why? What's up?'

'Every bloody thing!'

'Tell me,' stammered Ned, sitting on the bed with his powerful hands resting on his knees. The priest looked away.

'Do you remember that Scotch dame in Portona?'

'The young one – I do.'

'She was in town over Christmas.'

'Did you see her?'

'I did. I didn't let on to you I was in town. For your own sake.'

'I know, I know. Ye got friendly, so.'

'We did. She's a damned nice girl – worse luck. She wouldn't take no for an answer.'

Ned gave his brother a slow look of intense understanding and sympathy. The small, smouldering eyes were fixed on him in challenge.

'I suppose you think I'm a nice sort of fellow to talk like this?'

'I d–do not. I'd think worse if you didn't. I'm very sorry.'

'I'm a damned sight sorrier. And this is only the beginning of it. I thought I'd come here and forget it for a few days. Forget it! Lord God, yesterday put the tin hat on it. I thought my brain would burst, over there in Carriganassa.'

''Twill take time.'

''Twill take more than time. 'Twill take what self-respect

I have. You don't know, nobody can know what it means to a man to have nothing to look forward to for thirty or forty years. It's not the woman so much as the companionship. And it isn't as if you could talk about it. Other people can be lonely and talk about it but wouldn't a priest look sweet telling people how lonely he was. . . I suppose I shouldn't have told you either.'

Again the same angry glare, and with an infinite compassion Ned realised that for years his brother had been living in the same state of suspicion and fear, and that for years to come he would live in the same way and perhaps never be caught like this again. He laughed softly, wistfully.

'You needn't be afraid that I'll talk. If it was nothing else I daren't. The family would die of shame.'

'Don't I know it?' said Tom between his teeth. 'Sweet God, don't I know it?'

Ned rose and crossed gently to the window, his hands in the pockets of his trousers. His brows were raised; the unruly lock of black hair fell very low, obscuring his eyes.

'I was thinking,' he said slowly, 'wouldn't it have been better for us if we stopped at home and married girls like Cait Deignan?'

'I used to court her long ago,' said the priest, and it seemed as if the words were being dragged out of him. 'It's not too late for you.'

Ned shook his head slowly and gently, his eyes fixed on the brightening roadway outside. Then, without speaking, he went into the kitchen. His mother, the coloured shawl about her head, was blowing the fire. The bedroom door was opened and he could see Tomas in his shirtsleeves kneeling at the bed-side. He unbolted the half door, went through the garden and out on to the road. The spring wind ruffled his long black hair. There was a magical light upon everything. Through the

apple-green sky over the sea ran long streaks of crimson, so
still it might have been enamelled. The clouds swathed the
mountains fold on fold. Over there lay Carriganassa invisible
yet. It seemed as if only now, for the first time, was he saying
goodbye to it all.

NEWS FOR THE CHURCH

WHEN FATHER CASSIDY DREW BACK the shutter of the confessional he was a little surprised at the appearance of the girl at the other side of the grille. It was dark in the box but he could see she was young, of medium height and build, with a face that was full of animation and charm. What struck him most were her slightly freckled cheeks and long pale hair, pinned high up behind the grey-blue eyes, giving them a curiously oriental slant.

She wasn't a girl from the town, for he knew most of these by sight and many of them by something more, being notoriously an easy-going confessor. The other priests said that one of these days he'd give up hearing confessions altogether on the ground that there was no such thing as sin and that even if there was it didn't matter. This was part and parcel of his exceedingly angular character, for though he was kind enough to individual sinners, his mind was full of obscure abstract hatreds. He hated England; he hated the Irish government, and he particularly hated the middle classes, though so far as anyone knew none of them had ever done him the least bit of harm. He was a heavy-built man, slow-moving and slow-thinking, with no neck and a punchinello chin, a sour wine-coloured face, pouting crimson lips, and small blue hot-tempered eyes.

'Well, my child,' he grunted in a slow and mournful voice that sounded for all the world as if he had pebbles in his mouth, 'how long is it since your last confession?'

'A week, father,' she replied in a clear firm voice. It surprised him a little, for though she didn't look like one of the tough shots, neither did she look like the sort of girl who goes to confession every week. But with women you could never tell. They were all contrary, saints and sinners.

'And what sins did you commit since then?' he asked encouragingly.

'I told lies, father.'

'Anything else?'

'I used bad language, father.'

'I'm surprised at you,' he said with mock seriousness. 'An educated girl with the whole of the English language at your disposal! What sort of bad language?'

'I used the Holy Name, father.'

'Ach,' he said with a frown, 'you ought to know better than that. There's no great harm in damning and blasting but blasphemy is a different thing. To tell you the truth,' he added, being a man of great natural honesty, 'there isn't much harm in using the Holy Name either. Most of the time there's no intentional blasphemy but at the same time it coarsens the character. It's all the little temptations we don't indulge in that give us true refinement. Anything else?'

'I was tight, father.'

'Hm,' he grunted. This was rather more the sort of girl he had imagined her to be; plenty of devilment but no real badness. He liked her bold and candid manner. There was no hedging or false modesty about her as about most of his women penitents. 'When you say you were "tight" do you mean you were just merry or what?'

'Well, I mean I passed out,' she replied candidly with a shrug.

'I don't call that "tight", you know,' he said sternly. 'I call that beastly drunk. Are you often tight?'

'I'm a teacher in a convent school so I don't get much chance,' she replied ruefully.

'In a convent school?' he echoed with new interest. Convent schools and nuns were another of his phobias; he said they were turning the women of the country into imbeciles. 'Are you on holidays now?'

'Yes. I'm on my way home.'

'You don't live here then?'

'No, down the country.'

'And is it the convent that drives you to drink?' he asked with an air of unshakable gravity.

'Well,' she replied archly, 'you know what nuns are.'

'I do,' he agreed in a mournful voice while he smiled at her through the grille. 'Do you drink with your parents' knowledge?' he added anxiously.

'Oh, yes. Mummy is dead but Daddy doesn't mind. He lets us take a drink with him.'

'Does he do that on principle or because he's afraid of you?' the priest asked dryly.

'Ah, I suppose a little of both,' she answered gaily, responding to his queer dry humour. It wasn't often that women did, and he began to like this one a lot.

'Is your mother long dead?' he asked sympathetically.

'Seven years,' she replied, and he realised that she couldn't have been much more than a child at the time and had grown up without a mother's advice and care. Having worshipped his own mother, he was always sorry for people like that.

'Mind you,' he said paternally, his hands joined on his fat belly, 'I don't want you to think there's any harm in a drop of drink. I take it myself. But I wouldn't make a habit of it if I were you. You see, it's all very well for old jossers like me that have the worst of their temptations behind them, but yours are all ahead and drink is a thing that grows on you. You need never be afraid of going wrong if you remember that your mother may be watching you from heaven.'

'Thanks, father,' she said, and he saw at once that his gruff appeal had touched some deep and genuine spring of feeling in her. 'I'll cut it out altogether.'

'You know, I think I would,' he said gravely, letting his eyes rest on her for a moment. 'You're an intelligent girl. You can get all the excitement you want out of life without that. What else?'

'I had bad thoughts, father.'

'Ach,' he said regretfully, 'we all have them. Did you indulge them?'

'Yes, father.'

'Have you a boy?'

'Not a regular: just a couple of fellows hanging round.'

'Ah, that's worse than none at all,' he said crossly. 'You ought to have a boy of your own. I know there's old cranks that will tell you different, but sure, that's plain foolishness. Those things are only fancies, and the best cure for them is something real. Anything else?'

There was a moment's hesitation before she replied but it was enough to prepare him for what was coming.

'I had carnal intercourse with a man, father,' she said quietly and deliberately.

'You what?' he cried, turning on her incredulously. 'You had carnal intercourse with a man? At your age?'

'I know,' she said with a look of distress. 'It's awful.'

'It is awful,' he replied slowly and solemnly. 'And how often did it take place?'

'Once, father – I mean twice, but on the same occasion.'

'Was it a married man?' he asked, frowning.

'No, father, single. At least I think he was single,' she added with sudden doubt.

'You had carnal intercourse with a man,' he said accusingly, 'and you don't know if he was married or single!'

'I assumed he was single,' she said with real distress. 'He was the last time I met him but, of course, that was five years ago.'

'Five years ago? But you must have been only a child then.'

'That's all, of course,' she admitted. 'He was courting my sister, Kate, but she wouldn't have him. She was running round with her present husband at the time and she only kept him on a string for amusement. I knew that and I hated her because he was always so nice to me. He was the only one that came to the house who treated me like a grown-up. But I was only fourteen, and I suppose he thought I was too young for him.'

'And were you?' Father Cassidy asked ironically. For some reason he had the idea that this young lady had no proper idea of the enormity of her sin and he didn't like it.

'I suppose so,' she replied modestly. 'But I used to feel awful, being sent to up to bed and leaving him downstairs with Kate when I knew she didn't care for him. And then when I met him again the whole thing came back. I sort of went all soft inside. It's never the same with another fellow as it is with the first fellow you fall for. It's exactly as if he had some sort of hold over you.'

'If you were fourteen at the time,' said Father Cassidy, setting aside the obvious invitation to discuss the power of first love, 'you're only nineteen now.'

'That's all.'

'And do you know,' he went on broodingly, 'that unless you can break yourself of this terrible vice once for all it'll go on like that till you're fifty?'

'I suppose so,' she said doubtfully, but he saw that she didn't suppose anything of the kind.

'You suppose so!' he snorted angrily. 'I'm telling you so. And what's more,' he went on, speaking with all the earnestness at his command, 'it won't be just one man but dozens of men, and it won't be decent men but whatever low-class pups you can find who'll take advantage of you – the same horrible, mortal sin, week in week out till you're an old woman.'

'Ah, still, I don't know,' she said eagerly, hunching her shoulders ingratiatingly, 'I think people do it as much from curiosity as anything else.'

'Curiosity?' he repeated in bewilderment.

'Ah, you know what I mean,' she said with a touch of impatience. 'People make such a mystery of it!'

'And what do you think they should do?' he asked ironically. 'Publish it in the papers?'

'Well, God knows, 'twould be better than the way some of them go on,' she said in a rush. 'Take my sister, Kate, for instance. I admit she's a couple of years older than me and she brought me up and all the rest of it, but in spite of that we were always good friends. She showed me her love letters and I showed her mine. I mean, we discussed things as equals, but ever since that girl got married you'd hardly recognise her. She talks to no one only other married women, and they get in a huddle in a corner and whisper, whisper, whisper, and the moment you come into the room they begin to talk about the weather, exactly as if you were a blooming kid! I mean you can't help feeling 'tis something extraordinary.'

'Don't you try and tell me anything about immorality,' said Father Cassidy angrily. 'I know all about it already. It may begin as curiosity but it ends as debauchery. There's no vice you could think of that gets a grip on you quicker and degrades you worse, and don't you make any mistake about it, young woman! Did this man say anything about marrying you?'

'I don't think so,' she replied thoughtfully, 'but of course that doesn't mean anything. He's an airy, light-hearted sort of fellow and it mightn't occur to him.'

'I never supposed it would,' said Father Cassidy grimly. 'Is he in a position to marry?'

'I suppose he must be since he wanted to marry Kate,' she replied with fading interest.

'And is your father the sort of man that can be trusted to talk to him?'

'Daddy?' she exclaimed aghast. 'But I don't want Daddy brought into it.'

'What you want, young woman,' said Father Cassidy with sudden exasperation, 'is beside the point. Are you prepared to talk to this man yourself?'

'I suppose so,' she said with a wondering smile. 'But about what?'

'About what?' repeated the priest angrily. 'About the little matter he so conveniently overlooked, of course.'

'You mean ask him to marry me?' she cried incredulously. 'But I don't want to marry him.'

Father Cassidy paused for a moment and looked at her anxiously through the grille. It was growing dark inside the church, and for one horrible moment he had the feeling that somebody was playing an elaborate and most tasteless joke on him.

'Do you mind telling me,' he inquired politely, 'am I mad or are you?'

'But I mean it, father,' she said eagerly. 'It's all over and done with now. It's something I used to dream about, and it was grand, but you can't do a thing like that a second time.'

'You can't what?' he asked sternly.

'I mean, I suppose you can, really,' she said, waving her

piously joined hands at him as if she were handcuffed, 'but you can't get back the magic of it. Terry is light-hearted and good-natured, but I couldn't live with him. He's completely irresponsible.'

'And what do you think you are?' cried Father Cassidy, at the end of his patience. 'Have you thought of all the dangers you're running, girl? If you have a child who'll give you work? If you have to leave this country to earn a living what's going to become of you? I tell you it's your bounden duty to marry this man if he can be got to marry you – which, let me tell you,' he added with a toss of his great head, 'I very much doubt.'

'To tell you the truth I doubt it myself,' she replied with a shrug that fully expressed her feelings about Terry and nearly drove Father Cassidy insane. He looked at her for a moment or two and then an incredible idea began to dawn on his bothered old brain. He sighed and covered his face with his hand.

'Tell me,' he asked in a faraway voice, 'when did this take place?'

'Last night, father,' she said gently, almost as if she were glad to see him come to his senses again.

'My God,' he thought despairingly, 'I was right!'

'In town, was it?' he went on.

'Yes, father. We met on the train coming down.'

'And where is he now?'

'He went home this morning, father.'

'Why didn't you do the same?'

'I don't know, father,' she replied doubtfully as though the question had now only struck herself for the first time.

'Why didn't you go home this morning?' he repeated angrily. 'What were you doing round town all day?'

'I suppose I was walking,' she replied uncertainly.

'And of course you didn't tell anyone?'

'I hadn't anyone to tell,' she said plaintively. 'Anyway,' she added with a shrug, 'it's not the sort of thing you can tell people.'

'No, of course,' said Father Cassidy. 'Only a priest,' he added grimly to himself. He saw now how he had been taken in. This little trollop, wandering about town in a daze of bliss, had to tell someone her secret, and he, a good-natured old fool of sixty, had allowed her to use him as a confidant. A philosopher of sixty letting Eve, aged nineteen, tell him all about the apple! He could never live it down.

Then the fighting blood of the Cassidys began to warm in him. Oh, couldn't he, though? He had never tasted the apple himself, but he knew a few things about apples in general and that apple in particular that little Miss Eve wouldn't learn in a whole lifetime of apple-eating. Theory might have its drawbacks but there were times when it was better than practice. 'All right, my lass,' he thought grimly, 'we'll see which of us knows most!'

In a casual tone he began to ask her questions. They were rather intimate questions, such as doctor or priest may ask, and, feeling broadminded and worldly-wise in her new experience, she answered courageously and straightforwardly, trying to suppress all signs of her embarrassment. It emerged only once or twice, in a brief pause before she replied. He stole a furtive look at her to see how she was taking it, and once more he couldn't withhold his admiration. But she couldn't keep it up. First she grew uncomfortable and then alarmed, frowning and shaking herself in her clothes as if something were biting her. He grew graver and more personal. She didn't see his purpose; she only saw that he was stripping off veil after veil of romance, leaving her with nothing but a cold, sordid, cynical adventure like a bit of greasy meat on a plate.

'And what did he do next?' he asked.

'Ah,' she said in disgust, 'I didn't notice.'

'You didn't notice!' he repeated ironically.

'But does it make any difference?' she burst out despairingly, trying to pull the few shreds of illusion she had left more tightly about her.

'I presume you thought so when you came to confess it,' he replied sternly.

'But you're making it sound so beastly!' she wailed.

'And wasn't it?' he whispered, bending closer, lips pursed and brows raised. He had her now, he knew.

'Ah, it wasn't, father,' she said earnestly. 'Honest to God it wasn't. At least at the time I didn't think it was.'

'No,' he said grimly, 'you thought it was a nice little story to run and tell your sister. You won't be in such a hurry to tell her now. Say an Act of Contrition.'

She said it.

'And for your penance say three Our Fathers and three Hail Marys.'

He knew that was hitting below the belt, but he couldn't resist the parting shot of a penance such as he might have given a child. He knew it would rankle in that fanciful little head of hers when all his other warnings were forgotten. Then he drew the shutter and didn't open the farther one. There was a noisy woman behind, groaning in an excess of contrition. The mere volume of sound told him it was drink. He felt he needed a breath of fresh air.

He went down the aisle creakily on his heavy policeman's-feet and in the dusk walked up and down the path before the presbytery, head bowed, hands behind his back. He saw the girl come out and descend the steps under the massive fluted columns of the portico, a tiny, limp, dejected figure. As she reached the pavement she pulled herself together with a jaunty twitch of her shoulders and then collapsed again. The city lights went on and made globes of coloured light in the mist. As he returned to the church he suddenly began to chuckle, a fat good-natured chuckle, and as he passed the statue of St Anne, patron of marriageable girls, he almost found himself giving her a wink.

THE SENTRY

FATHER MACENERNEY WAS FINDING it hard to keep Sister Margaret quiet. The woman was lonesome, but he was lonesome himself. He liked his little parish outside the big military camp near Salisbury; he liked the country and the people, and he liked his little garden (even if it was raided twice a week by the soldiers), but he suffered from the lack of friends. Apart from his housekeeper and a couple of private soldiers in the camp, the only Irish people he had to talk to were the three nuns in the convent, and that was why he went there so frequently for his supper and to say his office in the convent garden.

But even here his peace was being threatened by Sister Margaret's obstreperousness. The trouble was, of course, that before the war fathers, mothers, sisters and brothers, as well as innumerable aunts and cousins, had looked into the convent or spent a few days at the inn, and every week long, juicy letters had arrived from home, telling the nuns by what political intrigue Paddy Dunphy had had himself appointed warble-fly inspector for the Benlicky area, but now it was years since anyone from Ireland had called and the letters from home were censored at both sides of the channel by inquisitive girls with a taste for scandal until a sort of creeping paralysis had descended on every form of intimacy. Sister Margaret was the worst hit, because a girl from her own town was in the Dublin censorship, and, according to Sister Margaret, she was a scandalmonger of the most objectionable kind. He had a job keeping her contented.

'Oh, Father Michael,' she sighed one evening as they were walking round the garden, 'I'm afraid I made a great mistake. A terrible mistake! I don't know how it is, but the English seem to me to have no nature.'

'Ah, now, I wouldn't say that,' protested Father Michael in his deep, sombre voice. 'They have their little ways, and we have ours, and if we both knew more about one another we'd like one another better.'

Then, to illustrate what he meant, he told her the story of old Father Dan Murphy, a Tipperary priest who had spent his life on the mission, and the Bishop. The Bishop was a decent, honourable little man, but quite unable to understand the ways of his Irish priests. One evening old Father Dan had called on Father Michael to tell him he would have to go home. The old man was terribly shaken. He had just received a letter from the Bishop, a terrible letter, a letter so bad that he couldn't even show it. It wasn't so much what the Bishop had said as the way he put it! And when Father Michael had pressed him the old man had whispered that the Bishop had begun his letter: 'Dear Murphy'.

'Oh!' cried Sister Margaret, clapping her hand to her mouth. 'He didn't, Father Michael?'

So, seeing that she didn't understand the situation any more than Father Dan had done, Father Michael explained that this was how an Englishman would address anyone except a particular friend. It was a convention; nothing more.

'Oh, I wouldn't say that at all,' Sister Margaret exclaimed indignantly. '"Dear Murphy"? Oh, I'm surprised at you, Father

Michael! What way is that to write to a priest? How can they expect people to have respect for religion when they show no respect for it themselves? Oh, that's the English all out! Listen, I have it every day of my life from them. I don't know how anyone can stand them.'

Sister Margaret was his best friend in the community; he knew the other nuns relied on him to handle her, and it was a genuine worry to him to see her getting into this unreasonable state.

'Oh, come! Come!' he said reproachfully. 'How well Sister Teresa and Sister Bonaventura get on with them!'

'I suppose I shouldn't say it,' she replied in a low, brooding voice, 'but, God forgive me, I can't help it. I'm afraid Sister Teresa and Sister Bonaventura are not *genuine*.'

'Now, you're not being fair,' he said gravely.

'Oh, now, it's no good you talking,' she cried, waving her hand petulantly. 'They're not genuine, and you know they're not genuine. They're lickspittles. They give in to the English nuns in everything. Oh, they have no independence! You wouldn't believe it.'

'We all have to give in to things for the sake of charity,' he said.

'I don't call that charity at all, father,' she replied obstinately. 'I call that moral cowardice. Why should the English have it all their own way? Even in religion they go on as if they owned the earth. They tell me I'm disloyal and a pro–German, and I say to them: "What did you ever do to make me anything else?" Then they pretend that we were savages, and they came over and civilised us! Did you ever in all your life hear such impudence? People that couldn't even keep their religion when they had it, and now they have to send for us to teach it to them again.'

'Well, of course, that's all true enough,' he said, 'but

we must remember what they're going through.'

'And what did we have to go through?' she asked shortly. 'Oh, now, father, it's all very well to be talking, but I don't see why we should have to make all the sacrifices. Why don't they think of all the terrible things they did to us? And all because we were true to our religion when they weren't! I'm after sending home for an Irish history, father, and, mark my words, the next time one of them begins picking at me, I'll give her her answer. The impudence!'

Suddenly Father Michael stopped and frowned.

'What is it, father?' she asked anxiously.

'I just got a queer feeling,' he muttered. 'I was wondering was there someone at my onions.'

The sudden sensation was quite genuine, though it might have happened in a normal way, for his onions were the greatest anxiety of Father Michael's life. He could grow them when the convent gardener failed, but, unlike the convent gardener, he grew them where they were a constant temptation to the soldiers at the other side of his wall.

'They only wait till they get me out of their sight,' he said, and then got on one knee and laid his ear to the earth. As a country boy he knew what a conductor of sound the earth is.

'I was right,' he shouted triumphantly as he sprang to his feet and made for his bicycle. 'If I catch them at it they'll leave me alone for the future. I'll give you a ring, sister.'

A moment later, doubled over the handlebars, he was pedalling down the hill towards his house. As he passed the camp gate he noticed that there was no sentry on duty, and it didn't take him long to see why. With a whoop of rage he threw his bicycle down by the gate and rushed across the garden. The sentry, a small man with fair hair, blue eyes and a worried expression, dropped the handful of onions he was holding. His rifle was standing beside the wall.

'Aha!' shouted Father Michael. 'So you're the man I was waiting for! You're the fellow that was stealing my onions!' He caught the sentry by the arm and twisted it viciously behind his back. 'Now you can come up to the camp with me and explain yourself.'

'I'm going, I'm going,' the sentry cried in alarm, trying to wrench himself free.

'Oh, yes, you're going all right,' Father Michael said grimly, urging him forward with his knee.

'Here!' the sentry cried in alarm. 'You let me go! I haven't done anything, have I?'

'You haven't done anything?' echoed the priest, giving his wrist another spin. 'You weren't stealing my onions!'

'Don't twist my wrist!' screamed the sentry, swinging round on him. 'Try to behave like a civilised human being. I didn't take your onions. I don't even know what you're talking about.'

'You dirty little English liar!' shouted Father Michael, beside himself with rage. He dropped the man's wrist and pointed at the onions. 'Hadn't you them there, in your hand, when I came in? Didn't I see them with you, God blast you!'

'Oh, those things?' exclaimed the sentry, as though he had suddenly seen a great light. 'Some kids dropped them and I picked them up.'

'You picked them up,' echoed Father Michael savagely, drawing back his fist and making the sentry duck. 'You didn't even know they were onions!'

'I didn't have much time to look, did I?' the sentry asked hysterically. 'I seen some kids in your bleeding garden, pulling the bleeding things. I told them get out and they defied me. Then I chased them and they dropped these. What do you mean, twisting my bleeding wrist like that? I was only trying to do you a good turn. I've a good mind to give you in charge.'

The impudence of the fellow was too much for the priest, who couldn't have thought up a yarn like that to save his life. He never had liked liars.

'You what?' he shouted incredulously, tearing off his coat. 'You'd give me in charge? I'd take ten little sprats like you and break you across my knee. Bloody little English thief! Take off your tunic!'

'I can't,' the sentry said in alarm.

'Why not?'

'I'm on duty.'

'On duty! You're afraid.'

'I'm not afraid.'

'Then take off your tunic and fight like a man.' He gave the sentry a punch that sent him staggering against the wall. 'Now will you fight, you dirty little English coward?'

'You know I can't fight you,' panted the sentry, putting up his hands to protect himself. 'If I wasn't on duty I'd soon show you whether I'm a coward or not. You're the coward, not me, you Irish bully! You know I'm on duty. You know I'm not allowed to protect myself. You're mighty cocky, just because you're in a privileged position, you mean, bullying bastard!'

Something in the sentry's tone halted the priest. He was almost hysterical. Father Michael couldn't hit him in that state.

'Get out of this so, God blast you!' he said furiously.

The sentry gave him a murderous look, then took up his rifle and walked back up the road to the camp gate. Father Michael stood and stared after him. He was furious. He wanted a fight and if only the sentry had hit back he would certainly have smashed him up. All the MacEnerneys were like that. His father was the quietest man in County Clare, but if you gave him occasion he'd fight in a bag, tied up.

He went in but found himself too upset to settle down. He sat in his big chair and found himself trembling all over with frustrated violence. 'I'm too soft,' he thought despairingly. 'Too soft. It was my one opportunity and I didn't take advantage of it. Now they'll all know that they can do what they like with me. I might as well give up trying to garden. I might as well go back to Ireland. This is no country for anyone.' At last he went to the telephone and rang up Sister Margaret. Her voice, when she answered, was trembling with eagerness.

'Oh, father,' she cried, 'did you catch them?'

'Yes,' he replied in an expressionless voice. 'One of the sentries.'

'And what did you do?'

'Gave him a clout,' he replied in the same tone.

'Oh,' she cried, 'if 'twas me I'd have killed him!'

'I would, only he wouldn't fight,' Father Michael said gloomily. 'If I'm shot from behind a hedge one of these days you'll know who did it.'

'Oh, isn't that the English all out?' she said in disgust. 'They have so much old talk about their bravery, and then when anyone stands up to them, they won't fight.'

'That's right,' he said, meaning it was wrong. He realised that for once he and Sister Margaret were thinking alike, and that the woman wasn't normal. Suddenly his conduct appeared to him in its true light. He had behaved disgracefully. After all his talk of charity, he had insulted another man about his nationality, had hit him when he couldn't hit back, and, only for that, might have done him a serious injury – all for a handful of onions worth about sixpence! There was nice behaviour for a priest! There was good example for non-Catholics! He wondered what the Bishop would say to that.

He sat back again in his chair, plunged in dejection. His atrocious temper had betrayed him again. One of these days it would land him in really serious trouble, he knew. And there were no amends he could make. He couldn't even go up to the camp, find the man, and apologise. He faithfully promised himself to do so if he saw him again. That eased his mind a little, and after saying Mass next morning he didn't feel quite so bad. The run across the downs in the early morning always gave him pleasure, the little red-brick village below in the hollow with the white spire rising out of black trees which resembled a stagnant pool, and the pale chalk-green of the hills with the barrows of old Celts showing on their polished surface. They, poor devils, had had trouble with the English too! He was nearly in good humour again when Elsie, the maid, told him that an officer from the camp wished to see him. His guilty conscience started up again like an aching tooth. What the hell was it now?

The officer was a tall, good-looking young man about his own age. He had a long, dark face with an obstinate jaw that stuck out like some advertisement for a shaving-soap, and a pleasant, jerky, conciliatory manner.

'Good morning, padre,' he said in a harsh voice. 'My name is Howe. I called about your garden. I believe our chaps have been giving you some trouble.'

By this time Father Michael would cheerfully have made him a present of the garden.

'Ah,' he said with a smile, 'wasn't it my own fault for putting temptation in their way?'

'Well, it's very nice of you to take it like that,' Howe said in a tone of mild surprise, 'but the CO is rather indignant. He suggested barbed wire.'

'Electrified?' Father Michael asked ironically.

'No,' Howe said. 'Ordinary barbed wire. Pretty effective, you know.'

'Useless,' Father Michael said promptly. 'Don't worry any

more about it. You'll have a drop of Irish? And ice in it. Go on, you will!'

'A bit early for me, I'm afraid,' Howe said, glancing at his watch.

'Coffee, so,' said the priest authoritatively. 'No one leaves this house without some nourishment.'

He shouted to Elsie for coffee and handed Howe a cigarette. Howe knocked it briskly on the chair and lit it.

'Now,' he said in a businesslike tone, 'this chap you caught last night – how much damage had he done?'

The question threw Father Michael more than ever on his guard. He wondered how the captain knew.

'Which chap was this?' he asked noncommittally.

'The chap you beat up.'

'That I beat up?' echoed Father Michael wonderingly. 'Who said I beat him up?'

'He did,' Howe replied laconically. 'He expected you to report him, so he decided to give himself up. You seem to have scared him pretty badly,' he added with a laugh.

However much Father Michael might have scared the sentry, the sentry had now scared him worse. It seemed the thing was anything but over, and if he wasn't careful, he might soon find himself involved as a witness against the sentry. It was like the English to expect people to report them! They took everything literally, even to a fit of bad temper.

'But why did he expect me to report him?' he asked in bewilderment. 'When do you say this happened? Last night?'

'So I'm informed,' Howe said shortly. 'Do you do it regularly? . . . I mean Collins, the man you caught stealing onions last evening,' he went on, raising his voice as though he thought Father Michael might be slightly deaf, or stupid, or both.

'Oh, was that his name?' the priest asked watchfully. 'Of course, I couldn't be sure he stole them. There were onions stolen all right, but that's a different thing.'

'But I understand you caught him at it,' Howe said with a frown.

'Oh, no,' replied Father Michael gravely. 'I didn't actually catch him at anything. I admit I charged him with it, but he denied it at once. At once!' he repeated earnestly as though this were an important point in the sentry's favour. 'It seems, according to what he told me, that he saw some children in my garden and chased them away, and, as they were running, they dropped the onions I found. Those could be kids from the village, of course.'

'First I've heard of anybody from the village,' Howe said in astonishment. 'Did you see any kids around, padre?'

'No,' Father Michael admitted with some hesitation. 'I didn't, but that wouldn't mean they weren't there.'

'I'll have to ask him about that,' said Howe. 'It's a point in his favour. Afraid it won't make much difference though. Naturally, what we're really concerned with is that he deserted his post. He could be shot for that, of course.'

'Deserted his post?' repeated Father Michael in consternation. This was worse than anything he had ever imagined. The wretched man might lose his life and for no other reason but his own evil temper. He felt he was being well punished for it. 'How did he desert his post?' he faltered.

'Well, you caught him in your garden,' Howe replied brusquely. 'You see, padre, in that time the whole camp could have been surprised and taken.'

In his distress, Father Michael nearly asked him not to talk nonsense. As if a military camp in the heart of England was going to be surprised while the sentry nipped into the next garden for a few onions! But that was the English all out. They had to reduce everything to the most literal terms.

'Oh, hold on now!' he said, raising a commanding hand.

'I think there must be a mistake. I never said I caught him in the garden.'

'No,' Howe snapped irritably. 'He said that. Didn't you?'

'No,' said Father Michael stubbornly, feeling that casuistry was no longer any use. 'I did not. Are you quite sure that man is right in his head?'

Fortunately, at this moment Elsie appeared with the coffee and Father Michael was able to watch her and the coffee-pot instead of Howe, who, he knew, was studying him closely. If he looked as he felt, he thought, he should be worth studying.

'Thanks,' Howe said, sitting back with his coffee-cup in his hand, and then went on remorselessly: 'Am I to understand that you beat this chap up across the garden wall?'

'Listen, my friend,' Father Michael said desperately, 'I tell you that fellow is never right in the head. He must be a hopeless neurotic. They get like that, you know. He'd never talk that way if he had any experience of being beaten up. I give you my word of honour it's the wildest exaggeration. I don't often raise my fist to a man, but when I do I leave evidence of it.'

'I believe that,' Howe said with a cheeky grin.

'I admit I did threaten to knock this fellow's head off,' continued Father Michael, 'but that was only when I thought he'd taken my onions.' In his excitement he drew closer to Howe till he was standing over him, a big, bulky figure of a man, and suddenly he felt the tears in his eyes. 'Between ourselves,' he said emotionally, 'I behaved badly. I don't mind admitting that to you. He threatened to give me in charge.'

'The little bastard!' said Howe incredulously.

'And he'd have been justified,' the priest said earnestly. 'I had no right whatever to accuse him without a scrap of evidence. I behaved shockingly.'

'I shouldn't let it worry me too much,' Howe said cheerfully.

'I can't help it,' said Father Michael brokenly. 'I'm sorry

to say the language I used was shocking. As a matter of fact, I'd made up my mind to aplogise to the man.'

He stopped and returned to his chair. He was surprised to notice that he was almost weeping.

'This is one of the strangest cases I've ever dealt with,' Howe said. 'I wonder if we're not talking at cross purposes. This fellow you mean was tall and dark with a small moustache, isn't that right?'

For one moment Father Michael felt a rush of relief at the thought that after all it might be merely a case of mistaken identity. To mix it up a bit more was the first thought that came to his mind. He didn't see the trap until it was too late.

'That's right,' he said.

'Listen, padre,' Howe said, leaning forward in his chair while his long jaw suddenly shot up like a rat-trap, 'why are you telling me all these lies?'

'Lies?' shouted Father Michael, flushing.

'Lies, of course,' said Howe without rancour. 'Damned lies, transparent lies! You've been trying to fool me for the last ten minutes, and you very nearly succeeded.'

'Ah, how could I remember?' Father Michael said wearily. 'I don't attach all that importance to a few onions.'

'I'd like to know what importance you attach to the rig-marole you've just told me,' snorted Howe. 'I presume you're trying to shield Collins, but I'm blessed if I see why.'

Father Michael didn't reply. If Howe had been Irish, he wouldn't have asked such a silly question, and as he wasn't Irish, he wouldn't understand the answer. The MacEnerneys had all been like that. Father Michael's father, the most truthful, Godfearing man in County Clare, had been threatened with a prosecution for perjury committed in the interest of a neighbour.

'Anyway,' Howe said sarcastically, 'what really happened

was that you came home, found your garden robbed, said "Good night" to the sentry, and asked him who did it. He said it was some kids from the village. Then you probably had a talk about the beautiful, beautiful moonlight. Now that's done, what about coming up to the mess some night for dinner?'

'I'd love it,' Father Michael said boyishly. 'I'm destroyed here for someone to talk to.'

'Come on Thursday. And don't expect too much in the way of grub. Our mess is a form of psychological conditioning for modern warfare. But we'll give you lots of onions. Hope you don't recognise them.'

And he went off, laughing his harsh but merry laugh. Father Michael laughed too, but he didn't laugh long. It struck him that the English had very peculiar ideas of humour. The interview with Howe had been anything but a joke. He had accused the sentry of lying, but his own attempts at concealing the truth had been even more unsuccessful than Collins's. It did not look well from a priest. He rang up the convent and asked for Sister Margaret. She was his principal confidante.

'Remember the sentry last night?' he asked expressionlessly.

'Yes, father,' she said nervously. 'What about him?'

'He's after being arrested.'

'Oh!' she said, and then, after a long pause: 'For what, father?'

'Stealing my onions and being absent from duty. I had an officer here, making inquiries. It seems he might be shot.'

'Oh,' she gasped. 'Isn't that awful?'

"Tis bad.'

'Oh!' she cried. 'Isn't that the English all out? The rich can do what they like, but a poor man can be shot for stealing a few onions! I suppose it never crossed their minds that he might be hungry. What did you say?'

'Nothing.'

'You did right, I'd have told them a pack of lies.'

'I did,' said Father Michael.

'Oh!' she cried. 'I don't believe for an instant that 'tis a sin, father. I don't care what anybody says. I'm sure 'tis an act of charity.'

'That's what I thought too,' he said, 'but it didn't go down too well. I liked the officer, though. I'll be seeing him again and I might be able to get round him. The English are very good like that, when they know you.'

'I'll start a novena at once,' she said firmly.

THE OLD FAITH

IT WAS A GREAT DAY WHEN, on the occasion of the Pattern at Kilmulpeter, Mass was said in the ruined cathedral and the old Bishop, Dr Gallogly, preached. It was Father Devine, who was a bit of an antiquarian, who looked up the details of the life of St Mulpeter for him. There were a lot of these, mostly contradictory and all queer. It seemed that, like most of the saints of that remote period, St Mulpeter had put to sea on a flagstone and floated ashore in Cornwall. There, the seven harpers of the King had just been put to death through the curses of the Druids and the machinations of the King's bad wife. St Mulpeter miraculously brought them all back to life, and, through the great mercy of God, they were permitted to sing a song about the Queen's behaviour, which resulted in St Mulpeter's turning her into a pillarstone and converting the King to the one true faith.

The Bishop had once been Professor of Dogmatic Theology in a seminary; a subject that came quite naturally to him, for he was a man who would have dogmatised in any station of life. He was a tall, powerfully built, handsome old man with a face that was both long and broad, with high cheekbones that gave the lower half of his face an air of unnatural immobility but drew attention to the fine blue, anxious eyes that moved slowly and never far. He was a quiet man who generally spoke in a low voice, but with the emphasising effect of a pile-driver.

For a dogmatic theologian, he showed great restraint on reading Father Devine's digest of the saint's life. He raised his brows a few times and then read it again with an air of resignation. 'I suppose that's what you'd call allegorical, father,' he said gravely.

He was a man who rarely showed signs of emotion. He seemed to be quite unaffected by the scene in the ruined cathedral, though it deeply impressed Father Devine, with the crowds of country people kneeling on the wet grass among the tottering crosses and headstones, the wild countryside framed in the mullioned windows, and the big, deeply moulded clouds drifting overhead. The Bishop disposed neatly of the patron by saying that though we couldn't all go to sea on flagstones, a feat that required great faith in anyone who attempted it, we could all have the family Rosary at night.

After Mass, Father Devine was showing the Bishop and some of the other clergy round the ruins, pointing out features of archaeological interest, when a couple of men who had been hiding in the remains of a twelfth-century chapel bolted. One of them stood on a low wall, looking down on the little group of priests with a scared expression. At once the Bishop raised his umbrella and pointed it accusingly at him.

'Father Devine,' he said in a commanding tone, 'see what that fellow has.'

'I have nothing, Your Eminence,' wailed the man on the wall.'

'You have a bottle behind your back,' said the Bishop grimly. 'What's in that?'

'Nothing, Your Eminence, only a drop of water from the Holy Well.'

'Give it here to me till I see,' ordered the Bishop, and when Father Devine passed him the bottle he removed the cork and sniffed.

'Hah!' he said with great satisfaction. 'I'd like to see the Holy Well that came out of. Is it any use my preaching about poteen year in year out when ye never pay any attention to me?'

"Tis a cold, windy quarter, Your Eminence,' said the man, 'and I have the rheumatics bad.'

'I'd sooner have rheumatics than cirrhosis,' said the Bishop. 'Bring it with you, father,' he added to Devine, and stalked on with his umbrella pressed against his spine.

The same night they all had dinner in the palace: Father Whelan, a dim-witted, good-natured old parish priest; his fiery Republican curate, Father Fogarty, who was responsible for the Mass in the ruined cathedral as he was for most other manifestations of life in that wild part, and Canon Lanigan. The Bishop and the Canon never got on, partly because the Canon was an obvious choice for the Bishop's job and he and his supporters were giving it out that the Bishop was getting old and needed a coadjutor, but mainly because he gave himself so many airs. He was tall and thin, with a punchinello chin and a long nose, and let on to be an authority on Church history and on food and wine. That last was enough to damn anyone in the Bishop's eyes, for he maintained almost *ex cathedra* that the best food and wine in the world were to be had on the restaurant car from Holyhead to Euston. The moment Lanigan got on to his favourite topic and mentioned Châteauneuf-du-Pape, the Bishop turned to Father Devine.

'Talking about drink, father,' he said with his anxious glare, 'what happened the bottle of poteen you took off that fellow?'

'I suppose it's in the hall,' said Father Devine. 'I need hardly say I wasn't indulging in it.'

'You could indulge in worse,' said the Bishop with a sideglance at the Canon. 'There was many a good man raised on it. Nellie,' he added, going so far as to turn his head a few inches, 'bring in that bottle of poteen, wherever it is . . . You can have it with your tea,' he added graciously to the Canon. 'Or is it coffee you want?'

'Oh, tea, tea,' sighed the Canon, offering it up. He had a good notion what the Bishop's coffee was like.

When Nellie brought in the poteen, the Bishop took out the cork and sniffed it again with his worried look.

'I hope 'tis all right,' he said in his expressionless voice. 'A pity we didn't find out who made it. When they can't get the rye, they make it out of turnips or any old thing.'

'You seem to know a lot about it, my lord,' said Devine with his waspish air.

'Why wouldn't I?' said the Bishop. 'Didn't I make it myself? My poor father – God rest him! – had a still of his own. But I didn't taste it in something like sixty years.'

He poured them out a stiff glass each and drank off his own in a gulp, without the least change of expression. Then he looked at the others anxiously to see how they responded. Lanigan made a wry face; as a member of the Food and Wine Society he probably felt it was expected of him. Father Fogarty drank it as if it were altar wine, but he was a nationalist and only did it on principle. Father Devine disgraced himself: spluttered, choked, and then went petulantly off to the bathroom.

Meanwhile the Bishop, who decided that it wasn't bad, was treating his guests to another round, which they seemed to feel it might be disrespectful to refuse. Father Devine did refuse, and with a crucified air that the Bishop didn't like. The Bishop, who like all bishops, knew everything and had one of the most venomously gossipy tongues in the diocese, was convinced that

he was a model of Christian charity and had spoken seriously
to Father Devine about his sharpness.

'Was it on an island you made this stuff?' the Canon asked
blandly.

'No,' replied the Bishop, who always managed to miss the
point of any remark that bordered on subtlety. 'A mountain.'

'Rather desolate, I fancy,' Lanigan said dreamily.

'It had to be if you didn't want the police coming down
on top of you,' said the Bishop. 'They'd have fifty men out
at a time, searching the mountains.'

'And bagpipes,' said the Canon, bursting into an old woman's
cackle as he thought of the hilly road from Beaune to Dijon
with the vineyards at each side. 'It seems to go with bagpipes.'

'There were no bagpipes,' the Bishop said contemptuously.
'As a matter of fact,' he continued with quiet satisfaction, 'it
was very nice up there on a summer's night, with the still in
a hollow on top of the mountain, and the men sitting round
the edges, talking and telling stories. Very queer stories some
of them were,' he added with an old man's complacent chuckle.

'Ah,' the Canon said deprecatingly, 'the people were half-
savage in those days.'

'They were not,' said the Bishop mildly, but from his tone
Father Devine knew he was very vexed. 'They were more
refined altogether.'

'Would you say so, my lord?' asked Father Fogarty, who,
as a good nationalist, was convinced that the people were
rushing to perdition and that the only hope for the nation was
to send them all back to whitewashed cabins fifty miles from
a town.

'Ah, a nicer class of people every way,' put in Father Whelan
mournfully. 'You wouldn't find the same nature at all in them
nowadays.'

'They had a lot of queer customs all the same, father,' said

the Bishop. 'They'd always put the first glass behind a rock.
Would that have something to do with the fairies?' he asked
of Father Devine.

'Well, at any rate,' the Canon said warmly, 'you can't deny
that the people today are more enlightened.'

'I deny it *in toto*,' the Bishop retorted promptly. 'There's
no comparison. The people were more intelligent altogether,
better balanced and better spoken. What would you say, Father
Whelan?'

'Oh, in every way, my lord,' said Father Whelan, taking
out his pipe.

'And the superstitions, my lord?' the Canon hissed super-
ciliously. 'The ghosts and the fairies and the spells?'

'They might have good reason,' said the Bishop with a flash
of his blue eyes.

'By Gor, you're right, my lord,' Father Fogarty said in a
loud voice, and then, realising the attention he had attracted,
he blushed and stopped short.

'"There are more things in heaven and earth, Horatio, than
are dreamt of in our philosophy",' added the Bishop with a
complacent smile.

'Omar Khayyám,' whispered Father Whelan to Father
Fogarty. 'He's a fellow you'd want to read. He said some very
good things.'

'That's a useful quotation,' said the Canon, seeing he was
getting the worst of it. 'I must remember that the next time
I'm preaching against fortune-tellers.'

'I wouldn't bother,' the Bishop said curtly. 'There's no
analogy. There was a parish priest in our place one time,' he
added reflectively. 'A man called Muldoon. Father Whelan
might remember him.'

'Con Muldoon,' defined Father Whelan. 'I do, well. His
nephew Peter was on the Chinese Mission.'

'He was a well-meaning man, but very coarse, I thought,' said the Bishop.

'That was his mother's side of the family,' explained Whelan. 'His mother was a Dempsey. The Dempseys were a rough lot.'

'Was she one of the Dempseys of Clasheen?' said the Bishop eagerly. 'I never knew that. Anyway, Muldoon was always preaching against superstition, and he had his knife in one poor old fellow up the Glen called Johnnie Ryan.'

'Johnnie the Fairies,' said Father Whelan with a nod. 'I knew him.'

'I knew him well,' said the Bishop. 'He was their Living Man.'

'Their what?' asked Father Devine in astonishment.

'Their Living Man,' repeated the Bishop. 'They had to take him with them wherever they were going, or they had no power. That was the way I heard it anyway. I remember him well playing the Fairy Music on his whistle.'

'You wouldn't remember how it went?' Father Fogarty asked eagerly.

'I was never much good at remembering music,' said the Bishop, to the eternal regret of Father Devine, who felt he would cheerfully have given five years of his life to hear the Bishop of Moyle whistle the Fairy Music. 'Anyway, I was only a child. Of course, there might be something in that. The mountain over our house, you'd often see queer lights on it that they used to say were a fairy funeral. They had some story of a man from our place that saw one on the mountain one night, and the fairies let down the coffin and ran away. He opened the coffin, and inside it there was a fine-looking girl, and when he bent over her she woke up. They said she was from the Tuam direction; a changeling or something. I never checked the truth of it.'

'From Galway, I believe, my lord,' said Father Whelan respectfully.

'Was it Galway?' said the Bishop.

'I dare say, if a man had enough poteen in, he could even believe that,' said the Canon indignantly.

'Still, Canon,' said Father Fogarty, 'strange things do happen.'

'Why then, indeed, they do,' said Father Whelan.

'Was this something that happened yourself, father?' the Bishop asked kindly, seeing the young man straining at the leash.

'It was, my lord,' said Fogarty. 'When I was a kid going to school. I got fever very bad, and the doctor gave me up. The mother, God rest her, was in a terrible state. Then my aunt came to stay with us. She was a real old countrywoman. I remember them to this day arguing downstairs in the kitchen, the mother saying we must be resigned to the will of God, and my aunt telling her not to be a fool; that everyone knew there were ways.'

'Well! Well! Well!' Father Whelan said, shaking his head.

'Then my aunt came up with the scissors,' Father Fogarty continued with suppressed excitement. 'First she cut off a bit of the tail of my shirt; then she cut a bit of hair from behind my ear, and the third time a bit of a fingernail, and threw them all into the fire, muttering something to herself, like an old witch.'

'My! My! My!' exclaimed Father Whelan.

'And you got better?' said the Bishop, with a quelling glance at the Canon.

'I did, my lord,' said Father Fogarty. 'But that wasn't the strangest part of it.' He leaned across the table, scowling, and dropped his eager, boyish voice to a whisper. 'I got better, but her two sons, my first cousins, two of the finest-looking lads you ever laid eyes on, died inside a year.' Then he sat back, took out a cigar, and scowled again. 'Now,' he asked, 'wasn't that extraordinary? I say, wasn't it extraordinary?'

'Ah, whatever was waiting to get you,' Father Whelan said philosophically, emptying his pipe on his plate, 'I suppose it had to get something. More or less the same thing happened to an old aunt of mine. The cock used to sleep in the house, on a perch over the door – you know, the old-fashioned way. One night the old woman had occasion to go out, and when she went to the door, the cock crowed three times and then dropped dead at her feet. Whatever was waiting for her, of course,' he added with a sigh.

'Well! Well! Well!' said the Canon. 'I'm astonished at you, Father Whelan. Absolutely astonished! I can't imagine how you can repeat these old wives' tales.'

'I don't see what there is to be astonished about, Canon,' said the Bishop. 'It wasn't anything worse than what happened to Father Muldoon.'

'That was a bad business,' muttered Father Whelan, shaking his head.

'What was it, exactly?' asked Father Devine.

'I told you he was always denouncing old Johnnie,' said the Bishop. 'One day, he went up the Glen to see him; they had words, and he struck the old man. Within a month he got a breaking-out on his knee.'

'He lost the leg after,' Father Whelan said, stuffing his pipe again.

'I suppose next you'll say it was the fairies' revenge,' said the Canon, throwing his discretion to the winds. It was too much for him; a man who knew Church history, had lived in France, and knew the best vintages backwards.

'That was what Father Muldoon thought,' said the Bishop grimly.

'More fool he,' the Canon said hotly.

'That's as may be, Canon,' the Bishop went on sternly. 'He went to the doctor, but treatment did him no good, so he went back up the valley to ask Johnnie what he ought to do. "I had nothing to do with that, father," said Johnnie, "and the curing of it isn't in my hands." "Then who was it?" asks Muldoon. "The Queen of the Fairies," said Johnnie, "and you might as well tell the doctor to take that leg off you while he's at it, for the Queen's wound is the wound that never heals." No more it did,' added the Bishop. 'The poor man ended his days on a peg leg.'

'He did, he did,' muttered Father Whelan mournfully, and there was a long pause. It was clear that the Canon was routed, and soon afterwards they all got up to go. It seemed that Father Fogarty had left his car outside the seminary, and the Bishop, in a benevolent mood, offered to take them across the field by the footpath.

'I'll take them,' said Father Devine.

'The little walk will do me good,' said the Bishop.

He, the Canon and Father Fogarty went first. Father Devine followed with Father Whelan, who went sideways down the steps with the skirts of his coat held up.

'As a matter of fact,' the Bishop was saying ahead of them, 'we're lucky to be able to walk so well. Bad poteen would deprive you of the use of your legs. I used to see them at home, talking quite nicely one minute and dropping off the chairs like bags of meal the next. You'd have to take them home on a door. The head might be quite clear, but the legs would be like gateposts.'

'Father Devine,' whispered Father Whelan girlishly, stopping in his tracks.

'Yes, what is it?' asked Father Devine gently.

'What His Lordship said,' whispered Father Whelan guiltily. 'That's the way I feel. Like gateposts.'

And before the young priest could do anything, he put out one of the gateposts, which didn't seem to alight properly on its base, the other leaned slowly towards it, and he fell in an ungraceful parody of a ballet dancer's final curtsy.

'Oh, my! My! My!' he exclaimed. Even in his liquor he was melancholy and gentle.

The other three turned slowly round. To Father Devine they looked like sleepwalkers.

'Hah!' said the Bishop with quiet satisfaction. 'That's the very thing I mean. We'll have to mind ourselves.'

And away the three of them went, very slowly, as though they owed no responsibility whatever towards the fallen guest. Paddy, the Bishop's 'boy', who was obviously expecting something of the sort, immediately appeared and, with the aid of Father Devine, put the old man on a bench and carried him back to the palace. Then, still carrying the bench between them, they set out after the others. They were just in time to see the collapse of the Canon, but in spite of it the other two went on. Father Fogarty had begun to chuckle hysterically. They could hear him across the field, and it seemed to Father Devine that he was already rehearsing the lovely story he would tell about 'the night I got drunk with the Bishop'.

Devine and Paddy left the Canon where he had fallen, and where he looked like being safe for a long time to come, and followed the other two. They had gone wildly astray, turning in a semicircle round the field till they were at the foot of the hill before a high fence round the plantation. The Bishop never hesitated, but immediately began to climb the wall.

'I must be gone wrong, father,' he said anxiously. 'I don't know what happened me tonight. I can usually do this easy enough. We'll go over the wall and up the wood.'

'I can't,' shouted Father Fogarty in a paroxysm of chuckles.

'Nonsense, man!' the Bishop said sternly, holding on to a bush and looking down at him from the top of the wall. 'Why can't you?'

'The fairies have me,' roared Father Fogarty.

'Pull yourself together, father,' the Bishop said sternly. 'You don't want to be making an exhibition of yourself.'

Next moment Father Fogarty was lying flat at the foot of the wall, roaring with laughter. Father Devine shouted to the Bishop, but he slid obstinately down at the other side of the wall. 'The ould divil!' Paddy exclaimed admiringly. 'That's more than we'll be able to do at his age, father.'

A few minutes later they found him flat under a tree in the starlight, quite powerless, but full of wisdom, resignation, and peace. They lifted him on a bench, where he reclined like the effigy on a tomb, his hands crossed meekly on his breast, and carried him back to bed.

'Since that evening,' Father Devine used to say in the waspish way the Bishop so much disliked, 'I feel there's nothing I don't know about fairies. I also have some idea about the sort of man who wrote the life of St Mulpeter of Moyle.'

THE MIRACLE

VANITY, ACCORDING TO THE BISHOP, was the Canon's great weakness, and there might be some truth in that. He was a tall, good-looking man, with a big chin, and a manner of deceptive humility. He deplored the fact that so many of the young priests came of poor homes where good manners weren't taught, and looked back regretfully to the old days when, according to him, every Irish priest read his Virgil. He went in a lot for being an authority on food and wine, and ground and brewed his own coffee. He refused to live in the ramshackle old presbytery which had served generations of priests, and had built for himself a residence that was second only to the Bishop's palace and that was furnished with considerably more taste and expense. His first innovation in the parish had been to alter the dues which, all over the Christian world, are paid at Christmas and Easter and have them paid four times a year instead. He said that this was because poor people couldn't afford large sums twice a year, and that it was easier for them to pay their dues like that; but in fact it was because he thought the dues that had been fixed were far too low to correspond in any way with the dignity of his office. When he was building his house he had them collected five times during the year, and as well as that, threw in a few

raffles and public subscriptions. He disliked getting into debt.
And there he ate his delicate meals with the right wines, brewed
coffee and drank green chartreuse, and occasionally dipped into
ecclesiastical history. He like to read about days when the clergy
were really well off.

It was distasteful to the Canon the way the lower classes
were creeping into the Church and gaining high office in it,
but it was a real heartbreak that its functions and privileges
were being usurped by new men and methods, and that
miracles were now being performed out of bottles and syringes.
He thought that a very undignified way of performing miracles
himself, and it was a real bewilderment of spirit to him when
some new drug was invented to make the medicine men more
indispensable than they were at present. He would have liked
surgeons to remain tradesmen and barbers as they were in the
good old days, and, though he would have been astonished
to hear it himself, was as jealous as a prima donna at the inter-
ference of Bobby Healy, the doctor, with his flock. He would
have liked to be able to do it all himself, and sometimes thought
regretfully that it was a peculiar dispensation of Providence
that when the Church was most menaced, it couldn't draw
upon some of its old grace and perform occasional miracles.
The Canon knew he would have performed a miracle with
a real air. He had the figure for it.

There was certainly some truth in the Bishop's criticism.
The Canon hated competition, he liked young Dr Devaney,
who affected to believe that medicine was all hocus-pocus
(which was what the Canon believed himself), and took a grave
view of Bobby Healy, which caused Bobby's practice to go
down quite a bit. When the Canon visited a dying man he
took care to ask: 'Who have you?' If he was told 'Dr Devaney',
he said: 'A good young man', but if it was 'Dr Healy' he merely
nodded and looked grave, and everyone understood that Bobby

had killed the unfortunate patient as usual. Whenever the two men met, the Canon was courteous and condescending, Bobby was respectful and obliging, and nobody could ever have told from the doctor's face whether or not he knew what was going on. But there was very little which Bobby didn't know. There is a certain sort of guile that goes deeper than any cleric's: the peasant's guile. Dr Healy had that.

But there was one person in his parish whom the Canon disliked even more than he disliked the doctor. That was a man called Bill Enright. Nominally, Bill was a farmer and breeder of greyhounds; really, he was the last of a family of bandits who had terrorised the countryside for generations. He was a tall, gaunt man with fair hair and a tiny, gold moustache; perfectly rosy skin, like a baby's, and a pair of bright blue eyes which seemed to expand into a wide unwinking, animal glare. His cheekbones were so high that they gave the impression of cutting his skin. They also gave his eyes an Oriental slant, and, with its low, sharp-sloping forehead, his whole face seemed to point outward to the sharp tip of his nose and then retreat again in a pair of high teeth, very sharp and very white, a drooping lower lip, and a small, weak, feminine chin.

Now, Bill, as he would be the first to tell you, was not a bad man. He was a traditionalist who did as his father and grand-father had done before him. He had gone to Mass and the Sacraments and even paid his dues four times a year, which was not traditional, and been prepared to treat the Canon as a bandit of similar dignity to himself. But the Canon had merely been incensed at the offer of parity with Bill and set out to demonstrate that the last of the Enrights was a common ruffian who should be sent to jail. Bill was notoriously living in sin with his housekeeper, Nellie Mahony from Doonamon, and the Canon ordered her to leave the house. When he failed in this he went to her brothers and demanded that they should drag her home, but her brothers had had too much experience of the Enrights to try such a risky experiment with them, and Nellie remained on, while Bill, declaring loudly that there was nothing in religion, ceased going to Mass. People agreed that it wasn't altogether Bill's fault, and that the Canon could not brook another authority than his own – a hasty man!

To Bobby Healy, on the other hand, Bill Enright was bound by the strongest tie that could bind an Enright, for the doctor had once cured a greyhound for him, the mother of King Kong. Four or five times a year he was summoned to treat Bill for an overdose of whiskey; Bill owed him as much money as it was fitting to owe to a friend, and all Bill's friends knew that when they were in trouble themselves, it would be better for them to avoid further trouble by having Dr Healy as well. Whatever the Canon might think, Bill was a man it paid to stand in well with.

One spring day Bobby got one of his usual summonses to the presence. Bill lived in a fine Georgian house a mile outside the town. It had once belonged to the Rowes, but Bill had got them out of it by the simple expedient of making their lives a hell for them. The avenue was overgrown, and the house with its fine Ionic portico looked dirty and dilapidated. Two dogs got up and barked at him in a neighbourly way. They hated it when Bill was sick, and they knew Bobby had the knack of putting him on his feet again.

Nellie Mahony opened the door. She was a small, fat, country girl with a rosy complexion and a mass of jet-black hair that shone almost as brilliantly as her eyes. The doctor, who was sometimes seized with these fits of amiable idiocy, took her by the waist, and she gave a shriek of laughter that broke off suddenly.

'Wisha, Dr Healy,' she said complainingly, 'oughtn't you to

be ashamed, and the state we're in!'

'How's that, Nellie?' he asked anxiously. 'Isn't it the usual thing?'

'The usual thing?' she shrieked. She had a trick of snatching up and repeating someone's final words in a brilliant tone, a full octave higher, like a fiddle repeating a phrase from the double bass. Then with dramatic abruptness she let her voice drop to a whisper and dabbed her eyes with her apron. 'He's dying, doctor,' she said.

'For God's sake!' whispered the doctor. Life had rubbed down his principles considerably, and the fact that Bill was suspected of a share in at least one murder didn't prejudice him in the least. 'What happened him? I saw him in town on Monday and he never looked better.'

'Never looked better?' echoed the fiddle, while Nellie's beautiful black eyes filled with a tragic emotion that was not far removed from joy. 'And then didn't he go out on the Tuesday morning on me, in the pouring rain, with three men and two dogs, and not come back till the Friday night, with the result' (this was a boss phrase of Nellie's, always followed by a dramatic pause and a change of key) 'that he caught a chill up through him and never left the bed since.'

'What are you saying to Bobby Healy?' screeched a man's voice from upstairs. It was nearly as high-pitched as Nellie's, but with a wild, nervous tremolo in it.

'What am I saying to Bobby Healy?' she echoed mechanically. 'I'm saying nothing at all to him.'

'Well, don't be keeping him down there, after I waiting all day for him.'

'There's nothing wrong with his lungs anyway,' the doctor said professionally as he went up the stairs. They were bare and damp. It was a lifelong grievance of Bill Enright's that the Rowes had been mean enough to take the furniture to

England with them.

He was sitting up in an iron bed, and the grey afternoon light and the white pillows threw up the brilliance of his colouring, already heightened with a touch of fever.

'What was she telling you?' he asked in his high-pitched voice – the sort of keen and unsentimental voice you'd attribute in fantasy to some cunning and swift-footed beast of prey, like a fox.

'What was I telling him?' Nellie echoed boldly, feeling the doctor's authority behind her. 'I was telling him you went out with three men and two dogs and never came back to me till Friday night.'

'Ah, Bill,' said the doctor reproachfully, 'how often did I tell you to stick to women and cats? What ails you?'

'I'm bloody bad, doctor,' whinnied Bill.

'You look it,' said Bobby candidly. 'That's all right, Nellie,' he added by way of dismissal.

'And make a lot of noise downstairs,' said Bill after her.

Bobby gave his patient a thorough examination. So far as he could see there was nothing wrong with him but a chill, though he realised from the way Bill's mad blue eyes followed him that the man was in a panic. He wondered whether, as he sometimes did, he shouldn't put him in a worse one. It was unprofessional, but it was the only treatment that ever worked, and with most of his men patients he was compelled to choose a moment, before it was too late and hadn't yet passed from fiction to fact, when the threat of heart disease or cirrhosis might reduce their drinking to some reasonable proportion. Then the inspiration came to him like heaven opening to poor sinners, and he sat for several moments in silence, working it out. Threats would be lost on Bill Enright. What Bill needed was a miracle, and miracles aren't things to be lightly undertaken. Properly performed, a miracle might do as much good to the doctor as to Bill.

'Well, Bobby?' asked Bill, on edge with nerves.

'How long is it since you were at Confession, Bill?' the doctor asked gravely.

Bill's rosy face turned the colour of wax, and the doctor, a kindly man, felt almost ashamed of himself.

'Is that the way it is, doctor?' Bill asked in a shrill, expressionless voice.

'I put it too strongly, Bill,' said the doctor, already relenting. 'Maybe I should have a second opinion.'

'Your opinion is good enough for me, Bobby,' said Bill wildly, pouring coals of fire on Bobby as he sat up in bed and pulled the clothes about him. 'Take a fag and light one for me. What the hell difference does it make? I lived my life and bred the best greyhound bitches in Europe.'

'And I hope you'll live to breed a good many more,' said the doctor. 'Will I go for the Canon?'

'The Half-Gent?' snorted Bill indignantly. 'You will not.'

'He has an unfortunate manner,' sighed the doctor. 'But I could bring you someone else.'

'Ah, what the hell do I want with any of them?' asked Bill. 'Aren't they all the same? Money! Money! That's all that's a trouble to them.'

'Ah, I wouldn't say that, Bill,' the doctor said thoughtfully as he paced the room, his wrinkled old face as grey as his homespun suit. 'I hope you won't think me intruding,' he added anxiously. 'I'm talking as a friend.'

'I know you mean it well, Bobby.'

'But you see, Bill,' the doctor went on, screwing up his left cheek as though it hurt him, 'the feeling I have is that you need a different sort of priest altogether. Of course, I'm not saying a word against the Canon, but, after all, he's only a secular. You never had a chat with a Jesuit, I suppose?'

The doctor asked it with an innocent air, as if he didn't know that the one thing a secular priest dreads after Old Nick himself is a Jesuit, and that a Jesuit was particularly hateful to the Canon, who considered that as much intellect and authority as could ever be needed by his flock was centred in himself.

'Never,' said Bill.

'They're a very cultured order,' said the doctor.

'What the hell do I want with a Jesuit?' Bill cried in protest. 'A drop of drink and a bit of skirt – what harm is there in that?'

'Oh, none in the world, man,' agreed Bobby cunningly. ''Tisn't as if you were ever a bad-living man.'

'I wasn't,' said Bill with unexpected self-pity. 'I was a good friend to anyone I liked.'

'And you know the Canon would take it as a personal compliment if anything happened you – I'm speaking as a friend.'

'You are, Bobby,' said Bill, his voice hardening under the injustice of it. 'You're speaking as a Christian. Anything to thwart a fellow like that! I could leave the Jesuits a few pounds for Masses, Bobby,' he added with growing enthusiasm. 'That's what would really break Lanigan's heart. Money is all he cares about.'

'Ah, I wouldn't say that, Bill,' Bobby said with a trace of alarm. His was a delicate undertaking, and Bill was altogether too apt a pupil for his taste.

'No,' said Bill with conviction, 'but that's what you mean. All right, Bobby. You're right as usual. Bring whoever you like and I'll let him talk. Talk never broke anyone's bones, Bobby.'

The doctor went downstairs and found Nellie waiting for him with an anxious air.

'I'm running over to Aharna for a priest, Nellie,' he whispered. 'You might get things ready while I'm away.'

'And is that the way it is?' she asked, growing pale.

'Ah, we'll hope for the best,' he said, again feeling ashamed.

In a very thoughtful frame of mind he drove off to Aharna, where an ancient Bishop called McGinty, whose name was remembered in clerical circles only with sorrow, had permitted the Jesuits to establish a house. There he had a friend called Father Finnegan, a stocky, middle-aged man with a tight mouth and little clumps of white hair in his ears. It is not to be supposed that Bobby told him all that was in his mind, or that Father Finnegan thought he did, but there is very little a Jesuit doesn't know, and Father Finnegan knew that this was an occasion.

As they drove up the avenue, Nellie rushed out to meet them.

'What is it, Nellie?' the doctor asked anxiously. He couldn't help dreading that at the last moment Bill would play a trick on him and die of shock.

'He's gone mad, doctor,' she replied reproachfully, as though she hadn't thought a professional man would do a thing like that to her.

'When did he go mad?' Bobby asked doubtfully.

'When he seen me putting up the altar. Now he's after barricading the door and says he'll shoot the first one that tries to get in.'

'That's quite all right, my dear young lady,' said Father Finnegan soothingly. 'Sick people often go on like that.'

'Has he a gun, Nellie?' Bobby asked cautiously.

'Did you ever know him without one?' retorted Nellie.

The doctor, who was of a rather timid disposition, admired his friend's coolness as they mounted the stair. While Bobby knocked, Father Finnegan stood beside the door, his hands behind his back and his head bowed in meditation.

'Who's there?' Bill cried shrilly.

''Tis only me, Bill,' the doctor replied soothingly. 'Can I

come in?'

'I'm too sick,' shouted Bill. 'I'm not seeing anyone.'

'One moment, doctor,' Father Finnegan said calmly, putting his shoulder to the door. The barricade gave way and they went in. One glance was enough to show Bobby that Bill had had time to get panic-stricken. He hadn't a gun, but this was the only thing that was lacking to remind Bobby of Two-Gun Joe's last stand. He was sitting well up, supported on his elbows, his head craned forward, his bright blue eyes flashing unseeingly from the priest to Bobby and from Bobby to the improvised altar. Bobby was sadly afraid that Bill was going to disappoint him. You might as well have tried to convert something in the zoo.

'I'm Father Finnegan, Mr Enright,' the Jesuit said, going up to him with his hand stretched out.

'I didn't send for you,' snapped Bill.

'I appreciate that, Mr Enright,' said the priest. 'But any friend of Dr Healy is a friend of mine. Won't you shake hands?'

'I don't mind,' whinnied Bill, letting him partake slightly of a limp paw but without looking at him. 'But I warn you I'm not a religious sort of bloke. I never went in for that at all. Anyone that thinks I'm not a hard nut to crack is in for a surprise.'

'If I went in for cracking nuts, I'd say the same,' said Father Finnegan gamely. 'You look well able to protect yourself.'

Bill gave a harsh snort indicative of how much could be said on that score if the occasion were more propitious; his eyes continued to wander unseeingly like a mirror in a child's hand, but Bobby felt the priest had struck the right note. He closed the door softly behind him and went down to the drawing room. The six windows opened on three landscapes. The lowing of distant cows pleased his ear. Then he swore and threw open the door to the hall. Nellie was sitting comfortably on the stairs with her ear cocked. He beckoned her down.

'What is it, doctor?' she asked in surprise.

'Get us a light. And don't forget the priest will want his supper.'

'You don't think I was listening?' she asked indignantly.

'No,' Bobby said dryly. 'You looked as if you were joining in the devotions.'

'Joining in the devotions?' she cried. 'I'm up since six, waiting hand and foot on him, with the result that I dropped down in a dead weakness on the stairs. Would you believe that now?'

'I would not,' said Bobby.

'You would not?' she repeated incredulously. 'Jesus!' she added after a moment. 'I'll bring you the lamp,' she said in a defeated tone.

Nearly an hour passed before there was any sound upstairs. Then Father Finnegan came down, rubbing his hands briskly and complaining of the cold. Bobby found the lamp lit in the bedroom and the patient lying with one arm under his head.

'How are you feeling now, Bill?' the doctor asked.

'Fine, Bobby,' said Bill. 'I'm feeling fine. You were right about the priest, Bobby. I was a fool to bother my head about the Canon. He's not educated at all, Bobby, not compared with that man.'

'I thought you'd like him,' said Bobby.

'I like a fellow to know his job, Bobby,' said Bill in the tone of one expert appraising another. 'There's nothing like the bit of education. I wish I met him sooner.' The wild blue eyes came to rest hauntingly on the doctor's face. 'I feel the better of it already, Bobby. What sign would that be?'

'I dare say 'tis the excitement,' said Bobby, giving nothing away. 'I'll have another look at you.'

'What's that she's frying, Bobby? Sausages and bacon?'

'It smells like it.'

'There's nothing I'm so fond of,' Bill said wistfully. 'Would it make me worse, Bobby? My stomach feels as if it was sandpapered.'

'I don't suppose so. But tea is all you can have with it.'

'Hah!' crowed Bill. ''Tis all I'm ever going to have if I live to be as old as Methuselah. But I'm not complaining, Bobby. I'm a man of my word. Oh, God, yes.'

'Go on!' said Bobby. 'Did you take the pledge?'

'Christ, Bobby,' said the patient, giving a wild heave in the bed, 'I took the whole bloody ship, masts and anchor . . . God forgive me for swearing!' he added piously. 'He made me promise to marry the Screech,' he said with a look which challenged the doctor to laugh if he dared.

'Ah, well, you might do worse, Bill,' said the doctor.

'How sure he is I'll have him!' bawled Nellie cheerfully, showing her moony face at the door.

'You see the way it is, Bobby,' said Bill without rancour. 'That's what I have to put up with.'

'Excuse me a minute, Nellie,' said the doctor. 'I'm having a look at Bill . . . You had a trying day of it,' he added, sitting on the bed and taking Bill's wrist. Then he took his temperature, and flashed the torch into his eyes and down his throat while Bill looked at him with a hypnotised glare.

'Begor, Bill, I wouldn't say but you're right,' the doctor said approvingly. 'I'd almost say you were a shade better.'

'But that's what I'm saying, man!' cried Bill, beginning to do physical exercises for him. 'Look at that, Bobby! I couldn't do that before. I call it a blooming miracle.'

'When you've seen as much as I have, you won't have so much belief in miracles,' said the doctor. 'Take a couple of these tablets anyway, and I'll have another look at you in the morning.'

It was almost too easy. The most up-to-date treatments were wasted on Bobby's patients. What they all secretly desired was to be rubbed with three pebbles from a Holy Well. Sometimes it left him depressed.

'Well, on the whole, Dr Healy,' Father Finnegan said as they drove off, 'that was a very satisfactory evening.'

'It was,' Bobby said guardedly. He had no intention of telling his friend how satisfactory it was from his point of view.

'People do make extraordinary rallies after the Sacraments,' went on Father Finnegan, and Bobby saw it wasn't even necessary to tell him. Educated men can understand one another without embarrassing admissions. His own conscience was quite easy. A little religion wouldn't do Bill the least bit of harm. The Jesuit's conscience, he felt, wasn't troubling him either. Even without a miracle Bill's conversion would have opened up the Canon's parish to the order. With a miracle, they'd have every old woman, male and female, for miles around calling them in.

'They do,' Bobby said wonderingly. 'I often noticed it.'

'And I'm afraid, Dr Healy, that the Canon won't like it,' added the Jesuit.

'He won't,' said the doctor as though the idea had only just occurred to himself. 'I'm afraid he won't like it at all.'

He was an honest man who gave credit where credit was due, and he knew it wasn't only the money – a couple of hundred a year at the least – that would upset the Canon. It was the thought that under his own very nose a miracle had been worked on one of his own parishioners by one of the hated Jesuits. Clerics are almost as cruel as small boys. The Canon wouldn't be allowed to forget the Jesuit miracle the longest day he lived.

But for the future he'd let Bobby alone.

ACHILLES' HEEL

IN ONE THING ONLY is the Catholic Church more vulnerable than any human institution, and that is in the type of woman who preys on celibates – particularly the priest's housekeeper. The priest's housekeeper is one of the supreme examples of Natural Selection, because it has been practically proved that when for any reason she is transferred to a male who is not celibate she pines away and dies. To say that she is sexless is to say both too much and too little, for, like the Church itself, she accepts chastity for a higher end – in her case, the subjection of some unfortunate man to a degree unparalleled in marriage. Wives, of course, have a similar ambition, but their purposes are mysteriously deflected by lovemaking, jealousy of other women, and children, and it is well known that many Irish wives go into hysterics of rage at the thought of the power vested in priests' housekeepers. *Their* victims, being celibate, have no children, and are automatically sealed off from other women, who might encourage them to greater independence.

But the most powerful among these are the housekeepers of bishops. Nellie Conneely, the Bishop of Moyle's housekeeper, had been with him since he was a canon, and even in those days he had been referred to by his parishioners as 'Nellie and the Canon'. 'Nellie and the Canon' didn't approve of all-night dances, so all-night dances were stopped. Half the population depended for patronage on 'Nellie and the Canon', and presents were encouraged – food for the Canon and something a little perishable for Nellie. The townspeople had no doubt as to which was the more important partner. She had even appeared on the altar steps on one occasion and announced that there would be no eight o'clock Mass because she was keeping the Canon in bed. She was a comparatively young woman for such a responsible position, and even at the time I speak of she was a well-preserved little body, with a fussy, humble, sugary air that concealed a cold intelligence. Her great rival was Canon Lanigan, who was the favourite in the succession of the diocese. In private he sniggered over her and called her La Maintenon, but when he visited the Bishop he was as sugary as herself and paid her flowery compliments on her cooking and even on her detestable bottled coffee. But Nellie, though she giggled and gushed in response, wasn't in the least taken in; she knew Lanigan preferred old French mish-mash to her own candid cooking, and she warned the Bishop not to trust him. 'God forgive me,' she said sadly, 'I don't know how it is I can't warm to Canon Lanigan. There is something about him that is not quite sincere. I know, of course, that I'm only a foolish old woman, and you don't have to mind me.'

But the Bishop had to mind her and he did. The poor man had one great fear, which was that he was fading away for lack of proper nourishment. He knew what the old-fashioned clerics were like, with their classical scholarship and their enormous appetites, and, comparing his own accomplishments and theirs, he couldn't see for the life of him how he was ever going to reach ninety. After eating a whole chicken for his dinner, he would sit in his study for hours, wondering what the connection was between serious scholarship and proper meals, till Nellie thrust her head in the door.

'You're all right?' she would ask coyly.

'I'm not, Nellie,' he would reply with a worried air. 'I'm feeling a bit low tonight.'

''Tis that chicken!' she would cry, making a dramatic entrance. 'I knew it. I said it to Tim Murphy. There wasn't a pick on it.'

'I was wondering about that myself,' he would say, fixing her with his anxious blue eyes. 'Murphy's chickens don't seem to be the same at all.'

'What you want is a nice grilled chop,' she would say authoritatively.

'I don't know,' he would mutter, measuring his idea of a chop against his idea of night starvation. 'There's a lot of eating in a chop.'

'Well, you could have cutlets,' she would say with a shrug, implying that she didn't think much of cutlets for a bad case like his own.

'Cutlets make a nice snack,' he agreed.

'Ah, they do, but they're too dry,' she would cry, waving them away in disgust. 'What you want is a good plate of nice curly rashers, with lots of fat on them. 'Twas my own fault. I knew there was nothing in that chicken. I should have served them with the chicken, but I declare to you my wits are wandering. I'm getting too old . . . And a couple of chips. Sure, 'twill be the making of you.'

One day, Nellie came in terrible trouble to the Bishop. She had just been visited by one of the local customs officers, Tim Leary. The Bishop's diocese was on the border between Northern and Southern Ireland, and since there was never a time when something that was plentiful on one side wasn't scarce on the other, there was constant smuggling in both directions. The South sent butter, eggs, ham and whiskey to the North, and the North sent back petrol, tea and sugar – all

without benefit of duty. The customs officials of the two
countries worked together in their efforts to prevent it. Nellie
seemed to have the greatest difficulty in explaining to the
Bishop what Tim Leary wanted of her. You'd have thought
she was not bright in the head.

'You said it yourself,' she said ingenuously. 'This diocese
was ever notorious for backbiting, but why do they pick on
me? I suppose they want to have their own housekeeper, someone that would do their whispering for them. It is something
I never would do, not even for your sake, and I will not do
it for them, even if they do say you're too old.'

'Who says I'm too old?' the Bishop asked mildly, but his
blue eyes had an angry light in them. He knew the people
who would say such things, and there were plenty of them.

'Don't, don't ask me to carry stories!' she begged, almost
in frenzy. 'I won't do it, even to save my life. Let Canon
Lanigan and the rest of them say what they like about me.'

'Never mind Canon Lanigan,' the Bishop said shortly. 'What
did Leary say about you?'

'But what could he say about me? What have he against
me only old *doorsha-dawrsha* he picked up in the low public
houses of the town? Oh, 'tisn't that at all, me lord, but the
questions he asked me. They put the heart across me. "Who
was the chief smuggler?" – wasn't that a nice thing for him
to ask me?'

'He thought you knew the chief smuggler?' the Bishop asked
incredulously.

'He thought I *was* the chief smuggler,' she replied with her
hand to her heart. 'He didn't say it, but I could read it in that
mean little mind of his. Whiskey, petrol, tea, and things, my
lord, that I declare to you and to my Maker, if I was to go
before Him at this minute of time, I never even knew the
names of.'

'He must be mad,' the Bishop said with a worried air. 'Which Learys is he belonged to? The ones from Clooneavullen?' The Bishop had a notion that most of the mysteries of human conduct could be solved by reference to heredity. He said he had never yet met a good man who came from a bad family.

'Aha!' Nellie cried triumphantly. 'Didn't I say it myself? That his own father couldn't read or write, and the joke of the countryside for his foolish talk!'

'Never mind his father,' the Bishop said sternly. 'He had an uncle in the lunatic asylum. All that family were touched. Tell him to come up here to me tomorrow, and I'll give him a bit of my mind.'

'You will to be sure, my lord,' she said complacently as she rose. Then at the door she stopped. 'But why would you talk to a little whippersnapper like that – a man like you, that has the ear of the government? I suppose someone put him up to it.'

The Bishop meditated on that for a moment. He saw Nellie's point about the impropriety of people's going over his head, and recognised that it might be the work of an enemy. Like Nellie, he knew the secrets of power and understood that the most important is never to deal directly with people you look down on.

'Give me my pen!' he said at last in a voice that made Nellie's heart flutter again. When some parish priest had been seen drunk in a public place, the Bishop would say in the same dry voice to his secretary, 'Give me my pen till I suspend Father Tom', or when some gang of wild young curates had started a card club in some remote village, 'Give me my pen till I scatter them!' It was the voice of ultimate authority, of the Church Militant personified in her own dear, simple man.

In spite of strenuous detective work, Nellie never did get to see the Bishop's letter to his friend in the government, Seumas Butcher, the Irish Minister of Revenue, but, on the other hand, neither did the Bishop ever get to see the Minister's reply. It was one of the features of Nellie's concern for him that she did not like him to know of anything that would upset his health, and she merely removed such letters from the hall. But even she had never seen a letter so likely to upset the Bishop as that from the Minister:

Dear Dr Gallogly:

It was a real pleasure to hear from you again. Mrs Butcher was only saying a week ago that it was ages since you paid us a visit. I have had careful inquiries made about the matter you mention, and I am very sorry indeed to inform you that the statements of the local Revenue Officer appear to be fully substantiated. Your housekeeper, Miss Ellen Conneely, is the owner of licensed premises at the other side of the Border which have long been known as the headquarters of a considerable smuggling organisation, whose base on this side appears to be the Episcopal Palace. You will realise that the Revenue Officers have no desire to take any steps that could be an embarrassment to you, but you will also appreciate that this traffic involves a considerable loss of revenue for both our country and the North of Ireland, and might, in the event of other gangs operating in the neighbourhood being tried and convicted, result in serious charges. I should be deeply grateful for Your Lordship's kind assistance in putting an early end to it.

Mise le meas
Seumas O. Buitseir
Aire

Nellie fully understood, when she had read this, the tone with which the Bishop said 'Give me my pen', as a father might say 'Give me my stick.' There were certain matters that could only be dealt with by a pen like a razor, and that evening she sat in her own room and wrote:

Dear Sir:

His Lordship, the Most Reverend Dr Gallogly, Bishop of Moyle, has handed me your letter of the 3rd inst. and asked me to reply to it on his behalf. He says it is a tissue of lies and that he does not want to be bothered any more with it. I suppose His Lordship would not know what is going on in his own house? Or is it a rogue and robber you think he is? I do not know how you can have the face to say such things to a bishop. All those lies were started by Tim Leary, and as His Lordship says, what better could you expect of a man whose uncle died in the Moyle Asylum, a wet and dirty case? The public house you talk about is only another of the lies. It does not belong to me at all but to my poor brother who, after long years of suffering for Ireland in English prisons, is now an incurable invalid with varicose veins and six children. How would the likes of him be a smuggler? Tim Leary will be thrown out if he calls here again. It is all lies. Did Tim Leary suffer for Ireland? Has Tim Leary six children? What has happened our Christian principles and what do we pay taxes for? We were better off when we had the English.

Yours sincerely,
Ellen Conneely

There was something about this letter that gave Nellie a real thrill of pride and satisfaction. Like all women of her kind, she had always had the secret desire to speak out boldly with the whole authority of the Church behind her, and now she had done it.

She had also illustrated to perfection the Achilles' heel of Catholicism, because, though Dr Gallogly would probably have had a heart attack if he had known the contents of her letter, no layman could be quite sure of this, and the Minister and his staff were left with a vague impression that, somehow or other, the Bishop of Moyle was now the ringleader of a smuggling gang. Being all of them good Catholics, they took the charitable view that the Bishop was no longer responsible for his actions and had taken to smuggling the way some old men take to other peculiar pursuits, but all the same it was a nasty situation. Whatever happened, you could not raid the palace for contraband. The very thought of what the newspapers would say about this made the Minister sick. The *Irish Times* would report it in full, with a smug suggestion that Protestant bishops never did things like that; the *Irish Independent* would assert that instructions for the raid had come direct from Moscow, through the local Communist cell; while the *Irish Press* would say, without fear of contradiction, that it was another British plot against the good name of Irishmen.

'Jesus, Joe!' the Minister said, with a moan, to his secretary. 'Forget it! Forget it, if you can!'

But the local customs officers could not forget it. Nellie didn't allow them. Scared by Tim Leary and the Minister's letter, she worked openly and feverishly to get rid of all the contraband in her possession, and the professional pride of the customs officers was mortified. Then, one day, a man was caught trying to cross the border into the North with a keg of whiskey under the seat of his car, and he swore by God and the Twelve Apostles that he had no notion how it had got there. But Tim Leary, who knew the man's friendship with Nellie, knew damn well how it had got there, and went to Paddy Clancy's liquor store in Moyle, from which it had originally come. Paddy, a crushed and quivering poor man, had to admit that the keg had been sold to the Bishop.

'Get me the Bishop's account, Paddy,' Tim said stiffly, and poor Paddy produced the ledger. It was an ugly moment, because Paddy was a man who made a point of never interfering with any man's business but he knew of old that the Bishop's liquor account was most peculiar. Tim Leary studied it in stupefaction.

'Honour of God!' he said angrily. 'Are you trying to tell me that the Bishop drinks all that?'

'Bishops have a lot of entertaining to do, Tim,' Paddy said meekly.

'Bishops don't have to have a bloody bonded store to entertain in!' shouted Tim.

'Well, Tim, 'tis a delicate matter,' Paddy said, sweating with anxiety. 'If a man is to have customers in this country, he cannot afford to ask questions.'

'Well, begod, I'm going to ask a few questions,' cried Tim, 'and I'm going to do it this very morning, what's more. Give me that ledger!'

Then, with the ledger under his arm, he went straight up to the palace. Nellie tried to head him off. First she said the Bishop was out; then she said the Bishop was ill; finally she said that the Bishop had given orders that Tim was not to be admitted.

'You try to stop me, Nellie, and I'll damn soon show you whether I'm going to be admitted or not,' said Tim, pushing past her, and at that moment the study door opened and the Bishop came out. It was no coincidence, and at that moment Nellie knew she was lost, for along with the appetite of a child, the Bishop had the curiosity of a child, and a beggar's voice at the door would be sufficient for him to get up and leave the door of his study ajar so that he could listen in comfort to the conversation.

'That will do, Nellie,' he said, and then came up to Tim with a menacing air – a handsome old man of six foot two, with a baby complexion and fierce blue eyes.

'What do you want?' he asked sternly, but on his own ground Tim could be as infallible as any bishop.

'I'm investigating the smuggling that's going on in this locality, and I want to ask you a few questions, my lord,' he replied grimly.

'So I heard,' said the Bishop. 'I told the Minister already I couldn't see why you had to do your investigating in my house.'

'I'm a public servant, my lord,' Tim said, his voice rising, 'and I'm entitled to make my investigations wherever I have to.'

'You're a very independent young man,' the Bishop said dryly but without rancour. 'Tell me, are you John Leary's son from Clooneavullen?'

'I'm nothing of the sort. Who said I was John Leary's son? My father was from Manister.'

'For God's sake!' the Bishop said softly. 'You're not Jim Leary's boy, by any chance?'

'I am, then,' said Tim with a shrug.

'Come on in,' the Bishop said, holding out his hand to Tim, while his eyes searched away into the distance beyond the front door. 'Your father was headmaster there when I was a canon. I must have seen you when you were a little fellow. Come in, anyway. No son of Jim Leary's is going to leave this house without a drink.'

'But I'm on duty, my lord,' said Tim, following him in.

'Aren't we all?' the Bishop asked mildly as he went to the sideboard. 'I'm as much a bishop now as I'll ever be.' With shaky hands he produced two glasses and a bottle of whiskey. He gave one tiny glass to Tim and took another himself. It

was obviously a duty rather than a pleasure. The Bishop did
not go in for drinking, because it seemed to ruin his appetite
and that was bad enough already.

'Now, tell me what all this is about,' he said comfortably.

Tim was beginning to realise that he really liked the man
– an old weakness of his, which, combined with his violent
temper, made him a bad investigator. He sometimes thought
the bad temper and the good nature were only two aspects
of the same thing.

'A man was caught trying to cross the Border a few days
ago with a keg of your whiskey in his car,' he said as firmly
as he could.

'A keg of my whiskey?' the Bishop repeated with real interest
and apparent enjoyment. 'But what would I be doing with
a keg of whiskey?'

'That's what I came to ask you,' replied Tim. 'You seem
to have bought enough of them in the past year.'

'I never bought a keg of whiskey in my whole life, boy,'
said the Bishop with amusement. 'Sure, if I take a drop of punch
before I go to bed, that's all the whiskey I ever see. It's bad
for a man of my age,' he added earnestly. 'I haven't the
constitution.'

'If you'll take one look at your account in Clancy's ledger,
you'll see you're supposed to have an iron constitution,' said
Tim and, as he opened the book, there was a knock and Nellie
came in modestly with a bundle of receipted bills in her hand.
'Or maybe this is the one with the iron constitution,' Tim
added fiercely. He still had not forgotten his unmannerly
reception.

'You need say no more,' she said briskly. 'I admit it, whatever
little harm I did to anyone. 'Twas only to keep my unfortunate angashore of a brother out of the workhouse. Between
drinking and politics, he was never much head to his poor

wife, God rest her. Not one penny did I ever make out of
it, and not one penny of His Lordship's money ever went astray.
I'll go if I have to, but I will not leave this house without a
character.'

'I'll give you the character,' Tim said savagely. 'And further-
more I'll see you have a place to go. You can do all the
smuggling you like there – if you're able.'

'That will do!' the Bishop said sternly. 'Go away, Nellie!'
he added over his shoulder, in the tone he used when he asked
for his pen to suspend Father Tom.

Nellie looked at him for a moment in stupefaction and then
burst into a howl of grief and went out, sobbing to herself
about 'the fifteen good years of my life that I wasted on him
and there's his gratitude'. The Bishop waited imperturbably
till her sobs had subsided in the kitchen before he spoke again.

'How many people know about this?'

'Begod, my lord, by this time I think you might say 'twas
common property,' said Tom with a laugh.

The Bishop did not laugh. 'I was afraid of that,' he said.
'What do they think of it?'

'Well, of course, they all have a great regard for you,' Tim
replied, in some embarrassment.

'I'm sure of that,' the Bishop said without a hint of irony.
'They have so much regard for me that they don't care if I
turn my house into a smuggler's den. They didn't suggest what
I might be doing with the Cathedral?'

Tim saw that the Bishop was more cut up than he affected
to be.

'Ah, I wouldn't worry about that,' he said anxiously.

'I'm not worrying. What will they do to Nellie?'

'Oh, she'll get the jail,' said Tim. 'As well as a bloody big
fine that'll be worse to her.'

'A fine? What sort of a fine?'

'That will be calculated on the value of the contraband,' said Tim. 'But if you ask me quietly, 'twill run well into the thousands.'

'Into the thousands?' the Bishop asked in alarm. 'But where would either of us get that sort of money, boy?'

'You may be damn full sure she has it,' Tim said grimly. 'Nellie?'

'Aye, and more along with it,' said Tim.

'For God's sake!' the Bishop exclaimed softly. He had put away his glass, and his long, fine fingers were intertwined. Then he gave a little snort that might have passed for laughter. 'And me thinking she was an old fool! Which of us was the fool? I wonder. After this, they'll be saying I'm not able to look after myself. They'll be putting in a coadjutor over me, as sure as you're there!'

'They wouldn't do that?' Tim asked in astonishment. It had never occurred to him before that there might be anybody who could interfere with a bishop.

'Oh, indeed they would,' the Bishop said, almost with enjoyment. 'And I wouldn't mind that itself if only they'd leave me my housekeeper. The jail won't take much out of her, but 'twill kill me. At my age I'm not going to be able to find another woman to look after me the way she does. Unless they'd let me go to jail along with her.'

Tim was an emotional young man, and he could hardly contemplate the personal problems that the Bishop set up in that casual way of his.

'There's nobody in this place would do anything to upset you,' he said, growing red. 'I'm sure they'll be well satisfied if she paid the fine, without sending her to jail. The only thing is, from my point of view, could you control her?'

'I could do nothing of the kind,' the Bishop replied in his blank way. 'If I was to give you my oath to control her for the future, would you believe me? You would not, I couldn't control her. You might be able to do it.'

'I'd damn soon do it if I had a free hand,' Tim said loyally.

'I'd give you all the hand you want,' the Bishop said placidly. 'I'd give you quarters here if you wanted them. You see, 'tis more in my interest than yours to stop the scandal, before they have me married to her.' From the dryness of his tone, the Bishop, an unemotional man, seemed to be suffering. 'I wouldn't forget it for you,' he added anxiously. 'Anyway, I'll have a talk to Butcher, and see if he can't do something for you. Not that that poor fool knows what he's doing, most of the time.'

That afternoon, the Bishop sat on by his window and watched as a lorry drove up before his palace and Tim Leary loaded it with commodities the Bishop had thought long gone from the world – chests of tea, bags of sugar, boxes of butter. There seemed to be no end to them. He felt crushed and humbled. Like all bishops, he was addicted to power, but he saw now that a bishop's power, like a bishop's knowledge, was little better than a shadow. He was just a lonely old man who was dependent on women, exactly as when they had changed his napkin and he had crowed and kicked his heels. There was no escape.

Mercifully, Nellie herself didn't put in an appearance as the premises were gone through. That evening, when she opened the door and said meekly, 'Dinner is served, my lord', the Bishop went in to a royal spread – the juiciest of roast beef, with roast potatoes and tender young peas drowned in butter. The Bishop ate stolidly through it, reading the book in front of his plate and never addressing a word to her. He was too bitter. He went to his study and took down the history of the diocese, which had so often consoled him in earlier griefs, but that night there was no consolation in it. It seemed that none

of the men who had held the see before him was of the sort
to be dominated by an old housekeeper, except for an
eighteenth-century bishop who, in order to inherit a legacy,
had become a Protestant. The door opened, and Nellie looked
shyly in.

'What are you feeling now?' she whispered.

'Let me alone,' he said in a dry voice, without looking at
her. 'My heart is broken!'

''Tisn't your heart at all,' she said shamefastly. ''Tis that beef.
'Twasn't hung long enough, that's all. There isn't a butcher
in this town will be bothered to hang beef. Would I get you
a couple of scrambled eggs?'

'Go away, I said.'

'You're right, my lord. There's nothing in eggs. Would I
fry you a couple of rashers?'

'I don't want anything, woman!' he said, almost shouting
at her.

'The dear knows, the rashers aren't worth it,' she admitted
with a heavy sigh. 'Nothing only old bones, and the hair still
sprouting on them. What you want is a nice little juicy bit
of Limerick ham with a couple of mashed potatoes and milk
sauce with parsley. That'll make a new man of you.'

'All right, all right,' he said angrily. 'But go away and let
me alone.'

His mouth was already watering, but he knew that there
was no ham in Limerick or out of it that could lift his sorrow;
that whenever a woman says something will make a new man
of you, all she means is that, like the rest of her crooked devices,
it will make an old man of you before your time.

THE SHEPHERDS

FATHER WHELAN, THE PARISH PRIEST, called on his curate,
Father Devine, one evening in autumn. Father Whelan
was a tall, stout man with a broad chest, a head that didn't
detach itself too clearly from the rest of his body, bushes of
wild hair in his ears, and the rosy, innocent, good-natured face
of a pious old countrywoman who made a living by selling eggs.

Devine was pale and worn-looking, with a gentle, dreamy
face which had the soft gleam of an old piano keyboard, and
he wore pince-nez perched on his unhappy, insignificant little
nose. He and Whelan got on very well, considering – considering, that is to say, that Devine, who didn't know when he
was well off, had fathered a dramatic society and an annual
festival on Whelan, who had to put in an attendance at both;
and that whenever the curate's name was mentioned, the parish
priest, a charitable old man who never said an unkind word
about anybody, tapped his forehead and said poor Devine's
poor father was just the same. 'A national teacher – sure, I
knew him well, poor man!'

What Devine said about Whelan in that crucified drawl of
his consisted mostly of the old man's words, with just the
faintest inflection which isolated and underlined their fatuity.
'I know some of the clergy are very opposed to books, but

I like a book myself. I'm very fond of Zane Grey. Even poetry I like. Some of the poems you see on advertisements are very clever.' And then Devine, who didn't often laugh, broke into a thin little cackle at the thought of Whelan representing the intellect and majesty of the Church. Devine was clever; he was lonely; he had a few good original water-colours and a bookcase full of works that were a constant source of wonder to Whelan. The old man stood in front of them now, his hat in his hands, lifting his warty old nose, while his eyes held a blank, hopeless, charitable look.

'Nothing there in your line, I'm afraid,' said Devine with his maddeningly respectful, deprecating air, as if he put the parish priest's tastes on a level with his own.

''Tisn't that,' said Whelan in a hollow faraway voice, 'but I see you have a lot of foreign books. I suppose you know the languages well.'

'Well enough to read,' Devine said wearily, his handsome head on one side. 'Why?'

'That foreign boat at the jetties,' Whelan said without looking round. 'What is it? French or German? There's terrible scandal about it.'

'Is that so?' drawled Devine, his dark eyebrows going up his narrow, slanting forehead. 'I didn't hear.'

'Terrible,' Whelan said mournfully, turning on him the full battery of his round, rosy old face and shining spectacles. 'There's girls on it every night. I told Sullivan I'd go round tonight and give them the hunt. It occurred to me we might want someone to speak the language.'

'I'm afraid my French would hardly rise to that,' Devine said dryly, but he made no other objection, for, except for his old womanly fits of virtue, Whelan was all right as parish priests go. Devine had had sad experience of how they could go. He put on his faded old coat and clamped his battered hat down over his pince-nez, and the two priests went down the Main Street to the post-office corner. It was deserted but for two out-of-works supporting either side of the door like ornaments, and a few others hanging hypnotised over the bridge while they studied the foaming waters of the weir. Devine had taken up carpentry himself in order to lure them into the technical classes, but it hadn't worked too well.

'The dear knows,' he said thoughtfully, 'you'd hardly wonder where those girls would go.'

'Ah,' said the parish priest, holding his head as though it were a flowerpot that might fall and break, 'what do they want to go anywhere for? They're mad on pleasure. That girl Nora Fitzpatrick is one of them, and her mother at home dying.'

'That might be her reason,' said Devine, who visited the Fitzpatricks and knew what their home was like, with six children, and a mother dying of cancer.

'Ah, the girl's place is at home,' said Whelan without rancour.

They went down past the Technical School to the quays, these too, deserted but for a coal boat and the big foreign grain boat, rising high and dark above the edge of the quay on a full tide. The town was historically reputed to have been a great place – well, about a hundred years ago – and had masses of grey stone warehouses, all staring with sightless eyes across the river. Two men who had been standing against the wall, looking up at the grain boat, came to join them. One was a tall, gaunt man with a long, sour, melancholy face which looked particularly hideous because it sported a youthful pink-and-white complexion and looked exactly like the face of an old hag, heavily made up. He wore a wig and carried a rolled-up umbrella behind his back. His name was Sullivan; he was the manager of a shop in town, and was forever in and out of the church. Devine hated him. The other, Joe Sheridan, was a small, fat, Jewish-looking man with dark skin and an excitable manner. Devine didn't dislike him so much. He was merely the inevitable local windbag, who got drunk on his own self-importance. As the four men met, Devine looked up and saw two young foreign faces, propped on their hands, peering at them over the edge of the boat.

'Well, boys?' asked Whelan.

'There's two aboard at present, father,' Sullivan said in a shrill, scolding voice. 'Nora Fitzpatrick and Phillie O'Malley.'

'Well, you'd better go aboard and tell them come off,' Whelan said tranquilly.

'I wonder what our legal position is, father?' Sheridan asked, scowling. 'I mean, have we any sort of *locus standi*?'

'Oh, in the event of your being stabbed, I think they could be tried,' Devine replied with bland malice. 'Of course, I don't know if your wife and children could claim compensation.'

The malice was lost on Whelan, who laid one hairy paw on Devine's shoulder and the other on Sheridan's to calm the fears of both. He exuded a feeling of pious confidence. It was the eggs all over again. God would look after His hens.

'Never mind about the legal position,' he said paternally. 'I'll be answerable for that.'

'That's good enough for me, father,' Sheridan said, and, pulling his hat down over his eyes and joining his hands behind his back, he strode up the gangway, with the air of a detective in a bad American film, while Sullivan, clutching his umbrella against the small of his back, followed him, head in air. A lovely pair, Devine thought. They went up to the two sailors.

'Two girls,' Sullivan said in his shrill, scolding voice. 'We're looking for the two girls that came aboard half an hour ago.'

Neither of the sailors stirred. One of them turned his eyes lazily and looked Sullivan up and down.

'Not this boat,' he said impudently. 'The other one. There's always girls on that.'

Then Sheridan, who had glanced downstairs through an open doorway, began to beckon.

'Phillie O'Malley!' he shouted in a raucous voice. 'Father Whelan and Father Devine are out here. Come on! They want to talk to you.'

'Tell her if she doesn't come I'll go and bring her,' the parish priest called anxiously.

'He says if you don't he'll come and bring you,' repeated Sheridan.

Nothing happened for a moment or two. Then a tall girl with a consumptive face emerged on deck with a handker-chief pressed to her eyes. Devine couldn't help feeling sick at the sight of her wretched finery, her cheap hat and bead necklace. He was angry and ashamed and a cold fury of sarcasm rose in him. The Good Shepherd indeed!

'Come on, lads,' the parish priest said encouragingly. 'What about the second one?'

Sheridan, flushed with triumph, was about to disappear down the companionway when one of the sailors gave him a heave which threw him to the edge of the ship. Then the sailor stood nonchalantly in the doorway, blocking the way. Whelan's face grew red with anger and he only waited for the girl to leave the gangway before going up himself. Devine paused to whisper a word to her.

'Get off home as quick as you can, Phillie,' he said, 'and don't upset yourself.'

At the tenderness in his voice she took the handkerchief from her face and began to weep in earnest. Then Devine went up after the others. It was a ridiculous scene with the fat old priest, his head in the air, trembling with senile anger and astonishment.

'Get out of the way at once!' he said.

'Don't be a fool, man!' Devine said with quiet ferocity. 'They're not accustomed to being spoken to like that. If you got a knife in your ribs, it would be your own fault. We want to talk to the captain.' And then, bending forward with his eyebrows raised in a humble, deprecating manner, he asked: 'I wonder if you'd be good enough to tell the captain we'd like to see him.'

The sailor who was blocking their way looked at him for a moment and then nodded in the direction of the upper deck. Taking his parish priest's arm and telling Sullivan and Sheridan to stay behind, Devine went up the ship. When they had gone a little way the second sailor passed them out, knocked at a door, and said something Devine did not catch. Then, with a scowl, he held open the door for them. The captain was a middle-aged man with a heavily lined, sallow face, close-cropped black hair, and a black moustache. There was something Mediterranean about his air.

'Bonsoir, messieurs,' he said in a loud, businesslike tone which did not conceal a certain nervousness.

'Bonsoir, monsieur le capitaine,' Devine said with the same plaintive, ingratiating air as he bowed and raised his battered old hat. 'Est-ce que nous vous dérangeons?'

'Mais, pas du tout; entrez, je vous prie,' the captain said heartily, clearly relieved by Devine's amiability. 'Vous parlez français alors?'

'Un peu, monsieur le capitaine,' Devine said deprecatingly. 'Vous savez, ici en Irlande on n'a pas souvent l'occasion.'

'Ah, well,' the captain said cheerfully. 'I speak English too, so we will understand one another. Won't you sit down?'

'I wish my French were anything like as good as your English,' Devine said as he sat.

'One travels a good deal,' the captain replied with a

flattered air. 'You'll have a drink? Some brandy, eh?'

'I'd be delighted, of course,' Devine said regretfully, 'but I'm afraid we have a favour to ask you first.'

'A favour?' the captain said enthusiastically. 'Certainly, certainly. Anything you like. Have a cigar?'

'Never smoke them,' Whelan said in a dull stubborn voice, looking first at the cigar-case and then looking away; and, to mask his rudeness, Devine, who never smoked cigars, took one and lit it.

'I'd better explain who we are,' he said, sitting back, his head on one side, his long, delicate hands hanging over the arms of the chair. 'This is Father Whelan, the parish priest. My name is Devine; I'm the curate.'

'And mine,' the captain said proudly, 'is Platon Demarrais. I bet you never before heard of a fellow called Platon?'

'A relation of the philospher, I presume,' said Devine.

'The very man! And I have two brothers, Zenon and Plotin.'

'What an intellectual family!'

'Pagans, of course,' the captain explained complacently. 'Greeks. My father was a schoolteacher. He called us that to annoy the priest. He was anticlerical.'

'That's not confined to schoolteachers in France,' Devine said, dryly. 'My father was a schoolteacher, but he never got round to calling me Aristotle. Which might be as well,' he added with a chuckle. 'At any rate, there's a girl called Fitzpatrick on the ship, with some sailor, I suppose. She's one of Father Whelan's parishioners, and we'd be grateful to you if you'd have her put off.'

'Speak for yourself, father,' said Whelan, raising his stubborn, old peasant head and quelling fraternisation with a glance. 'I wouldn't be grateful to any man for doing what 'tis only his duty to do.'

'Then, perhaps you'd better explain your errand yourself,

Father Whelan,' Devine said with an abnegation not far removed from waspishness.

'I think so, father,' Whelan said stubbornly. 'That girl, Captain Whatever-your-name-is,' he went on slowly, 'has no business to be on your ship at all. It is no place for a young unmarried girl to be at this hour of night.'

'I don't understand,' the captain said uneasily, with a sideways glance at Devine. 'Is she a relative of yours?'

'No, sir,' Whelan said emphatically. 'She's nothing whatever to me.'

'Then I don't see what you want her for,' said the captain.

'That's as I'd expect, sir,' Whelan said stolidly, studying his nails.

'Oh, for Heaven's sake!' exclaimed Devine, exasperated by the old man's boorishness. 'You see, captain,' he said patiently, bending forward with his worried air, his head tilted back as though he feared his pince-nez might fall off, 'this girl is one of Father Whelan's parishioners. She's not a very good girl – not that I mean there's much harm in her,' he added hastily, catching a note of unction in his own tone which embarrassed him, 'but she's a bit wild. It's Father Whelan's duty to keep her as far as he can from temptation. He is the shepherd, and she is one of his stray sheep,' he added with a faint smile at his own eloquence.

The captain bent forward and touched him lightly on the knee.

'You're a funny race,' he said with interest. 'I've travelled the whole world and met with Englishmen everywhere, and I will never understand you. Never!'

'We're not English, man,' Whelan said with the first trace of interest he had so far displayed. 'Don't you know what country you're in? This is Ireland.'

'Same thing,' said the captain.

'It is not the same thing,' said Whelan.

'Surely, captain,' Devine protested gently with his head cocked, sizing up his man, 'we admit some distinction?'

'Distinction?' the captain said. 'Pooh!'

'At the Battle of the Boyne you fought for us,' Devine said persuasively. 'We fought for you at Fontenoy and Ramillies.

> When on Ramillies bloody field
> The baffled French were forced to yield,
> The victor Saxon backward reeled
> Before the shock of Clare's Dragoons.'

He recited the lines with the same apologetic smile he had worn when speaking of sheep and shepherds, as though to excuse his momentary lapse into literature, but the captain waved him aside impatiently.

'Your beard!' he said with a groan and a shrug. 'I know all that. You call yourselves Irish, and the others call themselves Scotch, but you are all English. There is no difference. It is always the same; always women, always hypocrisy; always the plaster saint. Who is this girl? The *curé*'s daughter?'

'The *curé*'s daughter?' Devine exclaimed in surprise.

'Whose daughter?' asked Whelan with his mouth hanging.

'Yours, I gather,' Devine said dryly.

'Well, well, well!' the old man said blushing. 'What sort of upbringing do they have? Does he even know we can't get married?'

'I should say he takes it for granted,' replied Devine over his shoulder, more dryly even than before. 'Elle n'est pas sa fille,' he added with amusement to the captain.

'C'est sûr?'

'C'est certain.'

'Sa maîtresse alors?'

'Ni cela non plus,' Devine replied evenly with only the faintest of smiles on the worn shell of his face.

'Ah, bon, bon, bon!' the captain exclaimed excitedly, springing from his seat and striding about the cabin, scowling and waving his arms. 'Bon. C'est bon. Vous vous moquez de moi, monsieur le curé. Comprenez donc, c'est seulement par politesse que j'ai voulu faire croire que c'était sa fille. On voit bien que le vieux est jaloux. Est-ce que je n'ai pas vu les flics qui surveillent mon bateau toute la semaine? Mais croyez-moi, monsieur, je me fiche de lui et de ses agents.'

'He seems to be very excited,' Whelan said with distaste. 'What is he saying?'

'I'm trying to persuade him that she isn't your mistress,' Devine couldn't refrain from saying with quiet malice.

'My what?'

'Your mistress; the woman you live with. He says you're jealous and that you've had detectives watching his ship for a week.'

The blush which had risen to the old man's face began to spread to his neck and ears, and when he spoke, his voice quavered with emotion.

'Well, well, well!' he said. 'We'd better go home, Devine. 'Tis no good talking to that man. He's not right in the head.'

'He probably thinks the same of us,' Devine said as he rose. 'Venez manger demain soir et je vous expliquerai tout,' he added to the captain.

'Je vous remercie, monsieur,' the captain replied with a shrug, 'mais je n'ai pas besoin d'explications. Il n'y a rien d'inattendu, mais vous en faites toute une histoire.' He clapped his hand jovially on Devine's shoulder and almost embraced him. 'Naturellement je vous rends la fille, parce que vous la demandez, mais comprenez bien que je le fais à cause de vous, et non pas à cause de monsieur et de ses agents.' He drew himself up to his full height and glared at the parish priest, who stood in a dumb stupor.

'Oh, quant à moi,' Devine said with weary humour, 'vous feriez mieux en l'emmenant où vous allez. Et moi-même aussi.'

'Quoi?' shouted the captain in desperation, clutching his forehead. 'Vous l'aimez aussi?'

'No, no, no, no,' Devine said good-humouredly, patting him on the arm. 'It's all too complicated, I wouldn't try to understand if I were you.'

'What's he saying now?' asked Whelan with sour suspicion.

'Oh, he seems to think she's my mistress as well,' Devine replied pleasantly. 'He thinks we're sharing her, so far as I can see.'

'Come on, come on!' said Whelan despairingly, making for the gangway. 'My goodness, even I never thought they were as bad as that. And we sending missions to the blacks!'

Meanwhile, the captain had rushed aft and shouted down the stairway. The second girl appeared, small, plump, and weeping too, and the captain, quite moved, slapped her encouragingly on the shoulder and said something in a gruff voice which Devine suspected must be in the nature of advice to choose younger lovers for the future. Then the captain went up bristling to Sullivan, who stood by the gangway, leaning on his folded umbrella, and with fluttering hands and imperious nods ordered him off the vessel.

'Allez-vous-en!' he said curtly. 'Allez, allez, allez!'

Sullivan and Sheridan went first. Dusk had crept suddenly along the quays and lay heaped there the colour of blown sand. Over the bright river-mouth, shining under a bank of dark cloud, a star twinkled. 'The star that bids the shepherd fold,' Devine thought with sad humour. He felt hopeless and lost, as though he were returning to the prison-house of his youth. The parish priest preceded him down the gangway with his old woman's dull face sunk in his broad chest. At the foot he stopped and gazed back at the captain, who was scowling fiercely at him over the ship's side.

'Anyway,' he said heavily, 'thanks be to the Almighty God, your accursed race is withering off the face of the earth.'

Devine, with a bitter smile, raised his battered old hat and pulled the skirts of his coat about him as he stepped on the gangway.

'Vous viendrez demain, monsieur le capitaine?' he asked in his most ingratiating tone.

'Avec plaisir. A demain, monsieur le berger,' replied the captain with a knowing look.

PEASANTS

WHEN MICHAEL JOHN CRONIN STOLE THE FUNDS of the Carricknabreena Hurling, Football and Temperance Association, commonly called the Club, everyone said: 'Devil's cure to him!' ''Tis the price of him!' 'Kind father for him!' 'What did I tell you?' and the rest of the things people say when an acquaintance has got what is coming to him.

And not only Michael John but the whole Cronin family, seed, breed, and generation, came in for it; there wasn't one of them for twenty miles round or a hundred years back but his deeds and sayings were remembered and examined by the light of this fresh scandal. Michael John's father (the heavens be his bed!) was a drunkard who beat his wife, and his father before him a landgrabber. Then there was an uncle or grand-uncle who had been a policeman and taken a hand in the bloody work at Mitchelstown long ago, and an unmarried sister of the same whose good name it would by all accounts have needed a regiment of husbands to restore. It was a grand shaking-up the Cronins got altogether, and anyone who had a grudge in for them, even if it was no more than a thirty-third cousin, had rare sport, dropping a friendly word about it and saying how sorry he was for the poor mother till he had the blood lighting in the Cronin eyes.

There was only one thing for them to do with Michael John; that was to send him to America and let the thing blow over, and that, no doubt, is what they would have done but for a certain unpleasant and extraordinary incident.

Father Crowley, the parish priest, was chairman of the committee. He was a remarkable man, even in appearance; tall, powerfully built, but very stooped, with shrewd, loveless eyes that rarely softened to anyone except two or three old people. He was a strange man, well on in years, noted for his strong political views, which never happened to coincide with those of any party, and as obstinate as the devil himself. Now what should Father Crowley do but try to force the committee to prosecute Michael John?

The committee were all religious men who up to this had never as much as dared to question the judgments of a man of God: yes, faith, and if the priest had been a bully, which to give him his due he wasn't, he might have danced a jig on their backs and they wouldn't have complained. But a man has principles, and the like of this had never been heard of in the parish before. What? Put the police on a boy and he in trouble?

One by one the committee spoke up and said so. 'But he did wrong,' said Father Crowley, thumping the table. 'He did wrong and he should be punished.'

'Maybe so, father,' said Con Norton, the vice-chairman, who acted as spokesman. 'Maybe you're right, but you wouldn't say his poor mother should be punished too and she a widow woman?'

'True for you!' chorused the others.

'Serve his mother right!' said the priest shortly. 'There's none of you but knows better than I do the way that young man was brought up. He's a rogue and his mother is a fool. Why didn't she beat Christian principles into him when she had him on her knee?'

'That might be, too,' Norton agreed mildly. 'I wouldn't say but you're right, but is that any reason his Uncle Peter should be punished?'

'Or his Uncle Dan?' asked another.

'Or his Uncle James?' asked a third.

'Or his cousins, the Dwyers, that keep the little shop in Lissnacarriga, as decent a living family as there is in County Cork?' asked a fourth.

'No, father,' said Norton, 'the argument is against you.'

'Is it indeed?' exclaimed the priest, growing cross. 'Is it so? What the devil has it to do with his Uncle Dan or his Uncle James? What are ye talking about? What punishment is it to them, will ye tell me that? Ye'll be telling me next 'tis a punishment to me and I a child of Adam like himself.'

'Wisha now, father,' asked Norton incredulously, 'do you mean 'tis no punishment to them having one of their own blood made a public show? Is it mad you think we are? Maybe 'tis a thing you'd like done to yourself?'

'There was none of my family ever a thief,' replied Father Crowley shortly.

'Begor, we don't know whether there was or not,' snapped a little man called Daly, a hot-tempered character from the hills.

'Easy, now! Easy, Phil!' said Norton warningly.

'What do you mean by that?' asked Father Crowley, rising and grabbing his hat and stick.

'What I mean,' said Daly, blazing up, 'is that I won't sit here and listen to insinuations about my native place from any foreigner. There are as many rogues and thieves and vagabonds and liars in Cullough as ever there were in Carricknabreena – ay, begod, and more, and bigger! That's what I mean.'

'No, no, no, no,' Norton said soothingly. 'That's not what he means at all, father. We don't want any bad blood between

Cullough and Carricknabreena. What he means is that the
Crowleys may be a fine substantial family in their own country,
but that's fifteen long miles away, and this isn't their country,
and the Cronins are neighbours of ours since the dawn of
history and time, and 'twould be a very queer thing if at this
hour we handed one of them over to the police . . . And now,
listen to me, father,' he went on, forgetting his role of pacifi-
cator and hitting the table as hard as the rest, 'if a cow of mine
got sick in the morning, 'tisn't a Cremin or a Crowley I'd be
asking for help, and damn the bit of use 'twould be to me
if I did. And everyone knows I'm no enemy of the Church
but a respectable farmer that pays his dues and goes to his
duties regularly.'

'True for you! True for you!' agreed the committee.

'I don't give a snap of my finger what you are,' retorted
the priest. 'And now listen to me, Con Norton. I bear young
Cronin no grudge, which is more than some of you can say,
but I know my duty and I'll do it in spite of the lot of you.'

He stood at the door and looked back. They were gazing
blankly at one another, not knowing what to say to such an
impossible man. He shook his fist at them.

'Ye all know me,' he said. 'Ye know that all my life I'm
fighting the long-tailed families. Now, with the help of God,
I'll shorten the tail of one of them.'

Father Crowley's threat frightened them. They knew he
was an obstinate man and had spent his time attacking what
he called the 'corruption' of councils and committees, which
was all very well as long as it happened outside your own parish.
They dared not oppose him openly because he knew too much
about all of them and, in public at least, had a lacerating tongue.
The solution they favoured was a tactful one. They formed
themselves into a Michael John Cronin Fund Committee and
canvassed the parishioners for subscriptions to pay off what

Michael John had stolen. Regretfully they decided that Father
Crowley would hardly countenance a football match for the
purpose.

Then with the defaulting treasurer, who wore a suitably
contrite air, they marched up to the presbytery. Father Crowley
was at his dinner but he told the housekeeper to show them
in. He looked up in astonishment as his dining room filled
with the seven committeemen, pushing before them the cowed
Michael John.

'Who the blazes are ye?' he asked, glaring at them over the
lamp.

'We're the Club Committee, father,' replied Norton.

'Oh, are ye?'

'And this is the treasurer – the ex-treasurer, I should say.'

'I won't pretend I'm glad to see him,' said Father Crowley
grimly.

'He came to say he's sorry, father,' went on Norton. 'He
is sorry, and that's as true as God, and I'll tell you no lie . . .'
Norton made two steps forward and in a dramatic silence laid
a heap of notes and silver on the table.

'What's that?' asked Father Crowley.

'The money, father. 'Tis all paid back now and there's
nothing more between us. Any little crossness there was, we'll
say no more about it, in the name of God.'

The priest looked at the money and then at Norton.

'Con,' he said, 'you'd better keep the soft word for the judge.
Maybe he'll think more of it than I do.'

'The judge, father?'

'Ay, Con, the judge.'

There was a long silence. The committee stood with open
mouths, unable to believe it.

'And is that what you're doing to us, father?' asked Norton
in a trembling voice. 'After all the years, and all we done for

you, is it you're going to show us up before the whole country as a lot of robbers?'

'Ah, ye idiots, I'm not showing ye up.'

'You are then, father, and you're showing up every man, woman and child in the parish,' said Norton. 'And mark my words, 'twon't be forgotten for you.'

The following Sunday Father Crowley spoke of the matter from the altar. He spoke for a full half hour without a trace of emotion on his grim old face, but his sermon was one long, venomous denunciation of the 'long-tailed families' who, according to him, were the ruination of the country and made a mockery of truth, justice, and charity. He was, as his congregation agreed, a shockingly obstinate old man who never knew when he was in the wrong.

After Mass he was visited in his sacristy by the committee. He gave Norton a terrible look from under his shaggy eyebrows, which made that respectable farmer flinch.

'Father,' Norton said appealingly, 'we only want one word with you. One word and then we'll go. You're a hard character, and you said some bitter things to us this morning; things we never deserved from you. But we're quiet, peaceable poor men and we don't want to cross you.'

Father Crowley made a sound like a snort.

'We came to make a bargain with you, father,' said Norton, beginning to smile.

'A bargain?'

'We'll say no more about the whole business if you'll do one little thing – just one little thing – to oblige us.'

'The bargain!' the priest said impatiently. 'What's the bargain?'

'We'll leave the matter drop for good and all if you'll give the boy a character.'

'Yes, father,' cried the committee in chorus. 'Give him

a character! Give him a character!'

'Give him a what?' cried the priest.

'Give him a character, father, for the love of God,' said Norton emotionally. 'If you speak up for him, the judge will leave him off and there'll be no stain on the parish.'

'Is it out of your minds you are, you halfwitted angashores?' asked Father Crowley, his face suffused with blood, his head trembling. 'Here am I all these years preaching to ye about decency and justice and truth and ye no more understand me than that wall there. Is it the way ye want me to perjure myself? Is it the way ye want me to tell a damned lie with the name of Almighty God on my lips? Answer me, is it?'

'Ah, what perjure!' Norton replied wearily. 'Sure, can't you say a few words for the boy? No one is asking you to say much. What harm will it do you to tell the judge he's an honest, good-living, upright lad, and that he took the money without meaning any harm?'

'My God!' muttered the priest, running his hands distractedly through his grey hair. 'There's no talking to ye, no talking to ye, ye lot of sheep.'

When he was gone the committeemen turned and looked at one another in bewilderment.

'That man is a terrible trial,' said one.

'He's a tyrant,' said Daly vindictively.

'He is, indeed,' sighed Norton, scratching his head. 'But in God's holy name, boys, before we do anything, we'll give him one more chance.'

That evening when he was at his tea the committeemen called again. This time they looked very spruce, businesslike, and independent. Father Crowley glared at them.

'Are ye back?' he asked bitterly. 'I was thinking ye would be. I declare to my goodness, I'm sick of ye and yeer old committee.'

'Oh, we're not the committee, father,' said Norton stiffly.

'Ye're not?'

'We're not.'

'All I can say is, ye look mighty like it. And, if I'm not being impertinent, who the deuce are ye?'

'We're a deputation, father.'

'Oh, a deputation! Fancy that, now. And a deputation from what?'

'A deputation from the parish, father. Now, maybe you'll listen to us.'

'Oh, go on! I'm listening, I'm listening.'

'Well, now, 'tis like this, father,' said Norton, dropping his airs and graces and leaning against the table. ''Tis about that little business this morning. Now, father, maybe you don't understand us and we don't understand you. There's a lot of misunderstanding in the world today, father. But we're quiet simple poor men that want to do the best we can for everybody, and a few words or a few pounds wouldn't stand in our way. Now, do you follow me?'

'I declare,' said Father Crowley, resting his elbows on the table, 'I don't know whether I do or not.'

'Well, 'tis like this, father. We don't want any blame on the parish or on the Cronins, and you're the one that can save us. Now all we ask of you is to give the boy a character –'

'Yes, father,' interrupted the chorus, 'give him a character! Give him a character!'

'Give him a character, father, and you won't be troubled by him again. Don't say no to me now till you hear what I have to say. We won't ask you to go next, nigh or near the court. You have pen and ink beside you and one couple of lines is all you need write. When 'tis over you can hand Michael John his ticket to America and tell him not to show his face in Carricknabreena again. There's the price of his ticket, father,' he added, clapping a bundle of notes on the table. 'The Cronins themselves made it up, and we have his mother's word and his own word that he'll clear out the minute 'tis all over.'

'He can go to pot!' retorted the priest. 'What is it to me where he goes?'

'Now, father, can't you be patient?' Norton asked reproachfully. 'Can't you let me finish what I'm saying? We know 'tis no advantage to you, and that's the very thing we came to talk about. Now, supposing – just supposing for the sake of argument – that you do what we say, there's a few of us here, and between us, we'd raise whatever little contribution to the parish fund you'd think would be reasonable to cover the expense and trouble to yourself. Now do you follow me?'

'Con Norton,' said Father Crowley, rising and holding the edge of the table, 'I follow you. This morning it was perjury, and now 'tis bribery, and the Lord knows what 'twill be next. I see I've been wasting my breath ... And I see too,' he added savagely, leaning across the table towards them, 'a pedigree bull would be more use to ye than a priest.'

'What do you mean by that, father?' asked Norton in a low voice.

'What I say.'

'And that's a saying that will be remembered for you the longest day you live,' hissed Norton, leaning towards him till they were glaring at one another over the table.

'A bull,' gasped Father Crowley. 'Not a priest.'

''Twill be remembered.'

'Will it? Then remember this too. I'm an old man now. I'm forty years a priest, and I'm not a priest for the money or power or glory of it, like others I know. I gave the best that was in me – maybe 'twasn't much but 'twas more than many a better man would give, and at the end of my days ...' lowering his voice to a whisper he searched them with his terrible eyes, '. . . at the end of my days, if I did a wrong thing, or a bad thing, or an unjust thing, there isn't a man or woman in this parish that would brave me to my face and call me a villain. And isn't that a poor story for an old man that tried to be a good priest?' His voice changed again and he raised his head defiantly. 'Now get out before I kick you out!'

And true to his word and character not one word did he say in Michael John's favour the day of the trial, no more than if he was a black. Three months Michael John got and by all accounts he got off light.

He was a changed man when he came out of jail, downcast and dark in himself. Everyone was sorry for him, and people who had never spoken to him before spoke to him then. To all of them he said modestly: 'I'm very grateful to you, friend, for overlooking my misfortune.' As he wouldn't go to America, the committee made another whip-round and between what they had collected before and what the Cronins had made up to send him to America, he found himself with enough to open a small shop. Then he got a job in the County Council, and an agency for some shipping company, till at last he was able to buy a public-house.

As for Father Crowley, till he was shifted twelve months later, he never did a day's good in the parish. The dues went down and the presents went down, and people with money to spend on Masses took it fifty miles away sooner than leave it to him. They said it broke his heart.

He has left unpleasant memories behind him. Only for him, people say, Michael John would be in America now. Only for him he would never have married a girl with money, or had it to lend to poor people in the hard times, or ever sucked the blood of Christians. For, as an old man said to me of him: 'A robber he is and was, and a grabber like his grandfather before him, and an enemy of the people like his uncle, the

policeman; and though some say he'll dip his hand where he
dipped it before, for myself I have no hope unless the mercy
of God would send us another Moses or Brian Boru to cast
him down and hammer him in the dust.'

SONG WITHOUT WORDS

EVEN IF THERE WERE ONLY two men left in the world and both of them saints they wouldn't be happy. One of them would be bound to try and improve the other. That is the nature of things.

I am not, of course, suggesting that either Brother Arnold or Brother Michael was a saint. In private life Brother Arnold was a postman, but as he had a great name as a cattle doctor they had put him in charge of the monastery cows. He had the sort of face you would expect to see advertising somebody's tobacco: a big, innocent, contented face with a pair of blue eyes that were always twinkling. According to the Rule he was supposed to look sedate and go about in a composed and measured way, but he could not keep his eyes downcast for any length of time and wherever his eyes glanced they twinkled, and his hands slipped out of his long white sleeves and dropped some remark in sign language. Most of the monks were good at the deaf and dumb language; it was their way of getting round the Rule of Silence, and it was remarkable how much information they managed to pick up and pass on.

Now, one day it happened that Brother Arnold was looking for a bottle of castor oil and he remembered that he had lent it to Brother Michael, who was in charge of the stables. Brother

Michael was a man he did not get on too well with; a dour, dull sort of man who kept to himself. He was a man of no great appearance, with a mournful wizened little face and a pair of weak red-rimmed eyes – for all the world the sort of man who, if you clapped a bowler hat on his head and a cigarette in his mouth, would need no other reference to get a job in a stable.

There was no sign of him about the stable yard, but this was only natural because he would not be wanted till the other monks returned from the fields, so Brother Arnold pushed in the stable door to look for the bottle himself. He did not see the bottle, but he saw something which made him wish he had not come. Brother Michael was hiding in one of the horse-boxes; standing against the partition with something hidden behind his back and wearing the look of a little boy who has been caught at the jam. Something told Brother Arnold that at that moment he was the most unwelcome man in the world. He grew red, waved his hand to indicate that he did not wish to be involved, and returned to his own quarters.

It came as a shock to him. It was plain enough that Brother Michael was up to some shady business, and Brother Arnold could not help wondering what it was. It was funny, he had noticed the same thing when he was in the world, it was always the quiet, sneaky fellows who were up to mischief. In chapel he looked at Brother Michael and got the impression that Brother Michael was looking at him, a furtive look to make sure he would not be noticed. Next day when they met in the yard he caught Brother Michael glancing at him and gave back a cold look and a nod.

The following day Brother Michael beckoned him to come over to the stables as though one of the horses was sick. Brother Arnold knew it wasn't that; he knew he was about to be given some sort of explanation and was curious to know what it would be. He was an inquisitive man; he knew it, and blamed himself a lot for it.

Brother Michael closed the door carefully after him and then leaned back against the jamb of the door with his legs crossed and his hands behind his back, a foxy pose. Then he nodded in the direction of the horse-box where Brother Arnold had almost caught him in the act, and raised his brows inquiringly. Brother Arnold nodded gravely. It was not an occasion he was likely to forget. Then Brother Michael put his hand up his sleeve and held out a folded newspaper. Brother Arnold shrugged his shoulders as though to say the matter had nothing to do with him, but the other man nodded and continued to press the newspaper on him.

He opened it without any great curiosity, thinking it might be some local paper Brother Michael smuggled in for the sake of the news from home and was now offering as the explanation of his own furtive behaviour. He glanced at the name and then a great light broke on him. His whole face lit up as though an electric torch had been switched on behind, and finally he burst out laughing. He couldn't help himself. Brother Michael did not laugh but gave a dry little cackle which was as near as he ever got to laughing. The name of the paper was the *Irish Racing News*.

Now that the worst was over Brother Michael grew more relaxed. He pointed to a heading about the Curragh and then at himself. Brother Arnold shook his head, glancing at him expectantly as though he were hoping for another laugh. Brother Michael scratched his head for some indication of what he meant. He was a slow-witted man and had never been good at the sign talk. Then he picked up the sweeping brush and straddled it. He pulled up his skirts, stretched out his left hand holding the handle of the brush, and with his right began flogging the air behind him, a grim look on his leather little face. Inquiringly he looked again and Brother Arnold nodded excitedly and put his thumbs up to show he understood. He saw now that the real reason Brother Michael had behaved so queerly was that he read racing papers on the sly and he did so because in private life he had been a jockey on the Curragh.

He was still laughing like mad, his blue eyes dancing, wishing only for an audience to tell it to, and then he suddenly remembered all the things he had thought about Brother Michael and bowed his head and beat his breast by way of asking pardon. Then he glanced at the paper again. A mischievous twinkle came into his eyes and he pointed the paper at himself. Brother Michael pointed back, a bit puzzled. Brother Arnold chuckled and stowed the paper up his sleeve. Then Brother Michael winked and gave the thumbs-up sign. In that slow cautious way of his he went down the stable and reached to the top of the wall where the roof sloped down on it. This, it seemed, was his hiding-hole. He took down several more papers and gave them to Brother Arnold.

For the rest of the day Brother Arnold was in the highest spirits. He winked and smiled at everyone till they all wondered what the joke was. He still pined for an audience. All that evening and long after he had retired to his cubicle he rubbed his hands and giggled with delight whenever he thought of it; it was like a window let into his loneliness; it gave him a warm, mellow feeling, as though his heart had expanded to embrace all humanity.

It was not until the following day that he had a chance of looking at the papers himself. He spread them on a rough desk under a feeble electric light bulb high in the roof. It was four years since he had seen a paper of any sort, and then it was only a scrap of local newspaper which one of the carters had brought wrapped about a bit of bread and butter. But Brother

Arnold had palmed it, hidden it in his desk, and studied it as if it were a bit of a lost Greek play. He had never known until then the modern appetite for words – printed words, regardless of their meaning. This was merely a County Council wrangle about the appointment of seven warble-fly inspectors, but by the time he was done with it he knew it by heart.

So he did not just glance at the racing papers as a man would in the train to pass the time. He nearly ate them. Blessed words like fragments of tunes coming to him out of a past life; paddocks and point-to-points and two-year-olds, and again he was in the middle of a race-course crowd on a spring day, with silver streamers of light floating down the sky like heavenly bunting. He had only to close his eyes and he could see the refreshment tent again with the golden light leaking like split honey through the rents in the canvas, and the girl he had been in love with sitting on an upturned lemonade box. 'Ah, Paddy,' she had said, 'sure there's bound to be racing in heaven!' She was fast, too fast for Brother Arnold, who was a steady-going fellow and had never got over the shock of discovering that all the time she had been running another man. But now all he could remember of her was her smile and the tone of her voice as she spoke the words which kept running through his head, and afterwards whenever his eyes met Brother Michael's he longed to give him a hearty slap on the back and say: 'Michael, boy, there's bound to be racing in heaven.' Then he grinned and Brother Michael, though he didn't hear the words or the tone of voice, without once losing his casual melancholy air, replied with a wall-faced flicker of the horny eyelid, a tick-tack man's signal, a real, expressionless, horsey look of complete understanding.

One day Brother Michael brought in a few papers. On one he pointed to the horses he had marked, on the other to the horses who had won. He showed no signs of his jubilation.

He just winked, a leathery sort of wink, and Brother Arnold gaped as he saw the list of winners. It filled him with wonder and pride to think that when so many rich and clever people had lost, a simple little monk living hundreds of miles away could work it all out. The more he thought of it the more excited he grew. For one wild moment he felt it might be his duty to tell the Abbot, so that the monastery could have the full advantage of Brother Michael's intellect, but he realised that it wouldn't do. Even if Brother Michael could restore the whole abbey from top to bottom with his winnings, the ecclesiastical authorities would disapprove of it. But more than ever he felt the need of an audience.

He went to the door, reached up his long arm, and took down a loose stone from the wall above it. Brother Michael shook his head several times to indicate how impressed he was by Brother Arnold's ingenuity. Brother Arnold grinned. Then he took down a bottle and handed it to Brother Michael. The ex-jockey gave him a questioning look as though he were wondering if this wasn't cattle-medicine; his face did not change but he took out the cork and sniffed. Still his face did not change. All at once he went to the door, gave a quick glance up and a quick glance down and then raised the bottle to his lips. He reddened and coughed; it was good beer and he wasn't used to it. A shudder as of delight went through him and his little eyes grew moist as he watched Brother Arnold's throttle working on well-oiled hinges. The big man put the bottle back in its hiding-place and indicated by signs that Brother Michael could go there himself whenever he wanted and have a drink. Brother Michael shook his head doubtfully, but Brother Arnold nodded earnestly. His fingers moved like lightning while he explained how a farmer whose cow he had cured had it left in for him every week.

The two men were now fast friends. They no longer had

any secrets from one another. Each knew the full extent of the other's little weaknesses and liked him the more for it. Though they couldn't speak to one another they sought out one another's company and whenever other things failed they merely smiled. Brother Arnold felt happier than he had felt for years. Brother Michael's successes made him want to try his hand, and whenever Brother Michael gave him a racing paper with his own selections marked, Brother Arnold gave it back with his, and they waited impatiently till the results turned up three or four days late. It was also a new lease of life to Brother Michael, for what comfort is it to a man if he has all the winners when not a soul in the world can ever know whether he has or not. He felt now that if only he could have a bob each way on a horse he would ask no more of life.

It was Brother Arnold, the more resourceful of the pair, who solved that difficulty. He made out dockets, each valued for so many Hail Marys, and the loser had to pay up in prayers for the other man's intention. It was an ingenious scheme and it worked admirably. At first Brother Arnold had a run of luck. But it wasn't for nothing that Brother Michael had had the experience; he was too tough to make a fool of himself even over a few Hail Marys, and everything he did was carefully planned. Brother Arnold began by imitating him, but the moment he struck it lucky he began to gamble wildly. Brother Michael had often seen it happen on the Curragh and remembered the fate of those it had happened to. Men he had known with big houses and cars were now cadging drinks in the streets of Dublin. It struck him that God had been very good to Brother Arnold in calling him to a monastic life where he could do no harm to himself or to his family.

And this, by the way, was quite uncalled-for, because in the world Brother Arnold's only weakness had been for a bottle of stout and the only trouble he had ever caused his family was the discomfort of having to live with a man so good and gentle, but Brother Michael was rather given to a distrust of human nature, the sort of man who goes looking for a moral in everything even when there is no moral in it. He tried to make Brother Arnold take an interest in the scientific side of betting but the man seemed to treat it all as a great joke. A flighty sort of fellow! He bet more and more wildly with that foolish good-natured grin on his face, and after a while Brother Michael found himself being owed a deuce of a lot of prayers, which his literal mind insisted on translating into big houses and cars. He didn't like that either. It gave him scruples of conscience and finally turned him against betting altogether. He tried to get Brother Arnold to drop it, but as became an inventor, Brother Arnold only looked hurt and indignant, like a child who has been told to stop his play. Brother Michael had that weakness on his conscience too. It suggested that he was getting far too attached to Brother Arnold, as in fact he was. There was something warm and friendly about the man which you couldn't help liking.

Then one day he went in to Brother Arnold and found him with a pack of cards in his hand. They were a very old pack which had more than served their time in some farmhouse, but Brother Arnold was looking at them in rapture. The very sight of them gave Brother Michael a turn. Brother Arnold made the gesture of dealing, half playfully, and the other shook his head sternly. Brother Arnold blushed and bit his lip but he persisted, seriously enough now. All the doubts Brother Michael had been having for weeks turned to conviction. This was the primrose path with a vengeance, one thing leading to another. Brother Arnold grinned and shuffled the deck; Brother Michael, biding his time, cut for deal and Brother Arnold won. He dealt two hands of five and showed the five of hearts as trump. He wanted to play twenty-five. Still waiting for a sign, Brother Michael looked at his own hand. His face grew grimmer. It was not the sort of sign he had expected but it was a sign all the same; four hearts in a bunch; the ace, jack, two other trumps, and the three of spades. An unbeatable hand. Was that luck? Was that coincidence or was it the Adversary himself, taking a hand and trying to draw him deeper in the mire?

He liked to find a moral in things, and the moral in this was plain, though it went to his heart to admit it. He was a lonseome, melancholy man and the horses had meant a lot to him in his bad spells. At times it had seemed as if they were the only thing that kept him sane. How could he face twenty, perhaps thirty, years more of life, never knowing what horses were running or what jockeys were up – Derby Day, Punchestown, Leopardstown, and the Curragh all going by while he knew no more of them than if he were already dead?

'O Lord,' he thought bitterly, 'a man gives up the whole world for You, his chance of a wife and kids, his home and his family, his friends and his job, and goes off to a bare mountain where he can't even tell his troubles to the man alongside him, and still he keeps something back, some little thing to remind him of what he gave up. With me 'twas the sup of beer, and I dare say there are fellows inside who have a bit of a girl's hair hidden somewhere they can go and look at it now and again. I suppose we all have our little hiding-hole if the truth was known, but as small as it is, the whole world is in it, and bit by bit it grows on us again till the day You find us out.'

Brother Arnold was waiting for him to play. He sighed and put his hand on the desk. Brother Arnold looked at it and at him. Brother Michael idly took away the spade and added the heart and still Brother Arnold couldn't see. Then Brother Michael shook his head and pointed to the floor. Brother

Arnold bit his lip again as though he were on the point of crying, then threw down his hand and walked to the other end of the cowhouse. Brother Michael left him so for a few moments. He could see the struggle going on in the man, could almost hear the devil whisper in his ear that he (Brother Michael) was only an old woman – Brother Michael had heard that before; that life was long and a man might as well be dead and buried as not have some little innocent amusement – the sort of plausible whisper that put many a man on the gridiron. He knew, however hard it was now, that Brother Arnold would be grateful to him in the other world. 'Brother Michael,' he would say, 'I don't know what I'd ever have done without your example.'

Then Brother Michael went up and touched him gently on the shoulder. He pointed to the bottle, the racing paper, and the cards. Brother Arnold fluttered his hands despairingly but he nodded. They gathered them up between them, the cards, the bottle, and the papers, hid them under their habits to avoid all occasion of scandal, and went off to confess their guilt to the Prior.

LOST FATHERLANDS

ONE SPRING DAY, Father Felix in the monastery sent word down to Spike Ward, the motor driver, to pick up a gentleman for the four-fifteen train. Spike had no notion of who the gentleman was. All sorts came and went to that lonesome monastery up the mountain: people on pilgrimage, drunks going in for a cure, cures coming out for a drunk, men joining the novitiate, and others leaving it, some of them within twenty-four hours – they just took one good look at the place and bolted. One of the novices stole a suit of overalls left behind by a house painter and vanished across the mountain. As Spike often said, if it was him he wouldn't have waited to steal the overalls.

It lay across the mountainside, a gaunt, Victorian barracks. Spike drove up to the guesthouse, which stood away in by the end of the chapel. Father Felix, the Guestmaster, was waiting on the steps with the passenger – a tall, well-built, middle-aged man with greying hair. Father Felix himself inclined to fat; he wore big, shiny glasses, and his beard cascaded over his chest. Spike and the passenger loaded the trunk and bag, and Spike noticed that they were labelled for Canada. The liner was due at Cobh two days later.

'Goodbye now,' Father Felix said, shaking the passenger's

hand. 'And mind and don't lead Spike into bad ways on me. He's a fellow I have my eye on this long time. When are you coming up to us for good, Spike?' he asked gravely.

'When ye take a few women into the Order, father,' Spike replied in his thin drawl. 'What this place needs is a woman's hand.'

The passenger sat in front with Spike, and they chatted as they drove down the hill, glancing back at the monks working in the fields behind the monastery. You could see them from a long way off, like magpies.

'Was it on a holiday you were?' asked Spike, not meaning to be inquisitive, only to make conversation.

'A long holiday,' said the passenger, with a nod and a smile.

'Ah, well, everyone to his taste,' Spike said tolerantly. 'I suppose a lot depends on what you're used to. I prefer a bit of a change myself, like Father Felix's dipsos.'

'He has a few of them up there now,' said the passenger, with a quiet amusement that told Spike he wasn't one of them.

'Well, I'm sure I hope the poor souls are enjoying it,' said Spike with unction.

'They weren't enjoying it much at three this morning,' said the passenger in the same tone. 'One of them was calling for his mother. Father Felix was with him for over an hour, trying to calm him.'

'Not criticising the good man, 'tisn't the same thing at all,' Spike said joyously.

'Except for the feeding bottle,' said the passenger. And then, as though he were slightly ashamed of his own straight-faced humour: 'He does a wonderful job on them.'

'Well, they seem to have great faith in him,' Spike said, without undue credulity. 'He gets them from England and all parts – a decent little man.'

'And a saintly little man,' the passenger said, almost reproachfully.

'I dare say,' Spike said, without enthusiasm. 'He'd want to be, judging by the specimens I see.'

They reached town with about three-quarters of an hour to spare, and put the trunk and bag in the stationmaster's office. Old Mick Hurley, the stationmaster, was inside, and looked at the bags over his glasses. Even on a warm day, in his own office, he wore his braided frock-coat and uniform cap.

'This is a gent from the monastery, Mick,' said Spike. 'He's travelling by the four-fifteen. Would he have time for the pictures?'

But Spike might have known the joke would be lost on Mick, who gave a hasty glance at the clock behind him and looked alarmed. 'He'd hardly have time for that,' he said. 'She's only about twenty-five minutes late.'

'You have over an hour to put in,' said Spike as they left the office. 'You don't want to be sitting round there the whole time. Hanagan's lounge is comfortable enough, if you like a drink.'

'Will you have one with me?' asked the passenger.

'I don't know will I have the time,' Spike said. 'I have another call at four. I'll have one drink with you, anyway.'

They went into the bar, which was all done up in chromium, with concealed lighting. Tommy Hanagan, the Yank, was behind the bar himself. He was a tall, fresh-faced, rather handsome man, with fair hair of a dirty colour and smoke-blue eyes. His hat was perched far back on his head. Spike often said Tommy Hanagan was the only man he knew who could make a hat speak. He had earned the price of his public-house working in Boston and, according to him, had never ceased to regret his return. Tommy looked as though he lived in hopes that some day, when he did something as it should be done, it would turn out to be a convenience to somebody. So far, it had earned him nothing but mockery, and sometimes his blue eyes had a slightly bewildered expression, as though he were wondering what he was doing in that place at all.

Spike loved rousing him. All you had to do was give him one poke about America and the man was off, good for an hour's argument. America was the finest goddam country on the face of the earth, and the people that criticised it didn't know what they were talking about. In America, even the priests were friends: 'Tommy, where the hell am I going to get a hundred dollars?' 'I'll get it for you, Father Joe.' In Ireland, it was 'Mister Hanagan, don't you consider five pounds is a bit on the small side?' 'And I don't,' the Yank would say, pulling up his shirtsleeves. 'I'd sooner give a hundred dollars to a friend than fifteen to a bastard like that.' The same with the women. Over there, an Irishman would say, 'I'll do the washing up, Mary.' Here it was 'Where's that bloody tea, woman?' And then bawling her out for it! Not, as Spike noticed, that this ever prevented the Yank from bawling out his own wife twenty times a day. And Spike suspected that however he might enjoy rousing the Yank, the Yank enjoyed it more. It probably gave the poor man the illusion of being alive.

'What are you drinking?' the passenger asked in his low voice.

'Whiskey,' said Spike. 'I have to take whiskey every time I go up to that monastery. It's to restore the circulation.'

'Beer for me, please,' said the passenger.

'Your circulation is easily damaged, Spike,' said Hanagan as he turned to the whiskey bottle.

'If you knew as much about that place as I do, you'd be looking for whiskey, too.'

'Who said I don't know about it?' blustered Hanagan. 'I know as much about it as you do; maybe more.'

'You do,' Spike said mockingly. 'Yourself and the kids went up there two years ago, picking primroses. I heard about it. Ye brought the flask and had tea up the mountain two miles away. "Oh, what a lovely place the monks have! Oh, what a wonderful life they have up here!"Damn all you care about the poor unfortunates, getting up at half past one of a winter's morning and waiting till half five for a bit of breakfast.'

The Yank sprawled across the counter, pushing his hat back a shade farther. It was set for reasonable discussion. 'But what's that, only habit?' he asked.

'Habit!'

'What else is it?' the Yank asked appealingly. 'I have to get up at half past six every morning, winter and summer, and I have to worry about a wife and kids, and education and doctors for them, and paying income tax, which is more than the monks have to do.'

'Give me the income tax every time!' said Spike. 'Even the wife!'

'The remarkable thing about this country,' said Hanagan, 'is that they'll only get up in the morning when no one asks them to. I never asked the monks to get up at half past one. All I ask is that the people in this blooming town will get up at half past eight and open their shops by nine o'clock. And how many of them will do it?'

'And what the hell has that to do with the argument?' asked Spike, not that he thought it had anything to do with it. He knew only too well the Yank's capacity for getting carried away on a tide of his own eloquence.

'Well, what after all does the argument boil down to?' retorted Hanagan. 'The argument is that no one in this blooming country is respected for doing what he ought to do – only for doing what no one ever asked him to do.'

'Are people to sit down and wait for someone to ask them

to love God?' the passenger growled suddenly. Spike noticed that even though he mentioned God, he looked a nasty customer to cross in a discussion.

'I didn't say that,' Hanagan replied peaceably. 'But do you know this town?'

'No.'

'I do,' said Hanagan. 'I know it since I was a kid. I spent eighteen years out of it, and for all the difference it made to the town, I might have been out of it for a week. It's dead. The people are dead. They're no use to God or man.'

'You didn't answer my question.'

'You're talking about one sort of responsibility,' said Hanagan. 'I'm only saying there are other responsibilities. Why can't the people here see that they have a responsibility to the unfortunate women they marry? Why can't they see their responsibility to their own country?'

'What Tommy means is that people shouldn't be making pilgrimages to the monastery at all,' said Spike dryly. 'He thinks they should be making pilgrimages to him. He lights candles to himself every night – all because he doesn't beat his wife. Good luck to you now, and don't let him make you miss your train with his old guff.'

Spike and the passenger shook hands, and after that Spike put him out of his head completely. Meeting strangers like that, every day of the week, he couldn't remember the half of them. But three evenings later he was waiting in the car outside the station, hoping to pick up a fare from the four-fifteen, when Mick Hurley came flopping out to him with his spectacles down his nose.

'What am I going to do with them bags you left on Tuesday, Spike?' he asked.

What was he to do with the bags? Spike looked at him without comprehension. 'What bags, Mick?'

'Them bags for Canada.'

'Holy God!' exclaimed Spike, getting slowly out of the car. 'Do you mean he forgot his bags?'

'Forgot them?' Mick Hurley repeated indignantly. 'He never travelled at all, man.'

'Holy God!' repeated Spike. 'And the liner gone since yesterday! That's a nice state of affairs.'

'Why?' asked Mick. 'Who was it?'

'A man from the monastery.'

'One of Father Felix's drunks?'

'What the hell would a drunk be coming from Canada for?' asked Spike in exasperation.

'You'd never know,' said Mick. 'Where did you leave him?'

'Over in Tommy Hanagan's bar.'

'Then we'd better ask Tommy.'

Hanagan came out to them in his shirtsleeves, his cuffs rolled up and his hat well back.

'Tommy,' said Spike, 'you remember that passenger I left in your place on Tuesday?'

Tommy's eyes narrowed. 'The big, grey-haired bloke?' he said. 'What about him?'

'Mick Hurley here says he never took that train. You wouldn't know what happened him?'

Tommy rested one bare, powerful arm against the jamb of the door, leaned his head against it, and delicately tilted the hat forward over his eyes. 'That sounds bad,' he said. 'You're sure he didn't go off unknown to you?'

'How could he, man?' asked Mick excitedly, feeling that some slight on the railway company was implied. 'His bags are still there. No one but locals travelled on that train.'

'The man had a lot of money on him,' Hanagan said, looking at the ground.

'You're sure of that, Tommy?' Spike asked, in alarm. It was

bad enough for a motor driver to be mixed up in a mysterious disappearance without a murder coming into it as well.

'Up to a hundred pounds,' Hanagan said, giving a sharp glance up the street. 'I saw it when he paid for the drinks. I noticed Linehan, of the Guards, going in to his dinner. We might as well go over and ask him did he hear anything.'

They strode briskly in the direction of the policeman's house. Linehan came shuffling out, buttoning up his tunic – a fat, black-haired man who looked like something out of a butcher's shop.

'I didn't hear a word of it,' he said, looking from one to another, as though they might be concealing evidence. 'We'll ring up a few of the local stations. Some of them might have word of him.'

Hanagan went to get his coat. Mick Hurley had to leave them, to look after the four-fifteen, and at last Spike, Hanagan and Linehan went to the police station, where the others waited while Linehan had long, confidential chats about football and the weather with other policemen for ten miles around. Guards are lonely souls; they cannot trust their nearest and dearest, and can communicate only with one another, like mountaineers with signal fires. Hanagan sat on the table, pretending to read a paper, though every look and gesture betrayed impatience and disgust. Spike just sat, reflecting mournfully on the loss of his good time and money.

'We'll have to find out what his name was,' Linehan said, at last. 'The best thing we can do is drive up to the monastery and get more particulars.'

'The devil fly away with Mick Hurley!' Spike said bitterly. 'Wouldn't you think he'd tell us what happened without waiting three days? If he was after losing an express train, he'd wait a week to see would it turn up.'

The three of them got into Spike's car, and he drove off

up the mountain road, wondering how he was to get his fare
out of it and from whom. The monks were holy enough, but
they expected you to run a car on holy water, and a policeman
thought he was doing you a favour if he was seen in the car
with you. The veiled sunlight went out; they ran into thick
mist, and before they reached the mountain-top, it had turned
to rain. They could see it driving in for miles from the sea.
The lights were on in the chapel; there was some service on.
Spike noticed the Yank pause under the traceried window and
look away down the valley. Within the church, the choir
wailed, 'Et exspecto resurrectionem mortuorum. Et vitam
venturi saeculi.'

Father Felix came out and beckoned them in from the rain.
His face was very grave. 'You needn't tell me what you came
about, lads,' he said.

'You knew he was missing so, father?' said Linehan.

'We saw him,' said the priest.

'Where, father?' asked Spike.

'Out there,' Father Felix said, with a nod.

'On the mountain?'

'I dare say he's there still.'

'But what is he doing?'

'Oh, nothing. Nothing only staring. Staring at the monastery
and the monks working in the fields. Poor fellow! Poor
fellow!'

'But who is it?'

'One of our own men. One of the old monks. He's here
these fifteen years.'

'Fifteen years!' exclaimed Linehan. 'But what came over him
after all that time?'

'Some nervous trouble, I suppose,' said Father Felix in the
tone of a healthy man who has heard of nerves as a well-
recognised ailment of quite respectable people. 'A sort of mental

blackout, I heard them saying. He wouldn't know where he'd be for a few minutes at a time.'

'Ah, poor soul! Poor soul!' sighed Linehan, with a similar blankness of expression.

'But what was taking him to Canada?' asked Hanagan.

'Ah, well, we had to send him somewhere he wouldn't be known,' explained Father Felix sadly. 'He wanted to settle down in his own place in Kilkenny, but, of course, he couldn't.'

'Why not?' asked Hanagan.

'Oh, he couldn't, he couldn't,' Linehan said, with a sharp intake of breath as he strode to the window. 'Not after leaving the monastery. 'Twould cause terrible scandal.'

'That's why I hope you can get him away quietly,' Father Felix said. 'We did everything we could for him. Now the less talk there is, the better.'

'In that bleddy mist you might be searching the mountain for a week,' sighed Linehan, who had often shot it. 'If we knew where to look itself! We'll go up the road and see would any of Sullivan's boys have word of him.'

Sullivans' was the nearest farmhouse. The three men got into the car again and drove slowly down under the trees past the monastery. There was an iron railing, which seemed strangely out of place, and then a field, and then the bare mountain again. It was coming on to dark, and it struck Spike that they would find no one that night. He was sorry for that poor devil, and could not get over the casualness of Mick Hurley. A stationmaster! God, wouldn't you think he'd have some sense?

'It isn't Mick Hurley I blame at all,' Hanagan said angrily.

'Ah, well, Tommy, you can't be too hard on the poor monks,' Linehan said reasonably. 'I suppose they were hoping he'd go away and not cause any scandal.'

'A poor bloody loony!' snapped the Yank, his emotion

bringing out a strong Boston accent. 'Gahd, you wouldn't do it to a dawg!'

'How sure you are he was a loony!' Spike said, with a sneer. 'He didn't seem so very loony to me.'

'But you heard what Father Felix said!' Hanagan cried. 'Mental blackouts. That poor devil is somewhere out on that goddam mountain with his memory gone.'

'Ah, I'll believe all I hear when I eat all I get,' Spike said in the same tone.

It wasn't that he really disbelieved in the blackouts so much as that he had trained himself to take things lightly, and the Yank was getting on his nerves. At that moment he spotted the passenger out of the corner of his eye. The rain seemed to have caught him somewhere on top of a peak, and he was running, looking for shelter, from rock to rock. Without looking round, Spike stopped the car quietly and lit a cigarette.

'Don't turn round now, boys!' he said. 'He's just over there on our right.'

'What do you think we should do, Spike?' Linehan asked.

'Get out of the car quietly and break up, so that we can come round him from different directions,' said Spike.

'Then you'd scare him properly,' said Hanagan. 'Let me go and talk to him!'

Before they could hinder him, he was out of the car and running up the slope from the road. Spike swore. He knew if the monk took to his heels now, they might never catch him. Hanagan shouted and the monk halted, stared, then walked towards him.

'It looks as if he might come quietly,' said Linehan. He and Spike followed Hanagan slowly.

Hanagan stopped on a little hillock, hatless, his hands in his trousers pockets. The monk came up to him. He, too, was hatless; his raincoat was covered with mud; and he wore what looked like a week's growth of beard. He had a sullen, frightened look, like an old dog called to heel after doing something wrong.

'That's a bad evening now,' Hanagan said, with an awkward smile, which made him look unexpectedly boyish.

'I hope you're not taking all this trouble for me,' the monk said, looking first at Hanagan, then at Spike and the policeman, who stood a little apart from him.

'Ah, what trouble?' Hanagan said, with fictitious lightness. 'We were afraid you might be caught in the mist. It's bad enough even for those that know the mountain. You'd want to get those wet things off you quick.'

'I suppose so,' the monk said, looking down at his drenched clothes as though he were seeing them for the first time. Spike could now believe in the mental blackout, the man looked so stunned, like a sleepwalker.

'We'll stop at the pub and Spike can bring over whatever bags you want,' said Hanagan.

The public-house hotel looked uncannily bright after the loneliness of the mountain. Hanagan was at his most obnoxiously efficient. Linehan wanted to take a statement from the monk, but Hanagan stopped him. 'Is it a man in that state? How could he give you a statement?' He rushed in and out, his hat on the back of his head, producing hot whiskeys for them all, sending Spike to the station for the bag, and driving his wife and the maid mad seeing that there was hot water and shaving tackle in the bathroom and that a hot meal was prepared.

When the monk came down, shaved and in dry clothes, Hanagan sat opposite him, his legs spread and his hands on his thighs.

'What you'll do,' he said, with a commanding air, 'is rest here for a couple of days.'

'No thanks,' the monk said, shaking his head.

'It won't cost you anything,' Hanagan said, with a smile.

'It's not that,' said the monk in a low voice. 'I'd better get away from this.'

'But you can't, man. You'll have to see about getting your tickets changed. We can see to that for you. You might get pneumonia after being out so long.'

'I'll have to go on,' the monk said stubbornly. 'I have to get away.'

'You mean you're afraid you might do the same thing again?' Hanagan said in a disappointed tone. 'Maybe you're right. Though what anyone wants to go back to that place for beats me.'

'What do people want to go back anywhere for?' the monk asked in a dull tone.

Spike thought it was as close as ever he'd seen anyone get to knocking the Yank off his perch. Hanagan grew red, then rose and went in the direction of the door, suddenly changed his mind, and turned to grasp the monk's left hand in his own two. 'I'm a good one to talk,' he said in a thick voice. 'Eighteen years, and never a day without thinking of this place. You mightn't believe it, but there were nights I cried myself to sleep. And for what, I ask you? What did I expect?'

He had changed suddenly; no longer the bighearted, officious ward boss looking after someone in trouble, he had become humble and almost deferential. When they were leaving, he half opened the front door and halted. 'You're sure you won't stay?' he snapped over his shoulder.

'Sure,' said the monk, with a nod.

Hanagan waved his left arm, and they went out across the dark square to the station.

Spike and he saw the last of the monk, who waved to them till the train disappeared in the darkness. Hanagan followed it, waving, with a mawkish smile, as though he were seeing off a girl. Spike could see that he was deeply moved, but what it was all about was beyond him. Spike had never stood on the deck of a liner and watched his fatherland drop away behind him. He didn't know the sort of hurt it can leave in a boy's mind, a hurt that doesn't heal even when you try to conjure away the pain by returning. Nor did he realise, as Hanagan did at that moment, that there are other fatherlands, whose loss can hurt even more deeply.

A MOTHER'S WARNING

ONE WINTER EVENING Father Fogarty's housekeeper let in a strange young woman. She was tall and thin with a slight pale face, and her good manners barely contained a natural excitability of manner. Though he was normally shy of women he was attracted by her and offered her coffee.

'When you know what I came about you probably won't ask me to have coffee,' she replied with a rueful grin.

'In that case I'd better order it first,' he said, responding to her tone.

'You'd better hear what I have to confess and *then* order it,' she suggested slyly.

'By the way, it's not confession you want, is it?' he asked professionally.

'That comes afterwards too, like the coffee,' she replied.

'I don't know what your name is yet,' he said as she sat down.

'Sheila Moriarty.'

'You're not from this part of the world?'

'No. I'm from Limerick. I'm working here in Carr's Stores.'

'How do you like it?'

'The shop is all right. The place itself is fine. Too fine. I suppose that's what got me into the mess I'm in. Oh, I didn't realise it in time, but I was probably brought up too sheltered.'

'How many of you are there?' he asked.

'Six. Three boys, three girls. Daddy is an insurance agent; Mummy – well, I suppose Mummy is a saint.'

'A what?' he asked in surprise.

'Oh, I don't mean it that way, but she is, really. Trying to bring up six of us on Daddy's couple of quid and see that we had everything – education, music, religion. I'm damn full sure I couldn't do it. Now, here I am after less than a year away bringing disgrace on her!'

'What did you do?' he asked quietly.

'Stole stuff from the shop,' she replied sullenly. In Fogarty's experience there were two sorts of women criers, the ones who cried at once and the ones who got sullen. She was the sort who got sullen. 'Nice, aren't I?' she asked with a bitter little smile.

For a few moments he could say nothing. With her looks and temperament he would have expected her to say that she was pregnant, but you could never tell with women.

'How serious is it?' he asked gravely, and she opened her handbag and put a brooch on the little table beside her. It looked to him as silly as any other brooch – a sort of golden leaf that he couldn't imagine anyone's risking a job for.

'How much is it worth?' he asked doubtfully.

'Three quid,' she said.

'Can't you put it back?' he asked, and she shook her head slowly.

'I'm in a different department now.'

'Or put the price of it in the till?'

'Not without its being spotted.'

'All right,' he said. 'Send them a postal order anonymously. They won't ask any questions.'

'It's not as simple as that,' she said. 'Somebody knows I stole it.'

'Oh!' he exclaimed. 'Somebody in the shop?'

'Yes. An assistant manager. He encouraged me, in fact. He said the whole staff did it. Maybe they do; I don't know, but it doesn't matter anyhow. I should have known better.'

'I take it this manager fellow is a man?'

'Yes. His name is Michael Joyce. He lives in St Mary's Road.'

'Is he married by any chance?'

That did it. She began to sob dryly and bitterly. Then she dabbed her nose viciously with a handkerchief and went on talking as though at random.

'Cripes, and before I left home Mummy told me never to take anything that belonged to my employers. I went into hysterics on her. It shows you the way we were brought up. I didn't know people could do things like that. And *then* she told me not to have anything to do with married men because they weren't all like Daddy! We always thought she was so blooming innocent. She wasn't as innocent as we were, though.'

'You'd better tell me the rest of this,' Fogarty said sternly. 'How far has this thing gone?'

'Too far.'

'You mean you and he have been living together?'

'Near enough to it anyway. And that's what he wants.'

'But it's not what you want?'

'Not now,' she said almost angrily. 'At first, I suppose I let myself be dazzled. I must have when I let him persuade me to pinch that, mustn't I? Now that I know what he's like I'd sooner pitch myself in the river.'

'What is he like?' Fogarty asked.

'Oh, he's not what you think,' she said ruefully. 'He's clever. I know he's smooth and he's a liar, but he could probably get round you too if it was worth his while.'

'What do you mean when you say he's a liar?' Fogarty asked, weighing it up.

'I mean he told me things about his wife, and *they* were lies.'

'How do you know?'

'Because I met her.'

'Oh, so you know his wife?'

'I do. He made me come to his house one night after work for a bit of supper. It nearly choked me. That was when I turned against him. He brought me there deliberately to show me off to her. He watched us the whole time. And everything he'd said was wrong. She was decent and she was as frightened of him as I was. There's a devil in that man.'

'Is that all?' he asked.

'Isn't it enough?' she retorted. 'I think only for that last evening he could have done what he liked with me. But he isn't normal.'

'I mean, could we have the coffee in now?' he asked with an encouraging smile. Then he went to the head of the stairs and bellowed 'Mary! Coffee!' He shut the room door behind him and swaggered back to the mantelpiece. 'I'll have to think what's the best thing to do,' he said, sounding more confident than he felt. 'About this, to begin with,' he added, picking up the brooch. 'I gather you have no further use for it?'

'I wish to God I'd never seen it,' she said.

'You won't see it again,' he said, and put it in his coat pocket. 'I have to think about Mr Joyce as well. Meanwhile, whatever you do, don't go anywhere with him. Don't even talk to him. If he annoys you, tell him to go to hell. I suppose he's trying to blackmail you over the brooch?'

'I suppose so, in a way,' she replied uncertainly. 'He's not as crude as that, of course.'

'They never are,' he said from the depths of his worldy wisdom. 'But remember, there's nothing he can do to you that wouldn't injure himself a great deal worse.'

'I wouldn't be too sure of that,' she said doubtfully. 'A fellow in a position like that doesn't have to say "Miss Moriarty stole a brooch from the jewellery counter."'

'I don't think he'll say anything,' Fogarty said forcefully. 'Does he know you were coming to me?'

'No. I never told him anything.'

'If he starts anything, tell him I know everything about it,' he said. 'There's nothing these fellows dread more than a third party who's in on the game. Meanwhile forget about it. But remember, next time you meet a married man, what your mother told you. They're *not* all like your father. She was right there.'

When they had drunk their coffee he saw her to the door and held her hand for a moment.

'Give me two days to see what I can do,' he said. 'I'll be here on Friday night if you want me. Until then, forget about it.'

But this was more than he could do himself. Fogarty, partly because of his character, partly because of his circumstance, was a man who lived a great deal in his own imagination, and something about the girl had set his imagination on fire. Even the few words she had dropped had made him see the sort of home she came from, and the anxious, pious mother who tried to spread out her husband's little income into a full and comfortable life for six children who probably didn't even realise the sacrifices she was making for them, and wouldn't realise it till she was dead and buried. 'A saint', the girl had said, and she was probably right. He had known saints like that whose lives nobody would ever know about, much less write about. He could even see how a girl brought up in a poor, pious, cheerful home like that, where no quarrel was ever allowed to occur that could not be reported later as a joke to friends, and who was then left alone in a cheerless town would be readier than the next to grasp at whatever society offered itself. And he had no difficulty at all in imagining the sinister figure of Joyce, trying to lure the girl from one small misdemeanour to another until eventually he could exercise a moral blackmail on her. He had seen a few men like that as well. What would have happened to the girl if she hadn't had the sense to consult a priest required no imagination at all. But, in spite of his burning determination to frustrate Joyce, he wasn't at all sure what he should do.

Clearly, the first thing was to get some information, and the following evening he called on the curate in Joyce's parish. He was a tall, gentle young man called Rowlands, with whom Fogarty had spent a few months in another part of the diocese.

'Information, Ed!' Fogarty said. 'Information about one of your parishioners!'

'I'm sorry, Jerry, but the seal of the confessional is strictly observed in this parish,' Rowlands said with his old-maidish humour. 'Who is it, tell me?'

'A fellow called Joyce in St Mary's Road.'

'A manager in Carr's?' Rowlands said, stroking his long jaw thoughtfully. 'I know the man you mean. He's a small, bouncy little chap. It wouldn't be woman trouble, would it?'

'Why?' Fogarty asked keenly. 'Did he have woman trouble?'

'Oh, I heard something I didn't pay much attention to. About two years ago. He used to be a traveller for Carr's before he got the big job.'

'Anything else?'

'Let me see! It's coming back to me. Mind you, I couldn't say it was anything but old talk. He was supposed to be having something to do with a married woman called Trench. She was a Protestant, of course. Anyway, herself and her husband left in a hurry. Is that the sort of thing?'

'More or less,' Fogarty said grimly. 'This time it isn't a Protestant, and I see no reason why the woman should leave town in a hurry. Don't you think I'm right?'

'Oh, I'm sure you are, but all the same I'd be careful, Jerry. That sort of thing can get you into a nasty mess.'

'Ah, aren't I always careful?' Fogarty said with a jolly laugh.

'You are,' Rowlands said cautiously, 'but in unorthodox ways. I'm very orthodox, Jerry. I like to go by the books.'

But Fogarty had heard what he came to hear and his mind was made up. Next morning he rang Joyce up at the shop and suggested that it might be more convenient for both if they met at the presbytery. Joyce fell in with this enthusiastically and arrived that evening at the presbytery, looking as though he hoped to sell Fogarty a new suite of furniture. As a subtle touch Fogarty had left the stolen brooch lying on the little table where Sheila had placed it, but he was disappointed in his hope of seeing Joyce discountenanced. He smiled and picked up the brooch.

'That's a nice little article, father,' he said. 'Fifty bob in the store.'

'Three pounds, I believe,' Fogarty said sternly.

'As much as that?' Joyce said, in what appeared to be genuine surprise. 'Probably costs four and tuppence to make. But that's how we come to be millionaires, father.'

'It belongs to the store,' said Fogarty. 'It might help to make millionaires of you quicker if you took it back there.'

'Me, father?' Joyce asked innocently. 'Of course, I'll take it back if you like, but it might be a bit difficult to explain, mightn't it?'

'Oh, I wouldn't say so,' said Fogarty, beginning to lose his temper. 'You could tell them it was stolen at your instigation.'

'At my instigation?' Joyce repeated quietly. He took a few steps forward and faced Fogarty from the hearth, his arms folded. 'That's a very serious charge, father,' he went on after a moment. 'Are you sure you're in a position to prove it?'

Fogarty was taken aback. The scene wasn't going at all as he had planned it; he was in no position to prove anything, and because of it he began to bluster.

'Yes, and you know who the witness would be,' he said angrily. 'Sheila Moriarty.'

'Sheila Moriarty?' Joyce repeated phrases and names in the manner of one who thinks while he talks, to give himself time. 'And do you think seriously, father, that the Bishop is going to accept the story of a girl you say is a thief and consider that it entitled you to go round making wild charges against me?'

'You tried to seduce that girl,' shouted Fogarty, trying to brazen it out.

'And what else, father?' Joyce asked impudently.

'I believe there is also a lady called Trench, who may have something to say about it,' Fogarty said furiously.

'I see,' Joyce said, but he didn't; again he was only playing for time. Then he suddenly changed from defence to attack, but even then he was very much master of himself as Fogarty was not.

'Has it struck you, father, that Sheila is very well able to look after herself?'

'It hasn't,' Fogarty said shortly.

'Yet when she wants to be protected against me – that's her story, anyway, according to you – she goes to you and not the parish priest! Doesn't that seem peculiar?'

It didn't, so far as Fogarty was concerned. Whatever happened to Irish priests in the course of their career, young people who got into trouble always took care to avoid them when they became parish priests. And Dempsey, Fogarty's parish priest, was somebody whom anybody, old or young, would avoid.

'That's her business,' he said, raising his hand.

'You're trying to make it mine, father,' Joyce said

reproachfully. 'By the way, have you told the parish priest?'

'That's none of your business either,' Fogarty said, losing his temper again.

'Oh, but I might have to see the parish priest if this persecution went any farther, father.'

'Persecution?' Fogarty growled furiously.

'Yes, father, persecution,' Joyce said steadily. 'Hysterical young women with sex on the brain going to young priests, who accept everything they say without making proper inquiries! That is persecution, and I hope it doesn't go any farther. In the meantime,' Joyce added contemptuously, 'you'd be wise to put that brooch in the dustbin and forget about the whole business.' Then his tone changed again and became insolently personal. 'Before I go, father, did Sheila Moriarty ever tell you what her mother's advice was before she left home?'

'I'm not discussing her business with you,' said Fogarty.

'You should really ask her some time,' said Joyce, and then he turned on his heel and went jauntily down the stairs.

Fogarty was furious. He knew he had been out-manoeuvred all over the shop, and by somebody he thoroughly despised and believed to be an arrant coward. He had an aching regret that he hadn't hit the man when he had the opportunity. It was clearly a public duty on someone's part to hit him. But he had been foxed, and the result was that though he had summoned Joyce merely to warn him off, it was himself who had been warned off. And Fogarty was not a man who was accustomed to being warned off.

And yet, when he woke next morning, he was full of cheerfulness and bounce. When he analysed the scene all over again, everything about it seemed all right. An unpleasant duty had been done, no matter how inadequately. In spite of his bluff Joyce was a coward and much too afraid to pursue Sheila further. Above all, he would say nothing about the brooch. Sheila's word against his might not count, but Sheila's word and that of her priest would satisfy any reasonable person that he was at the bottom of any offence she had committed. But though Fogarty knew he had won, he realised too that for the future he must be more careful in his dealings with business-men and would have to get advice, if not from the parish priest, at least from some priest older than himself. It was all very well to know a few thousand sins theoretically, but to know a few of them practically gave the other fellow an immense advantage.

When Sheila Moriarty came that evening she saw at once from his manner that things had gone well. This time he told Mary to bring up the coffee at once and till it arrived he talked to Sheila about her native place. When he had poured out the coffee he smiled knowingly at her.

'I had a visitor last night,' he said.

'What did you think of him?' she asked ruefully.

'To tell you the truth, I didn't like him very much. Smooth, of course. A smart salesman. Not one you could do business with, though.'

'Do you think I don't know it?' she asked wearily. 'What did he say for himself?'

'Nothing much for himself, a lot for other people. I'll be quite honest with you, he was too smart for me altogether, not to mind you. But I'm sure of one thing. He'll give you no more trouble unless you make an opportunity for him.'

· 'I promise you I won't do that if I can avoid it.'

'You'll have to avoid it,' Fogarty said sternly. 'Anything you have to do with that man for the future is going to injure you. He's frightened and sore, and he'll hurt you in any way he can.'

'And the brooch?'

'Never mind about that. Tell it in Confession, of course,

but say you've taken steps to return it. I'll find a way myself sooner or later.'

'I'm not going to thank you,' she said. 'Only for you I don't know what would have happened me.'

'I did nothing only what I'd be bound to do for anyone,' he said. 'And even that much I mightn't have been able to do except that I knew something about him.'

'What was it?'

'Nothing much. Just an unfortunate married woman who found it advisable to leave town as a result of her association with him. That was something he didn't want brought up.'

'I suppose I should have guessed it,' she said despondently. 'It's our vanity that we can never bring ourselves to believe there could have been anyone else, isn't it? What else did he say?'

Fogarty realised with surprise that, bitter as she was, and perhaps because she was bitter, she could go on all night talking about Joyce.

'Oh, he told me to ask you what the advice was that your mother gave you,' Fogarty replied with a jolly laugh.

'He told you that?' she asked sharply, and at once he knew he had said the wrong thing. What there was wrong about it he couldn't see, unless it was that she was still so sore that every word she had uttered in confidence to a man she was in love with hurt her when it came from someone else.

'Naturally, I didn't say you'd already told me,' he added to comfort her.

'I'm glad of that anyway,' she said and got up.

'There's no need to go so soon,' he exclaimed. 'I can drive you wherever you want to go.'

'I think I'd better go just the same, father,' she said with a smile, but he could have sworn she was fighting back tears. Something had gone wrong, dreadfully wrong, but he had no idea what it was and felt a complete fool.

'You'll keep in touch with me anyway?' he said.

'Indeed I will.'

'And if that fellow annoys you again, don't waste any more time. Come straight out of the shop and let me know. You understand that?'

'I promise, father.'

Then she was gone and Fogarty felt let down. Let down, bewildered, frustrated, and he didn't know why. What her mother had said couldn't possibly have anything to do with it. It was advice that any mother might have given her daughter when she was leaving home for the first time, except for saying that 'all married men weren't like her Daddy', which only showed the ingenuousness of the poor woman.

But why then had Sheila withered up when he referred to it, and, above all, why had Joyce worn that complacent, insolent smile when *he* referred to it? Then he understood and he withered up too. Sheila's mother had said something else, something about not throwing temptation in the way of priests because they were more vulnerable than other men. And quite innocently she had thrown temptation in his way and quite innocently he had been tempted, and Joyce in his coarse worldy way had seen it all. Her mother had known she was a lonely vulnerable girl and realised where it might carry her. And where it might have carried her – and him – God only knew, if he had not accidentally shown her how it all looked in an enemy's eye.

Now, Fogarty had a strong impression that he would never meet the girl again and never know what her mother had really said to her about not associating with a priest, because priests were weaker than other men, because they were more un-protected than other men. And suddenly the loneliness he was for ever trying to banish descended on him in all its black bitterness and he added aloud, 'O God, we are, we are!'

THE FRYING-PAN

FATHER FOGARTY'S ONLY REAL FRIENDS in Kilmupeter were the Whittons. Whitton was the teacher there. He had been to the seminary and college with Fogarty, and, like him, intended to be a priest, but when the time came for him to take the vow of celibacy, he had contracted scruples of conscience and married the principal one. Fogarty, who had known her too, had to admit that she wasn't without justification, and now, in this lonely place where chance had thrown them together again, she formed the real centre of what little social life he had. With Tom Whitton he had a quiet friendship compounded of exchanges of opinion about books or wireless talks. He had the impression that Whitton didn't really like him and considered him a man who would have been better out of the Church. When they went to the races together, Fogarty felt that Whitton disapproved of having to put on bets for him and thought that priests should not bet at all. Like other outsiders, he knew perfectly what priests should be, without the necessity for having to be that way himself. He was sometimes savage in the things he said about the parish priest, old Father Whelan. On the other hand, he had a pleasant sense of humour and Fogarty enjoyed retailing his cracks against the cloth. Men as intelligent as Whitton were rare in country schools, and soon, too, he would grow stupid and wild for lack of educated society.

One evening Father Fogarty invited them to dinner to see some films he had taken at the races. Films were his latest hobby. Before this it had been fishing and shooting. Like all bachelors, he had a mania for adding to his possessions, and his lumber room was piled high with every possible sort of junk from chest-developers to field glasses, and his library cluttered with works on everything from Irish history to Freudian psychology. He passed from craze to craze, each the key to the universe.

He sprang up at the knock, and found Una at the door, all in furs, her shoulders about her ears, her big, bony, masculine face blue with cold but screwed up in an amiable monkey-grin. Tom, a handsome man, was tall and self-conscious. He had greying hair, brown eyes, a prominent jaw, and was quiet-spoken in a way that concealed passion. He and Una disagreed a lot about the way the children should be brought up. He thought she spoiled them.

'Come in, let ye, come in!' cried Fogarty hospitably, showing the way into his warm study with its roaring turf fire, deep leather chairs, and the Raphael print above the mantelpiece: a real bachelor's room. 'God above!' he exclaimed, holding Una's hand a moment longer than was necessary. 'You're perished! What'll you have to drink, Una?'

'Whi-hi-hi –' stammered Una excitedly, her eyes beginning to pop. 'I can't say the bloody word.'

'Call it malt, girl,' said the priest.

'That's enough! That's enough!' she cried laughingly, snatching the glass from him. 'You'll send me home on my ear, and then I'll hear about it from this fellow.'

'Whiskey, Tom?'

'Whiskey, Jerry,' Whitton said quietly with a quick

conciliatory glance. He kept his head very stiff and used his eyes a lot instead.

Meanwhile Una, unabashedly inquisitive, was making the tour of the room with the glass in her hand, to see if there was anything new in it. There usually was.

'Is this new, father?' she asked, halting before a pleasant eighteenth-century print.

'Ten bob,' the priest said promptly. 'Wasn't it a bargain?'

'I couldn't say. What is it?'

'The old courthouse in town.'

'Go on!' said Una.

Whitton came and studied the print closely. 'That place is gone these fifty years and I never saw a picture of it,' he said. 'This is a bargain all right.'

'I'd say so,' Fogarty said with quiet pride.

'And what's the sheet for?' Una asked, poking at a tablecloth pinned between the windows.

'That's not a sheet, woman!' Fogarty exclaimed. 'For God's sake, don't be displaying your ignorance!'

'Oh, I know,' she cried girlishly. 'For the pictures! I'd forgotten about them. That's grand!'

Then Bella, a coarse, good-looking country girl, announced dinner, and the curate, with a self-conscious, boyish swagger, led them into the dining room and opened the door of the sideboard. The dining room was even more ponderous than the sitting room. Everything in it was large, heavy, and dark.

'And now, what'll ye drink?' he asked over his shoulder, studying his array of bottles. 'There's some damn good Burgundy – 'pon my soul, 'tis great!'

'How much did it cost?' Whitton asked with poker-faced humour. 'The only way I have of identifying wines is by the price.'

'Eight bob a bottle,' Fogarty replied at once.

'That's a very good price,' said Whitton with a nod. 'We'll have some of that.'

'You can take a couple of bottles home with you,' said the curate, who, in the warmth of his heart, was always wanting to give his treasures away. 'The last two dozen he had – wasn't I lucky?'

'You have the appetite of a canon on the income of a curate,' Whitton said in the same tone of grave humour, but Fogarty caught the scarcely perceptible note of criticism in it. He did not allow this to upset him.

'Please God, we won't always be curates,' he said sunnily.

'Bella looks after you well,' said Una when the meal was nearly over. The compliment was deserved so far as it went, though it was a man's meal rather than a woman's.

'Doesn't she, though?' Fogarty exclaimed with pleasure. 'Isn't she damn good for a country girl?'

'How does she get on with Stasia?' asked Una – Stasia was Father Whelan's old housekeeper, and an affliction to the community.

'They don't talk. Stasia says she's an immoral woman.'

'And is she?' Una asked hopefully.

'If she isn't, she's wasting her own time and my whiskey,' said Fogarty. 'She entertains Paddy Coakley in the kitchen every Saturday night. I told her I wouldn't keep her unless she got a boy. And wasn't I right? One Stasia is enough for any parish. Father Whelan tells me I'm going too far.'

'And did you tell him to mind his own business?' Whitton asked with a penetrating look.

'I did, to be sure,' said Fogarty, who had done nothing of the sort.

'Ignorant, interfering old fool!' Whitton said quietly, the ferocity of his sentiments belied by the mildness of his manner.

'That's only because you'd like to do the interfering yourself,' said Una good-humouredly. She frequently had to act as peacemaker between the parish priest and her husband.

'And a robber,' Tom Whitton added to the curate, ignoring her. 'He's been collecting for new seats for the church for the last ten years. I'd like to know where that's going.'

'He had a collection for repairing my roof,' said the curate, 'and 'tis leaking still. He must be worth twenty thousand.'

'Now, that's not fair, father,' Una said flatly. 'You know yourself there's no harm in Father Whelan. It's just that he's certain he's going to die in the workhouse. It's like Bella and her boy. He has nothing more serious to worry about, and he worries about that.'

Fogarty knew there was a certain amount of truth in what Una said, and that the old man's miserliness was more symbolic than real, and at the same time he felt in her words criticism of a different kind from her husband's. Though Una wasn't aware of it she was implying that the priest's office made him an object of pity rather than blame. She was sorry for old Whelan, and, by implication, for him.

'Still, Tom is right, Una,' he said with sudden earnestness. 'It's not a question of what harm Father Whelan intends, but what harm he does. Scandal is scandal, whether you give it deliberately or through absent-mindedness.'

Tom grunted, to show his approval, but he said no more on the subject, as though he refused to enter into an argument with his wife about subjects she knew nothing of. They returned to the study for coffee, and Fogarty produced the film projector. At once the censoriousness of Tom Whitton's manner dropped away, and he behaved like a pleasant and intelligent boy of seventeen. Una, sitting by the fire with her legs crossed, watched them with amusement. Whenever they came to the priest's house, the same sort of thing happened.

Once it had been a microscope, and the pair of them had amused themselves with it for hours. Now they were kidding themselves that their real interest in the cinema was educational. She knew that within a month the cinema, like the microscope, would be lying in the lumber room with the rest of the junk.

Fogarty switched off the light and showed some films he had taken at the last race meeting. They were very patchy, mostly out of focus, and had to be interpreted by a running commentary, which was always a shot or two behind.

'I suppose ye wouldn't know who that is?' he said as the film showed Una, eating a sandwich and talking excitedly and demonstratively to a couple of wild-looking country boys.

'It looks like someone from the County Club,' her husband said dryly.

'But wasn't it good?' Fogarty asked innocently as he switched on the lights again. 'Now, wasn't it very interesting?' He was exactly like a small boy who had performed a conjuring trick.

'Marvellous, father,' Una said with a sly and affectionate grin.

He blushed and turned to pour them out more whiskey. He saw that she had noticed the pictures of herself. At the same time, he saw she was pleased. When he had driven them home, she held his hand and said they had had the best evening for years – a piece of flattery so gross and uncalled-for that it made her husband more tongue-tied than ever.

'Thursday, Jerry?' he said with a quick glance.

'Thursday, Tom,' said the priest.

The room looked terribly desolate after her; the crumpled cushions, the glasses, the screen and the film projector, everything had become frighteningly inert, while outside his window the desolate countryside had taken on even more of its supernatural animation; bogs, hills, and fields, full of ghosts and shadows. He sat by the fire, wondering what his own life might have been like with a girl like that, all furs and scent and laughter, and two bawling, irrepressible brats upstairs. When he tiptoed up to his bedroom he remembered that there would never be children there to wake, and it seemed to him that with all the things he bought to fill his home, he was merely trying desperately to stuff the yawning holes in his own big, empty heart.

On Thursday, when he went to their house, Ita and Brendan, though already in bed, were refusing to sleep till he said good-night to them. While he was taking off his coat the two of them rushed to the banisters and screamed: 'We want Father Fogey.' When he went upstairs they were sitting bolt upright in their cots, a little fat, fair-haired rowdy boy and a solemn baby girl.

'Father,' Brendan began at once, 'will I be your altar boy when I grow up?'

'You will to be sure, son,' replied Fogarty.

'Ladies first! Ladies first!' the baby shrieked in a frenzy of rage. 'Father, will I be your altar boy?'

'Go on!' Brendan said scornfully. 'Little girls can't be altar boys, sure they can't, father?'

'I can,' shrieked Ita, who in her excitement exactly resembled her mother. 'Can't I, father?'

'We might be able to get a dispensation for you,' said the curate. 'In a pair of trousers, you'd do fine.'

He was in a wistful frame of mind when he came downstairs again. Children would always be a worse temptation to him than women. Children were the devil! The house was gay and spotless. They had no fine mahogany suite like his, but Una managed to make the few coloured odds and ends they had seem deliberate. There wasn't a cigarette end in the ashtrays; the cushions had not been sat on. Tom, standing before the fireplace (not to disturb the cushions, thought Fogarty), looked as if someone had held his head under the tap, and was very self-consciously wearing a new brown tie. With his greying hair plastered flat, he looked schoolboyish, sulky, and resentful, as though he were meditating ways of restoring his authority over a mutinous household. The thought crossed Fogarty's mind that he and Una had probably quarrelled about the tie. It went altogether too well with his suit.

'We want Father Fogey!' the children began to chant monotonously from the bedroom.

'Shut up!' shouted Tom.

'We want Father Fogey,' the chant went on, but with a groan in it somewhere.

'Well, you're not going to get him. Go to sleep!'

The chant stopped. This was clearly serious.

'You don't mind if I drop down to a meeting tonight, Jerry?' Tom asked in his quiet, anxious way. 'I won't be more than half an hour.'

'Not at all, Tom,' said Fogarty heartily. 'Sure, I'll drive you.'

'No, thanks,' Whitton said with a smile of gratitude. 'It won't take me ten minutes to get there.'

It was clear that a lot of trouble had gone to the making of supper, but out of sheer perversity Tom let on not to recognise any of the dishes. When they had drunk their coffee, he rose and glanced at his watch.

'I won't be long,' he said.

'Tom, you're not going to that meeting?' Una asked appealingly.

'I tell you I have to,' he replied with unnecessary emphasis.

'I met Mick Mahoney this afternoon, and he said they didn't need you.'

'Mick Mahoney knows nothing about it.'

'I told him to tell the others you wouldn't be coming, that

Father Fogarty would be here,' she went on desperately, fighting for the success of her evening.

'Then you had no business to do it,' her husband retorted angrily, and even Fogarty saw that she had gone the worst way about it, by speaking to members of his committee behind his back. He began to feel uncomfortable. 'If they come to some damn fool decision while I'm away, it'll be my responsibility.'

'If you're late, you'd better knock,' she sang out gaily to cover up his bad manners. 'Will we go into the sitting room, father?' she asked over-eagerly. 'I'll be with you in two minutes. There are fags on the mantelpiece, and you know where to find the whi-hi-hi— blast that word!'

Fogarty lit a cigarette and sat down. He felt exceedingly uncomfortable. Whitton was an uncouth and irritable bastard, and always had been so. He heard Una upstairs, and then someone turned on the tap in the bathroom. 'Bloody brute!' he thought indignantly. There had been no need for him to insult her before a guest. Why the hell couldn't he have finished his quarrelling while they were alone? The tap stopped and he waited, listening, but Una didn't come. He was a warm-hearted man and could not bear the thought of her alone and miserable upstairs. He went softly up the stairs and stood on the landing. 'Una!' he called softly, afraid of waking the children. There was a light in the bedroom; the door was ajar and he pushed it in. She was sitting at the end of the bed and grinned at him dolefully.

'Sorry for the whine, father,' she said, making a brave attempt to smile. And then, with the street-urchin's humour which he found so attractive: 'Can I have a loan of your shoulder, please?'

'What the blazes ails Tom?' he asked, sitting beside her.

'He – he's jealous,' she stammered, and began to weep again with her head on his chest. He put his arm about her and patted her awkwardly.

'Jealous?' he asked incredulously, turning over in his mind the half-dozen men whom Una could meet at the best of times. 'Who the blazes is he jealous of?'

'You!'

'Me?' Fogarty exclaimed indignantly, and grew red, thinking of how he had given himself away with his pictures. 'He must be mad! I never gave him any cause for jealousy.'

'Oh, I know he's completely unreasonable,' she stammered. 'He always was.'

'But you didn't say anything to him, did you?' Fogarty asked anxiously.

'About what?' she asked in surprise, looking up at him and blinking back her tears.

'About me?' Fogarty mumbled in embarrassment.

'Oh, he doesn't know about that,' Una replied frantically. 'I never mentioned that to him at all. Besides, he doesn't care that much about me.'

And Fogarty realised that in the simplest way in the world he had been brought to admit to a married woman that he loved her and she to imply that she felt the same about him, without a word being said on either side. Obviously, these things happened more innocently that he had ever thought possible. He became more embarrassed than ever.

'But what is he jealous of so?' he added truculently.

'He's jealous of you because you're a priest. Surely, you saw that?'

'I certainly didn't. It never crossed my mind.'

Yet at the same time he wondered if this might not be the reason for the censoriousness he sometimes felt in Whitton against his harmless bets and his bottles of wine.

'But he's hardly ever out of your house, and he's always borrowing your books, and talking theology and Church history to you. He has shelves of them here – look!' And she pointed at a plain wooden bookcase, filled with solid-looking works. 'In my b–b–bedroom! That's why he really hates Father Whelan. Don't you see, Jerry,' she said, calling him for the first time by his Christian name, 'you have all the things he wants.'

'I have?' repeated Fogarty in astonishment. 'What things?'

'Oh, how do I know?' she replied with a shrug, relegating these to the same position as Whelan's bank-balance and his own gadgets, as things that meant nothing to her. 'Respect and responsibility and freedom from the worries of a family, I suppose.'

'He's welcome to them,' Fogarty said with wry humour. 'What's that the advertisements say? – owner having no further use for same.'

'Oh, I know,' she said with another shrug, and he saw that from the beginning she had realised how he felt about her and been sorry for him. He was sure that there was some contradiction here which he should be able to express to himself, between her almost inordinate piety and her light-hearted acceptance of his adoration for her – something that was exclusively feminine, but which he could not isolate with her there beside him, willing him to make love to her, offering herself to his kiss.

'It's a change to be kissed by someone who cares for you,' she said after a moment.

'Ah, now, Una, that's not true,' he protested gravely, the priest in him getting the upper hand of the lover who had still a considerable amount to learn. 'You only fancy that.'

'I don't, Jerry,' she replied with conviction. 'It's always been the same, from the first month of our marriage – always! I was a fool to marry him at all.'

'Even so,' Fogarty said manfully, doing his duty by his friend with a sort of schoolboy gravity, 'You know he's still fond of you. That's only his way.'

'It isn't, Jerry,' she went on obstinately. 'He wanted to be a priest and I stopped him.'

'But you didn't.'

'That's how he looks at it. I tempted him.'

'And damn glad he was to fall!'

'But he did fall, Jerry, and that's what he can never forgive. In his heart he despises me and despises himself for not being able to do without me.'

'But why should he despise himself? That's what I don't understand.'

'Because I'm only a woman, and he wants to be independent of me and every other woman as well. He has to teach to keep a home for me, and he doesn't want to teach. He wants to say Mass and hear confessions, and be God Almighty for seven days of the week.'

Fogary couldn't grasp it, but he realised that there was something in what she said, and that Whitton was really a lonely, frustrated man who felt he was forever excluded from the only things which interested him.

'I don't understand it,' he said angrily. 'It doesn't sound natural to me.'

'It doesn't sound natural to you because you have it, Jerry,' she said. 'I used to think Tom wasn't normal, either, but now I'm beginning to think there are more spoiled priests in the world than ever went into seminaries. You see, Jerry,' she went on in a rush, growing very red, 'I'm a constant reproach to him. He thinks he's a terrible blackguard because he wants to make love to me once a month ... I can talk like this to you because you're a priest.'

'You can, to be sure,' said Fogarty with more conviction

than he felt.

'And even when he does make love to me,' she went on, too full of her grievance even to notice the anguish she caused him, 'he manages to make me feel that I'm doing all the love-making.'

'And why shouldn't you?' asked Fogarty gallantly, concealing the way his heart turned over in him.

'Because it's a sin!' she cried tempestuously.

'Who said it's a sin?'

'He makes it a sin. He's like a bear with a sore head for days after. Don't you see, Jerry,' she cried, springing excitedly to her feet and shaking her head at him, 'it's never anything but adultery with him, and he goes away and curses himself because he hasn't the strength to resist it.'

'Adultery?' repeated Fogarty, the familiar word knocking at his conscience as if it were Tom Whitton himself at the door.

'Whatever you call it,' Una rushed on. 'It's always adultery, adultery, adultery, and I'm always a bad woman, and he always wants to show God that it wasn't him but me, and I'm sick and tired of it. I want a man to make me feel like a respectable married woman for once in my life. You see, I feel quite respectable with you, although I know I shouldn't.' She looked in the mirror of the dressing-table and her face fell. 'Oh, Lord!' she sighed. 'I don't look it . . . I'll be down in two minutes now, Jerry,' she said eagerly, thrusting out her lips to him, her old, brilliant, excitable self.

'You're grand,' he muttered.

As she went into the bathroom, she turned in another excess of emotion and threw her arms about him. As he kissed her, she pressed herself close to him till his head swam. There was a mawkish, girlish grin on her face. 'Darling!' she said in an agony of passion, and it was as if their loneliness enveloped them like a cloud.

THE TEACHER'S MASS

FATHER FOGARTY, the curate in Crislough, used to say in his cynical way that his greatest affliction was having to serve the teacher's Mass every morning. He referred, of course, to his own Mass, the curate's Mass, which was said early so that Father Fogarty could say Mass later in Costello. Nobody ever attended it, except occasionally in summer, when there were visitors at the hotel. The schoolteacher, old Considine, served as acolyte. He had been serving the early Mass long before Fogarty came, and the curate thought he would also probably be doing it long after he had left. Every morning, you saw him coming up the village street, a pedantically attired old man with a hollow face and a big moustache that was turning grey. Everything about him was abstract and angular, even to his voice, which was harsh and without modulation, and sometimes when he and Fogarty came out of the sacristy with Considine leading, carrying the book, his pace was so slow that Fogarty wondered what effect it would have if he gave him one good kick in the behind. It was exactly as Fogarty said – as though *he* was serving Considine's Mass, and the effect of it was to turn Fogarty into a more unruly acolyte than ever he had been in the days when he himself was serving the convent Mass.

Whatever was the cause, Considine always roused a bit of the devil in Fogarty, and he knew that Considine had no great affection for him, either. The old man had been headmaster of the Crislough school until his retirement, and all his life he had kept himself apart from the country people, like a parish priest or a policeman. He was not without learning; he had a quite respectable knowledge of local history, and a very good one of the ecclesiastical history of the Early Middle Ages in its local applications, but it was all book learning, and like his wing collar, utterly unrelated to the life about him. He had all the childish vanity of the man of dissociated scholarship, wrote occasional scurrilous letters to the local paper to correct some error in etymology, and expected everyone on that account to treat him as an oracle. As a schoolmaster he had sneered cruelly at the barefoot urchins he taught, describing them as 'illiterate peasants' who believed in the fairies and in spells, and when, twenty years later, some of them came back from Boston or Brooklyn and showed off before the neighbours, with their big American hats and high-powered cars, he still sneered at them. According to him, they went away illiterate and came home illiterate.

'I see young Carmody is home again,' he would say to the curate after Mass.

'Is that so?'

'And he has a car like a house,' Considine would add, with bitter amusement. 'A car with a grin on it. 'Twould do fine to cart home his mother's turf.'

'The blessings of God on him,' the curate would say cheerfully. 'I wish I had a decent car instead of the old yoke I have.'

'I dare say it was the fairies,' the old teacher would snarl, with an ugly smile that made his hollow, high-cheeked face look like a skull. 'It wasn't anything he ever learned here.'

'Maybe we're not giving the fairies their due, Mr Considine,' said the curate, with the private conviction that it would be easier to learn from them than from the schoolmaster.

The old man's scornful remarks irritated Fogarty because he liked the wild, barefooted, inarticulate brats from the mountainy farms, and felt that if they showed off a bit when they returned from America with a few dollars in their pockets, they were well entitled to do so. Whoever was entitled to the credit, it was nothing and nobody at home. The truth was he had periods of terrible gloom when he felt he had mistaken his vocation. Or, rather the vocation was all right, but the conditions under which he exercised it were all wrong, and those conditions, for him, were well represented by the factitious scholarship of old Considine. It was all in the air. Religion sometimes seemed no more to him than his own dotty old housekeeper, who, whatever he said, invested herself with the authority of a bishop and decided who was to see him and about what, and settled matters on her own whenever she got half a chance. Things were so bad with her that whenever the country people wanted to see him, they bribed one of the acolytes to go and ask him to come himself to their cottages. The law was represented by Sergeant Twomey, who raided the mountain pubs half an hour after closing time, in response to the order of some lunatic superintendent at the other side of the county, while as for culture, there was the library van every couple of months, from which Considine, who acted as librarian, selected a hundred books, mainly for his own amusement. He was partial to books dealing with voyages in the Congo or Tibet ('Tibet is a very interesting country, father'). The books that were for general circulation he censored to make sure there were no bad words like 'navel' in them that might corrupt the ignorant 'peasantry'. And then he came to Fogarty and told him he had been reading a very 'interesting' book about birdwatching in the South Seas, or something like that.

Fogarty's own temptation was toward action and energy, just as his depression was often no more than the expression of his frustration. He was an energetic and emotional man who in other circumstances would probably have become a successful businessman. Women were less of a temptation to him than the thought of an active instinctual life. All he wanted in the way of a holiday was to get rid of his collar and take a gun or rod or stand behind the bar of a country hotel. He ran the local hurling team for what it was worth, which wasn't much, and strayed down the shore with the boatmen or up the hills with the poachers and poteen-makers, who all trusted him and never tried to conceal any of their harmless misdemeanours from him. Once, for instance, in the late evening, he came unexpectedly on a party of scared poteen-makers on top of a mountain and sat down on the edge of the hollow where they were operating their still. 'Never mind me, lads!' he said, lighting a pipe. 'I'm not here at all.' 'Sure we know damn well you're not here, father,' one old man said, and chuckled. 'But how the hell can we offer a drink to a bloody ghost?'

These were his own people, the people he loved and admired, and it was principally the feeling that he could do little or nothing for them that plunged him into those suicidal fits of gloom in which he took to the bottle. When he heard of a dance being held in a farmhouse without the permission of the priest or the police, he said, 'The blessings of God on them' – though he had to say it discreetly, for fear it should get back.

Fogarty knew that in the teacher's eyes this was another black mark against him, for old Considine could not understand how any educated man could make so little of the cloth as to sit drinking with 'illiterate peasants' instead of talking to a fine, well-informed man like himself about the situation in the Far East or the relationship of the Irish dioceses to the old kingdoms of the Early Middle Ages.

Then one evening Fogarty was summoned to the teacher's house on a sick call. It only struck him when he saw it there at the end of the village – a newish, red-brick box of a house, with pebble dash on the front and a steep stairway up from the front door – that it was like the teacher himself. Maisie, the teacher's unmarried daughter, was a small, plump woman with a face that must once have been attractive, for it was still all in curves, with hair about it like Mona Lisa's, though now she had lost all her freshness, and her skin was red and hard and full of wrinkles. She had a sad smile, and Fogarty could not resist a pang of pity for her because he realised that she was probably another victim of Considine's dislike of 'illiterates'. How could an 'illiterate' boy come to a house like that, or how could the teacher's daughter go out walking with him?

She had got the old man to bed, and he lay there with the engaged look of a human being at grips with his destiny. From his narrow window there was a pleasant view of the sea road and a solitary tree by the water's edge. Beyond the bay was the mountain, with a cap on it – the sign of bad weather. Fogarty gave him the last Sacraments, and he confessed and received Communion with a devotion that touched Fogarty in spite of himself. He stayed on with the daughter until the doctor arrived, in case any special medicines were needed. They sat in the tiny box of a front room with a bay window and a high mahogany bookcase that filled one whole wall. She wanted to stay and make polite conversation for the priest, though all the time she was consumed with anxiety. When the doctor left, Fogarty left with him, and pressed Maisie's hand and told her to call on him for anything, at any time.

Dr Mulloy was more offhand. He was a tall, handsome young man of about Fogarty's own age. Outside, standing beside his car, he said to Fogarty, 'Ah, he might last a couple of years if he minded himself. They don't of course. You know the way it is. A wonder that daughter of his never married.'

'How could she?' Fogarty asked in a low voice, turning to glance again at the ill-designed, pretentious little suburban house. 'He'd think her too grand for any of the boys round this place.'

'Why then, indeed, if he pops off on her, she won't be too grand at all,' said the doctor. 'A wonder an educated man like that wouldn't have more sense. Sure he can't have anything to leave her?'

'No more than myself, I dare say,' said Fogarty, who saw that the doctor only wanted to find out how much they could pay; and he went off to summon one of the boy acolytes to take Considine's place at Mass next morning.

But the next morning when Fogarty reached the sacristy, instead of the boy he had spoken to, old Considine was waiting, with everything neatly arranged in his usual pedantic manner, and a wan old man's smile on his hollow face.

'Mr Considine!' Fogarty exclaimed indignantly. 'What's the meaning of this?'

'Ah, I'm fine this morning, father,' said the old man, with a sort of fictitious drunken excitement. 'I woke up as fresh as a daisy.' Then he smiled malevolently and added, 'Jimmy Leary thought he was after doing me out of a job, but Dr Mulloy was too smart for him.'

'But you know yourself what Dr Mulloy said,' Fogarty protested indignantly. 'I talked to him myself about it. He said you could live for years, but any exertion might make you go off any time.'

'And how can man die better?' retorted the teacher, with the triumphant air he wore whenever he managed to produce an apt quotation. 'You remember Macaulay, I suppose,' he added doubtfully, and then his face took on a morose look. ''Tisn't that at all,' he said. 'But 'tis the only thing I have to look forward to. The day wouldn't be the same to me if I had to miss Mass.'

Fogarty knew that he was up against an old man's stubbornness and love of habitual things, and that he was wasting his breath advising Considine himself. Instead, he talked to the parish priest, a holy and muddleheaded old man named Whelan. Whelan shook his head mournfully over the situation, but then he was a man who shook his head over everything. He had apparently decided many years ago that any form of action was hateful, and he took to his bed if people became too presssing.

'He's very obstinate, old John, but at the same time, you wouldn't like to cross him,' Whelan said.

'If you don't do something about it, you might as well put back the Costello Mass another half an hour,' Fogarty said. He was forever trying to induce Whelan to make up his mind. 'He's getting slower every day. One of these days he'll drop dead on me at the altar.'

'Oh, I'll mention it to him,' the parish priest said regretfully. 'But I don't know would it be wise to take too strong a line. You have to humour them when they're as old as that. I dare say we'll be the same ourselves, father.'

Fogarty knew he was wasting his breath on Whelan as well. Whelan would no doubt be as good as his word, and talk about the weather to Considine for an hour, and then end by dropping a hint, which might be entirely lost, that the old teacher shouldn't exert himself too much, and that would be all.

A month later, the old teacher had another attack, but this time Fogarty only heard of it from his mad housekeeper, who knew everything that went on in the village.

'But why didn't he send for me?' he asked sharply.

'Ah, I suppose he wasn't bad enough,' replied the housekeeper. 'Mrs MacCarthy said he got over it with pills and a sup of whiskey. They say whiskey is the best thing.'

'You're sure he didn't send for me?' Fogarty asked. There were times when he half expected the woman, in the exercise of her authority, to refuse the Last Rites to people she didn't approve of.

'Sure, of coure he didn't. It was probably nothing.'

All the same, Fogarty was not easy in his mind. He knew what it meant to old people to have the priest with them at the end, and he suspected that if Considine made light of his attack, it could only be because he was afraid Fogarty would take it as final proof that he was not fit to serve Mass. He felt vaguely guilty about it. He strode down the village street, saluting the fishermen who were sitting on the sea wall in the dusk. The teacher's cottage was dark when he reached it. The cobbler, a lively little man who lived next door, was standing outside.

'I hear the old master was sick again, Tom,' said the curate.

'Begor, he was, father,' said the cobbler. 'I hear Maisie found him crawling to the fire on his hands and knees. Terrible cold they get when they're like that. He's a sturdy old divil, though. You needn't be afraid you'll lose your altar boy for a long time yet.'

'I hope not, Tom,' said Fogarty, who knew that the cobbler, a knowledgeable man in his own way, thought there was something funny about the old schoolmaster's serving Mass. 'And I hope we're all as good when our own time comes.'

He went home, too thoughtful to chat with the fishermen. The cobbler's words had given him a sudden glimpse of old Considine's sufferings, and he was filled with the compassion that almost revolted him at times for sick bodies and suffering minds. He was an emotional man, and he knew it was partly the cause of his own savage gloom, but he could not restrain it.

Next morning, when he went to the sacristy, there was the old teacher, with his fawning smile, the smile of a guilty small boy who has done it again and this time knows he will not escape without punishment.

'You weren't too good last night, John,' the curate said, using Considine's Christian name for the first time.

'No, Father Jeremiah,' Considine replied, pronouncing the priest's name slowly and pedantically. 'I was a bit poorly in the early evening. But those pills of Dr Mulloy's are a wonder.'

'And isn't it a hard thing to say you never sent for me?' Fogarty went on.

Considine blushed furiously, and this time he looked really guilty and scared.

'But I wan't that bad, father,' he protested with senile intensity, his hands beginning to shake and his eyes to sparkle. 'I wasn't as frightened yesterday as I was the first time. It's the first time it frightens you. You feel sure you'll never last it out. But after that you get to expect it.'

'Will you promise me never to do a thing like that again?' the curate asked earnestly. 'Will you give me your word that you'll send for me, any hour of the day or night?'

'Very well, father,' Considine replied sullenly. ''Tis very good of you. I'll give you my word I'll send for you.'

And they both recognised the further, unspoken part of the compact between them. Considine would send for Fogarty, but nothing Fogarty saw or heard was to permit him again to try to deprive the old teacher of his office. Not that he any longer wished to do so. Now that he recognised the passion of will in the old man, Fogarty's profound humanity only made him anxious to second it and enable Considine to do what clearly he wished to do – die in harness. Fogarty had also begun to recognise that it was not mere obstinacy that got the old man out of his bed each morning and brought him shivering and sighing and shuffling up the village street. There was obstinacy there, and plenty of it, but there was something else, which the curate valued more; something he felt the lack of in himself. It wasn't easy to put a name on it. Faith was one name, but it was no more than a name and was used to cover too many excesses of devotion that the young priest found distasteful. This was something else, something that made him ashamed of his own human weakness and encouraged him to fight the depression, which seemed at times as if it would overwhelm him. It was more like the miracle of the Mass itself, metaphor become reality. Now when he thought of his own joke about serving the teacher's Mass, it didn't seem quite so much like a joke.

One morning in April, Fogarty noticed as he entered the sacristy that the old man was looking very ill. As he helped Fogarty, his hands shook piteously. Even his harsh voice had a quaver in it, and his lips were pale. Fogarty looked at him and wondered if he shouldn't say something, but decided against it. He went in, preceded by Considine, and noticed that though the teacher tried to hold himself erect, his walk was little more than a shuffle. He went up to the altar, but found it almost impossible to concentrate on what he was doing. He heard the labouring steps behind him, and as the old man started to raise the heavy book onto the altar, Fogarty paused for a moment and looked under his brows. Considine's face was now white as a sheet, and as he raised the book he sighed. Fogarty wanted to cry out, 'For God's sake, man, lie down!' He wanted to hold Considine's head on his knee and whisper into his ear. Yet he realised that to the strange old man behind him this would be no kindness. The only kindness he could do him was to crush down his own weak warmheartedness and continue the sacrifice. Never had he seemed farther away from the reality of the Mass. He heard the labouring steps, the panting breath, behind him, and it seemed as if they had lasted some timeless time before he heard another heavy sign as Considine managed to kneel.

At last, Fogarty found himself waiting for a response that did not come. He looked round quickly. The old man had fallen silently forward on to the altar steps. His arm was twisted beneath him and his head was turned sideways. His jaw had fallen, and his eyes were sightless.

'John!' Fogarty called, in a voice that rang through the church. 'Can you hear me? John!'

There was no reply, and the curate placed him on his back, with one of the altar cushions beneath his head. Fogarty felt under the surplice for his buttons and unloosed them. He felt for the heart. It had stopped; there was no trace of breathing. Through the big window at the west end he saw the church-yard trees and the sea beyond them bright in the morning light. The whole church seemed terribly still, so that the mere tick-ing of the clock filled it with its triumphant mocking of the machine of flesh and blood that had fallen silent.

Fogarty went quickly to the sacristy and returned with the sacred oils to anoint the teacher. He knew he had only to cross the road for help, to have the old man's body removed and get an acolyte to finish the Mass, but he wanted no help. He felt strangely light-headed. Instead, when he had done, he returned to the altar and resumed the Mass where he had left off, murmuring the responses to himself. As he did so, he realised that he was acutely aware of every detail, of every sound, he had no feeling that he was lacking in concentra-tion. When he turned to face the body of the church and said 'Dominus vobiscum', he saw as if for the first time the pros-trate form with its fallen jaw and weary eyes, under the light that came in from the sea through the trees in their first leaf, and murmured 'Et cum spiritu tuo' for the man whose spirit had flown. Then, when he had said the prayers after Mass beside the body, he took his biretta, donned it, and walked by the body, carrying his chalice, and feeling as he walked that some figure was walking before him, slowly, saying goobye. In his excited mind echoed the rubric: 'Then, having adored and thanked God for everything, he goes away.'

THE WREATH

WHEN FATHER FOGARTY READ OF THE DEATH of his friend, Father Devine, in a Dublin nursing home, he was stunned. He was a man who did not understand the irremediable. He took out an old seminary group, put it on the mantelpiece and spent the evening looking at it. Devine's clever, pale, shrunken face stood out from the rest, not very different from what it had been in his later years except for the absence of pince-nez. He and Fogarty had been boys together in a provincial town where Devine's father had been a schoolmaster and Fogarty's mother had kept a shop. Even then, everybody had known that Devine was marked out by nature for the priesthood. He was clever, docile and beautifully mannered. Fogarty's vocation had come later and proved a surprise, to himself as well as to others.

They had been friends over the years, affectionate when together, critical and sarcastic when apart. They had not seen one another for close on a year. Devine had been unlucky. As long as the old Bishop, Gallogly, lived, he had been fairly well sheltered, but Lanigan, the new one, disliked him. It was partly Devine's own fault. He could not keep his mouth shut. He was witty and waspish and said whatever came into his head about colleagues who had nothing like his gifts. Fogarty

remembered the things Devine had said about himself. Devine
had affected to believe that Fogarty was a man of many per-
sonalities, and asked with mock humility which he was now
dealing with – Nero, Napoleon or St Francis of Assisi.

It all came back: the occasional jaunts together, the plans
for holidays abroad that never took place; and now the warm
and genuine love for Devine which was so natural to Fogarty
welled up in him, and, realising that never again in this world
would he be able to express it, he began to weep. He was
as simple as a child in his emotions. When he was in high spirits
he devised practical jokes of the utmost crudity; when he was
depressed he brooded for days on imaginary injuries: he forgot
lightly, remembered suddenly and with exaggerated intensity,
and blamed himself cruelly and unjustly for his own shortcom-
ings. He would have been astonished to learn that, for all the
intrusions of Nero and Napoleon, his understanding had continued to develop when that of cleverer men had dried up,
and that he was a better and wiser man at forty than he had
been twenty years before.

But he did not understand the irremediable. He had to have
someone to talk to, and for want of a better, rang up Jackson,
a curate who had been Devine's other friend. He did not really
like Jackson, who was worldly, cynical and something of a
careerist, and he usually called him by the worst name in his
vocabulary – a Jesuit. Several times he had asked Devine what
he saw in Jackson but Devine's replies had not enlightened
him much. 'I wouldn't trust myself too far with the young
Loyola if I were you,' Fogarty had told Devine with his worldly
swagger. Now, he had no swagger left.

'That's terrible news about Devine, Jim, isn't it?' he said.

'Yes,' Jackson drawled in his usual cautious, cagey way, as
though he were afraid to commit himself even about that. 'I
suppose it's a happy release for the poor devil.'

That was the sort of tone that maddened Fogarty. It sounded as though Jackson were talking of an old family pet who had been sent to the vet's.

'I hope he appreciates it,' he said gruffly. 'I was thinking of going to Dublin and coming back with the funeral. You wouldn't come, I suppose?'

'I don't very well see how I could, Jerry,' Jackson replied in a tone of mild alarm. 'It's only a week since I was up last.'

'Ah, well, I'll go myself,' said Fogarty. 'You don't know what happened him, do you?'

'Ah, well, he was always anaemic,' Jackson said lightly. 'He should have looked after himself, but he didn't get much chance with old O'Leary.'

'He wasn't intended to,' Fogarty said darkly, indiscreet as usual.

'What?' Jackson asked in surprise. 'Oh no,' he added, resuming his worldly tone. 'It wasn't a sinecure, of course. He was fainting all over the shop. Last time was in the middle of Mass. By then, of course, it was too late. When I saw him last week I knew he was dying.'

'You saw him last week?' Fogarty repeated.

'Oh, just for a few minutes. He couldn't talk much.'

And again, the feeling of his own inadequacy descended on Fogarty. He realised that Jackson, who seemed to have as much feeling as a mowing machine, had kept in touch with Devine, and gone out of his way to see him at the end, while he, the devoted, warm-hearted friend, had let him slip from sight into eternity and was now wallowing in the sense of his own loss.

'I'll never forgive myself, Jim,' he said humbly. 'I never even knew he was sick.'

'I'd like to go to the funeral myself if I could,' said Jackson. 'I'll ring you up later if I can manage it.'

He did manage it, and that evening they set off in Fogarty's car for the city. They stayed in an old hotel in a side-street where porters and waiters all knew them. Jackson brought Fogarty to a very pleasant restaurant for dinner. The very sight of Jackson had been enough to renew Fogarty's doubts. He was a tall, thin man with a prim, watchful, clerical air, and he knew his way around. He spent at least ten minutes over the menu and the wine list, and the head waiter danced attendance on him as head waiters do only when they are either hopeful or intimidated.

'You needn't bother about me,' Fogarty said to cut short the rigmarole. 'I'm having steak.'

'Father Fogarty is having steak, Paddy,' Jackson said suavely, looking at the head waiter over his spectacles with what Fogarty called his 'Jesuit' air. 'Make it rare. And stout, I fancy. It's a favourite beverage of the natives.'

'I'll spare you the stout,' Fogarty said, enjoying the banter. 'Red wine will do me fine.'

'Mind, Paddy,' Jackson said in the same tone, 'Father Fogarty said *red* wine. You're in Ireland now, remember.'

Next morning they went to the parish church where the coffin was resting on trestles before the altar. Beside it, to Fogarty's surprise, was a large wreath of roses. When they got up from their knees, Devine's uncle, Ned, had arrived with his son. Ned was a broad-faced, dark-haired, nervous man, with the anaemic complexion of the family.

'I'm sorry for your trouble, Ned,' said Fogarty.

'I know that, father,' said Ned.

'I don't know if you know Father Jackson. He was a great friend of Father Willie's.'

'I heard him speak of him,' said Ned. 'He talked a lot about the pair of ye. Ye were his great friends. Poor Father Willie!' he added with a sigh. 'He had few enough.'

Just then the parish priest came in and spoke to Ned Devine.

His name was Martin. He was a tall man with a stern, unlined, wooden face and candid blue eyes like a baby's. He stood for a few minutes by the coffin, then studied the breastplate and wreath, looking closely at the tag. It was only then that he beckoned the two younger priests towards the door.

'Tell me, what are we going to do about that thing?' he asked with a professional air.

'What thing?' Fogarty asked in surprise.

'The wreath,' Martin replied with a nod over his shoulder.

'What's wrong with it?'

''Tis against the rubrics,' replied the parish priest in the complacent tone of a policeman who has looked up the law on the subject.

'For heaven's sake, what have the rubrics to do with it?' Fogarty asked impatiently.

'The rubrics have a whole lot to do with it,' Martin replied with a stern glance. 'And, apart from that, 'tis a bad custom.'

'You mean Masses bring in more money?' Fogarty asked with amused insolence.

'I do not mean Masses bring in more money,' replied Martin, who tended to answer every remark verbatim, like a solicitor's letter. It added to the impression of woodenness he gave. 'I mean that flowers are a pagan survival.' He looked at the two young priests with the same anxious, innocent, wooden air. 'And here am I, week in, week out, preaching against flowers, and a blooming big wreath of them in my own church. And on a priest's coffin, what's more! What am I to say about that?'

'Who asked you to say anything?' Fogarty asked angrily. 'The man wasn't from your diocese.'

'Now, that's all very well,' said Martin. 'That's bad enough by itself, but it isn't the whole story.'

'You mean because it's from a woman?' Jackson broke in

lightly in a tone that would have punctured any pose less substantial than Martin's.

'I mean, because it's from a woman, exactly.'

'A woman!' said Fogarty in astonishment. 'Does it say so?'

'It does not say so.'

'Then how do you know?'

'Because it's red roses.'

'And does that mean it's from a woman?'

'What else could it mean?'

'I suppose it could mean it's from somebody who didn't study the language of flowers the way you seem to have done,' Fogarty snapped.

He could feel Jackson's disapproval of him weighing on the air, but when Jackson spoke it was at the parish priest that his coldness and nonchalance were directed.

'Oh, well,' he said with a shrug. 'I'm afraid we know nothing about it, father. You'll have to make up your own mind.'

'I don't like doing anything when I wasn't acquainted with the man,' Martin grumbled, but he made no further attempt to interfere, and one of the undertaker's men took the wreath and put in on the hearse. Fogarty controlled himself with difficulty. As he banged open the door of his car and started the engine his face was flushed. He drove with his head bowed and his brows jutting down like rocks over his eyes. It was what Devine had called his Nero look. As they cleared the main streets he burst out.

'That's the sort of thing that makes me ashamed of myself, Jim. Flowers are a pagan survival! And they take it from him, what's worse. They take it from him. They listen to that sort of stuff instead of telling him to shut his big ignorant gob.'

'Oh, well,' Jackson said tolerantly, taking out his pipe, 'we're hardly being fair to him. After all, he didn't know Devine.'

'But that only makes it worse,' Fogarty said hotly. 'Only

for our being there he'd have thrown out that wreath. And for what? His own dirty, mean, suspicious mind!'

'Ah, I wouldn't go as far as that,' Jackson said, frowning. 'I think in his position I'd have asked somebody to take it away.'

'You would?'

'Wouldn't you?'

'But why, in God's name?'

'Oh, I suppose I'd be afraid of the scandal – I'm not a very courageous type.'

'Scandal?'

'Whatever you like to call it. After all, some woman sent it.'

'Yes. One of Devine's old maids.'

'Have you ever heard of an old maid sending a wreath of red roses to a funeral?' Jackson asked, raising his brows, his head cocked.

'To tell you the God's truth, I might have done it myself,' Fogarty confessed with boyish candour. 'It would never have struck me that there was anything wrong with it.'

'It would have struck the old maid all right, though.'

Fogarty turned his eyes for a moment to stare at Jackson. Jackson was staring back. Then he missed a turning and reversed with a muttered curse. To the left of them the Wicklow mountains stretched away southwards, and between the grey walls the fields were a ragged brilliant green under the tattered sky.

'You're not serious, Jim?' he said after a few minutes.

'Oh, I'm not suggesting that there was anything wrong,' Jackson said, gesturing widely with his pipe. 'Women get ideas. We all know that.'

'These things can happen in very innocent ways,' Fogarty said with ingenuous solemnity. Then he scowled again and a blush spread over his handsome craggy face. Like all those who live mainly in their imaginations, he was always astonished and shocked at the suggestions that reached him from the outside world: he could live with his fantasies only by assuming that they were nothing more. Jackson, whose own imagination was curbed and even timid, who never went at things like a thoroughbred at a gate, watched him with amusement and a certain envy. Just occasionally he felt that he himself would have liked to welcome a new idea with that boyish wonder and panic.

'I can't believe it,' Fogarty said angrily, tossing his head.

'You don't have to,' Jackson replied, nursing his pipe and swinging round in the seat with his arm close to Fogarty's shoulder. 'As I say, women get these queer ideas. There's usually nothing in them. At the same time, I must say *I* wouldn't be very scandalised if I found out that there was something in it. If ever a man needed someone to care for him, Devine did in the last year or two.'

'But not Devine, Jim,' Fogarty said, raising his voice. 'Not Devine! You could believe a thing like that about me. I suppose I could believe it about you. But I knew Devine since we were kids, and he wouldn't be capable of it.'

'I never knew him in that way,' Jackson admitted. 'In fact, I scarcely knew him at all, really. But I'd have said he was as capable of it as the rest of us. He was lonelier than the rest of us.'

'God, don't I know it?' Fogarty said in sudden self-reproach. 'I could understand if it was drink.'

'Oh, not drink!' Jackson said with distaste. 'He was too fastidious. Can you imagine him in the DTs like some old parish priest, trying to strangle the nurses?'

'But that's what I say, Jim. He wasn't the type.'

'Oh, you must make distinctions,' said Jackson. 'I could imagine him attracted by some intelligent woman. You know yourself how he'd appeal to her, the same way he appealed to us, a cultured man in a country town. I don't have to tell you the sort of life an intelligent woman leads, married to some lout of a shopkeeper or a gentleman farmer. Poor devils, it's a mercy that most of them aren't educated.'

'He didn't give you any hint who she was?' Fogarty asked incredulously. Jackson had spoken with such conviction that it impressed him as true.

'Oh, I don't even know if there was such a woman,' Jackson said hastily, and then he blushed too. Fogarty remained silent. He knew now that Jackson had been talking about himself, not Devine.

As the country grew wilder and furze bushes and ruined keeps took the place of pastures and old abbeys, Fogarty found his eyes attracted more and more to the wreath that swayed lightly with the hearse, the only spot of pure colour in the whole landscape with its watery greens and blues and greys. It seemed an image of the essential mystery of a priest's life. What, after all, did he really know of Devine? Only what his own temperament suggested, and mostly – when he wasn't being St Francis of Assisi – he had seen himself as the worldly one of the pair, the practical, coarse-grained man who cut corners, and Devine as the saint, racked by the fastidiousness and asceticism that exploded in his bitter little jests. Now his mind boggled at the idea of the agony that alone could have driven Devine into an entanglement with a woman; yet the measure of his incredulity was that of the conviction he would presently begin to feel. When once an unusual idea broke through his imagination, he hugged it, brooded on it, promoted it to the dignity of a revelation.

'God, don't we lead terrible lives?' he burst out at last. 'Here we are, probably the two people in the world who knew Devine best, and even we have no notion what that thing in front of us means.'

'Which might be as well for our peace of mind,' said Jackson.

'I'll engage it did damn little for Devine's,' Fogarty said

grimly. It was peculiar; he did not believe yet in the reality of the woman behind the wreath, but already he hated her.

'Oh, I don't know,' Jackson said in some surprise. 'Isn't that what we all really want from life?'

'Is it?' Fogarty asked in wonder. He had always thought of Jackson as a cold fish, and suddenly found himself wondering about that as well. After all, there must have been something in him that attracted Devine. He had the feeling that Jackson, who was, as he recognised, by far the subtler man, was probing him, and for the same reason. Each was looking in the other for the quality that had attracted Devine, and which, having made him their friend, might make them friends also. Each was trying to see how far he could go with the other. Fogarty, as usual, was the first with a confession.

'I couldn't do it, Jim,' he said earnestly. 'I was never even tempted, except once, and then it was the wife of one of the men who was in the seminary with me. I was crazy about her. But when I saw what her marriage to the other fellow was like, I changed my mind. She hated him like poison, Jim. I soon saw she might have hated me in the same way. It's only when you see what marriage is really like, as we do, that you realise how lucky we are.'

'Lucky?' Jackson repeated mockingly.

'Aren't we?'

'Did you ever know a seminary that wasn't full of men who thought they were lucky? They might be drinking themselves to death, but they never doubted their luck? Nonsense, man! Anyway, why do you think she'd have hated you?'

'I don't,' Fogarty replied with a boyish laugh. 'Naturally, I think I'd have been the perfect husband for her. That's the way Nature kids you.'

'Well, why shouldn't you have made her a perfect husband?' Jackson asked quizzically. 'There's nothing much wrong with you that I can see. Though I admit I can see you better as a devoted. father.'

'God knows you might be right,' Fogarty said, his face clouding again. It was as changeable as an Irish sky, Jackson thought with amusement. 'You could get on well enough without the woman, but the kids are hell. She had two. "Father Fogey" they used to call me. And my mother was as bad,' he burst out. 'She was wrapped up in the pair of us. She always wanted us to be better than everybody else, and when we weren't she used to cry. She said it was the Fogarty blood breaking out in us – the Fogartys were all horse dealers.' His handsome, happy face was black with all the old remorse and guilt. 'I'm afraid she died under the impression that I was a Fogarty after all.'

'If the Fogartys are any relation to the Martins, I'd say it was most unlikely,' Jackson said, half amused, half touched.

'I never knew till she was dead how much she meant to me,' Fogarty said broodingly. 'Hennessey warned me not to take the Burial Service myself, but I thought it was the last thing I could do for her. He knew what he was talking about, of course. I disgraced myself, bawling like a blooming kid, and he pushed me aside and finished it for me. My God, the way we gallop through that till it comes to our own turn! Every time I've read it since, I've read it as if it were for my mother.'

Jackson shook his head uncomprehendingly.

'You feel these things more than I do,' he said. 'I'm a cold fish.'

It struck Fogarty with some force that this was precisely what he had always believed himself and that now he could believe it no longer.

'Until then, I used to be a bit flighty,' he confessed. 'After that I knew it wasn't in me to care for another woman.'

'That's only more of your nonsense,' said Jackson

impatiently. 'Love is just one thing, not half a dozen. If I were a young fellow looking for a wife I'd go after some girl who felt like that about her father. You probably have too much of it. I haven't enough. When I was in Manister there was a shopkeeper's wife I used to see. I talked to her and lent her books. She was half crazy with loneliness. Then one morning I got home and found her standing outside my door in the pouring rain. She'd been there half the night. She wanted me to take her away, to "save" her, as she said. You can imagine what happened her after.'

'Went off with someone else, I suppose?'

'No such luck. She took to drinking and sleeping with racing men. Sometimes I blame myself for it. I feel I should have kidded her along. But I haven't enough love to go round. You have too much. With your enthusiastic nature you'd probably have run off with her.'

'I often wondered what I would do,' Fogarty said shyly.

He felt very close to tears. It was partly the wreath, brilliant in the sunlight, that had drawn him out of his habitual reserve and made him talk in that way with a man of even greater reserve. Partly, it was the emotion of returning to the little town where he had grown up. He hated and avoided it; it seemed to him to represent all the narrowness and meanness that he tried to banish from his thoughts, but at the same time it contained all the nostalgia and violence he had felt there; and when he drew near it again a tumult of emotions rose in him that half strangled him. He was watching for it already like a lover.

'There it is!' he said triumphantly, pointing to a valley where a tapering Franciscan tower rose on the edge of a clutter of low Georgian houses and thatched cabins. 'They'll be waiting for us at the bridge. That's how they'll be waiting for me when my turn comes, Jim.'

A considerable crowd had gathered at the farther side of the bridge to escort the hearse to the cemetery. Four men shouldered the shiny coffin over the bridge past the ruined castle and up the hilly Main Street. Shutters were up on the shop fronts, blinds were drawn, everything was at a standstill except where a curtain was lifted and an old woman peered out.

'Counting the mourners,' Fogarty said with a bitter laugh. 'They'll say I had nothing like as many as Devine. That place,' he added, lowering his voice, 'the second shop from the corner, that was ours.'

Jackson took it in at a glance. He was puzzled and touched by Fogarty's emotion because there was nothing to distinguish the little market town from a hundred others. A laneway led off the hilly road and they came to the abbey, a ruined tower and a few walls, with tombstones sown thickly in choir and nave. The hearse was already drawn up outside and people had gathered in a semicircle about it. Ned Devine came hastily up to the car where the two priests were donning their vestments. Fogarty knew at once that there was trouble brewing.

'Whisper, Father Jerry,' Ned muttered in a strained, excited voice. 'People are talking about that wreath. I wonder would you know who sent it?'

'I don't know the first thing about it, Ned,' Fogarty replied, and suddenly his heart began to beat violently.

'Come here a minute, Sheela,' Ned called, and a tall, pale girl with the stain of tears on her long bony face left the little group of mourners and joined them. Fogarty nodded to her. She was Devine's sister, a schoolteacher who had never married. 'This is Father Jackson, Father Willie's other friend. They don't know anything about it either.'

'Then I'd let them take it back,' she said doggedly.

'What would you say, father?' Ned asked, appealing to

Fogarty, and suddenly Fogarty felt his courage desert him. In disputing with Martin he had felt himself an equal on neutral ground, but now the passion and prejudice of the little town seemed to rise up and oppose him, and he felt himself again a boy, rebellious and terrified. You had to know the place to realise the hysteria that could be provoked by something like a funeral.

'I can only tell you what I told Father Martin already,' he said, growing red and angry.

'Did he talk about it too?' Ned asked sharply.

'There!' Sheela said vindictively. 'What did I tell you?'

'Well, the pair of you are cleverer than I am,' Fogarty said. 'I saw nothing wrong with it.'

'It was no proper thing to send to a priest's funeral,' she hissed with prim fury. 'And whoever sent it was no friend of my brother.'

'You saw nothing wrong with it, father?' Ned prompted appealingly.

'But I tell you, Uncle Ned, if that wreath goes into the graveyard we'll be the laughing stock of the town,' she said in an old-maidish frenzy. 'I'll throw it out myself if you won't.'

'Whisht, girl, whisht, and let Father Jerry talk!' Ned said furiously.

'It's entirely a matter for yourselves, Ned,' Fogarty said excitedly. He was really scared now. He knew he was in danger of behaving imprudently in public, and sooner or later, the story would get back to the Bishop, and it would be suggested that he knew more than he pretended.

'If you'll excuse me interrupting, father,' Jackson said suavely, giving Fogarty a warning glance over his spectacles. 'I know this is none of my business.'

'Not at all, father, not at all,' Ned said passionately. 'You were the boy's friend. All we want is for you to tell us what to do.'

'Oh, well, Mr Devine, that would be too great a responsibility for me to take,' Jackson replied with a cagey smile,
though Fogarty saw that his face was very flushed. 'Only someone who really knows the town could advise you about that.
I only know what things are like in my own place. Of course,
I entirely agree with Miss Devine,' he said, giving her a smile
that suggested that this, like crucifixion, was something he
preferred to avoid. 'Naturally, Father Fogarty and I have discussed it already. I think personally that it was entirely improper
to send a wreath.' Then his mild, clerical voice suddenly grew
menacing and he shrugged his shoulders with an air of con-
tempt. 'But, speaking as an outsider, I'd say if you were to
send that wreath back from the graveyard, you'd make yourself
something far worse than a laughing stock. You'd throw mud
on a dead man's name that would never be forgotten for you
the longest day you lived . . . Of course, that's only an outsider's opinion,' he added urbanely, drawing in his breath in
a positive hiss.

'Of course, of course, of course,' Ned Devine said, click-
ing his fingers and snapping into action. 'We should have
thought of it ourselves, father. 'Twould be giving tongues to
the stones.'

Then he lifted the wreath himself and carried it to the
graveside. Several of the men by the gate looked at him with
a questioning eye and fell in behind him. Some hysteria had
gone out of the air. Fogarty gently squeezed Jackson's hand.

'Good man, Jim!' he said in a whisper. 'Good man you are!'

He stood with Jackson at the head of the open grave beside
the local priests. As their voices rose in the psalms for the dead
and their vestments billowed about them, Fogarty's brooding
eyes swept the crowd of faces he had known since his childhood
and which were now caricatured by age and pain. Each time

they came to rest on the wreath which stood at one side of the open grave. It would lie there now above Devine when all the living had gone, his secret. And each time it came over him in a wave of emotion that what he and Jackson had protected was something more than a sentimental token. It was the thing that had linked them to Devine, and for the future would link them to one another – love. Not half a dozen things, but one thing, between son and mother, man and sweetheart, friend and friend.

An Act of Charity

THE PARISH PRIEST, Father Maginnis, did not like the second curate, Father Galvin, and Father Fogarty could see why. It was the dislike of the professional for the amateur, no matter how talented, and nobody could have said that Father Galvin had much in the way of talent. Maginnis was a professional to his fingertips. He drove the right car, knew the right people, and could suit his conversation to any company, even that of women. He even varied his accent to make people feel at home. With Deasy, the owner of the garage, he talked about 'the caw', but to Lavin, the garage hand, he said 'the cyarr', smiling benignly at the homeliness of his touch.

Galvin was thin, pale, irritable, and intense. When he should have kept a straight face he made some stupid joke that stopped the conversation dead; and when he laughed in the proper place at someone else's joke, it was with a slight air of vexation, as though he found it hard to put up with people who made him laugh at all. He worried himself over little embarrassments and what people would think of them, till Fogarty asked bluntly, 'What the hell difference does it make what they think?' Then Galvin looked away sadly and said, 'I suppose you're right.'

But Fogarty didn't mind his visits so much except when

he had asked other curates in for a drink and a game of cards. Then he took a glass of sherry or something equally harmless and twiddled it awkwardly for half an hour as though it were some sort of patent device for keeping his hands occupied. When one of the curates made a harmless dirty joke, Galvin pretended to be looking at a picture so that he didn't have to comment. Fogarty, who loved giving people nicknames, called him Father Mother's Boy. He called Maginnis the Old Pro, but when that nickname got back, as everything a priest says gets back, it did Fogarty no harm at all. Maginnis was glad he had a curate with so much sense.

He sometimes asked Fogarty to Sunday dinner, but he soon gave up on asking Galvin, and again Fogarty sympathised with him. Maginnis was a professional, even to his dinners. He basted his meat with one sort of wine and his chickens with another, and he liked a guest who could tell the difference. He also liked him to drink two large whiskeys before dinner and to make sensible remarks about the wine; and when he had exhausted the secrets of his kitchen he sat back, smoked his cigar, and told funny stories. They were very good stories, mostly about priests.

'Did I ever tell you the one about Canon Murphy, father?' he would bellow, his fat face beaming. 'Ah, that's damn good. Canon Murphy went on a pilgrimage to Rome, and when he came back he preached a sermon on it. "So I had a special audience with His Holiness, dearly beloved brethren, and he asked me, 'Canon Murphy, where are you now?' 'I'm in Dromod, Your Holiness,' said I. 'What sort of a parish is it, Canon Murphy?' says he. 'Ah, 'tis a nice, snug little parish, Your Holiness,' says I. 'Are they a good class of people?' says he. 'Well, they're not bad, Your Holiness,' said I. 'Are they good-living people?' says he. 'Well, they're as good as the next, Your Holiness,' says I. 'Except when they'd have a drop taken.'

'Tell me, Canon Murphy,' says he, 'do they pay their dues?'
And like that, I was nearly struck dumb. 'There you have me,
Your Holiness!' says I. 'There you have me!' " '

At heart Fogarty thought Maginnis was a bit of a sham and
that most of his stories were fabrications; but he never made
the mistake of underestimating him, and he enjoyed the feeling Maginnis gave him of belonging to a group, and that of
the best kind – well balanced, humane, and necessary.

At meals in the curates' house, Galvin had a tendency to
chatter brightly and aimlessly that irritated Fogarty. He was
full of scraps of undigested knowledge, picked up from
newspapers and magazines, about new plays and books that
he would never either see or read. Fogarty was a moody young
man who preferred either to keep silent or engage in long
emotional discussions about local scandals that grew murkier
and more romantic the more he described them. About such
things he was hopelessly indiscreet. 'And that fellow notoriously
killed his own father,' he said once, and Galvin looked at him
in distress. 'You mean he really killed him?' he asked – as
though Fogarty did not really mean everything at the moment
he was saying it – and then, to make things worse, added, 'It's
not something I'd care to repeat – not without evidence, I
mean.'

'The Romans used eunuchs for civil servants, but we're more
enlightened,' Fogarty said once to Maginnis. 'We prefer the
natural ones.' Maginnis gave a hearty laugh; it was the sort
of remark he liked to repeat. And when Galvin returned after
lunching austerely with some maiden ladies and offered half-
baked suggestions, Maginnis crushed him, and Fogarty
watched with malicious amusement. He knew it was turning
into persecution, but he wasn't quite sure which of the two
men suffered more.

When he heard the explosion in the middle of the night,

he waited for some further noise to interpret it, and then rose
and put on the light. The housekeeper was standing outside
her bedroom door in a raincoat, her hands joined. She was
a widow woman with a history of tragedy behind her, and
Fogarty did not like her; for some reason he felt she had the
evil eye, and he always addressed her in his most commanding tone.

'What was that, Mary?' he asked.

'I don't know, father,' she said in a whisper. 'It sounded
as if it was in Father Galvin's room.'

Fogarty listened again. There was no sound from Galvin's
room, and he knocked and pushed in the door. He closed the
door again immediately.

'Get Dr Carmody quick!' he said brusquely.

'What is it, father?' she asked. 'An accident?'

'Yes, a bad one. And when you're finished, run out and
ask Father Maginnis to come in.'

'Oh, that old gun!' she moaned softly. 'I dreaded it. I'll ring
Dr Carmody.' She went hastily down the stairs.

Fogarty followed her and went into the living room to pick
up the sacred oils from the cupboard where they were kept.
'I don't know, doctor,' he heard Mary moaning. 'Father
Fogarty said it was an accident.' He returned upstairs and lifted
the gun from the bed before anointing the dead man. He had
just concluded when the door opened and he saw the parish
priest come in, wearing a blue flowered dressing gown.

Maginnis went over to the bed and stared down at the figure
on it. Then he looked at Fogarty over his glasses, his face almost
expressionless. 'I was afraid of something like this,' he said
knowingly. 'I knew he was a bit unstable.'

'You don't think it could be an accident?' Fogarty asked,
though he knew the question sounded ridiculous.

'No,' Maginnis said, giving him a downward look through

the spectacles. 'Do you?'

'But how could he bring himself to do a thing like that?' Fogarty asked incredulously.

'Oh, who knows?'   ··d Maginnis, almost impatiently. 'With weak characters it's har₍ to tell. He doesn't seem to have left any message.'

'Not that I can see.'

'I'm sorry 'twas Carmody you sent for.'

'But he was Galvin's doctor.'

'I know, I know, but all the same he's young and a bit immature. I'd have preferred an older man. Make no mistake about it, father, we have a problem on our hands,' he added with sudden resolution. 'A very serious problem.'

Fogarty did not need to have the problem spelled out for him. The worst thing a priest could do was to commit suicide, since it seemed to deny everything that gave his vocation meaning – Divine Providence and Mercy, forgiveness, Heaven, Hell. That one of God's anointed could come to such a state of despair was something the Church could not admit. It would give too much scandal. It was simply an unacceptable act.

'That's his car now, I fancy,' Maginnis said.

Carmody came quickly up the stairs with his bag in his hand and his pink pyjamas showing under his tweed jacket. He was a tall, spectacled young man with a long, humorous clown's face, and in ordinary life adopted a manner that went with his face, but Fogarty knew he was both competent and conscientious. He had worked for some years in an English hospital and developed a bluntness of speech that Fogarty found refreshing.

'Christ!' he said as he took in the scene. Then he went over and looked closely at the body. 'Poor Peter!' he added. Then he took the shotgun from the bedside table, where Fogarty had put it and examined it. 'I should have kept a closer eye on him,' he said with chagrin. 'There isn't much I can do for him now.'

'On the contrary, doctor,' Maginnis said. 'There was never a time when you could do more for him.' Then he gave Fogarty a meaningful glance. 'I wonder if you'd mind getting Jack Fitzgerald for me, father? Talk to himself, and I needn't warn you to be creful what you say.'

'Oh, I'll be careful,' Fogarty said with gloomy determination. There was something in his nature that always responded to the touch of melodrama, and he knew Maginnis wanted to talk to Carmody alone. He telephoned to Fitzgerald, the undertaker, and then went back upstairs to dress. It was clear he wasn't going to get any more sleep that night.

He heard himself called and returned to Galvin's room. This time he really felt the full shock of it: the big bald parish priest in his dressing gown and the gaunt young doctor with his pyjama top open under the jacket. He could see the two men had been arguing.

'Perhaps you'd talk to Dr Carmody, father?' Maginnis suggested benignly.

'There's nothing to talk about, Father Fogarty,' Carmody said, adopting the formal title he ignored when they were among friends. 'I can't sign a certificate saying this was a natural death. You know I can't. It's too unprofessional.'

'Professional or not, Dr Carmody, someone will have to do it,' Maginnis said. 'I am the priest of this parish. In a manner of speaking I'm a professional man too, you know. And this unfortunate occurrence is something that doesn't concern only me and you. It has consequences that affect the whole parish.'

'Your profession doesn't require you to sign your name to a lie, father,' Carmody said angrily. 'That's what you want me to do.'

'Oh, I wouldn't call that a lie, Dr Carmody,' Maginnis said with dignity. 'In considering the nature of a lie we have to take account of its good and bad effects. I can see no possible good effect that might result from a scandal about the death of this poor boy. Not one! In fact, I can see unlimited harm.'

'So can I,' Fogarty burst out. His voice sounded too loud, too confident, even to his own ears.

'I see,' Carmody said sarcastically. 'And you think we should keep on denouncing the Swedes and Danes for their suicide statistics, just because they don't fake them the way we do. Ah, for God's sake, man, I'd never be able to respect myself again.'

Fogarty saw that Maginnis was right. In some ways Carmody was too immature. 'That's all very well, Jim, but Christian charity comes before statistics,' he said appealingly. 'Forget about the damn statistics, can't you? Father Galvin wasn't only a statistic. He was a human being – somebody we both knew. And what about his family?'

'What about his mother?' Maginnis asked with real pathos. 'I gather you have a mother yourself, Dr Carmody?'

'And you expect me to meet Mrs Galvin tomorrow and tell her her son was a suicide and can't be buried in consecrated ground?' Fogarty went on emotionally. 'Would you like us to do that to your mother if it was your case?'

'A doctor has unpleasant things to do as well, Jerry,' said Carmody.

'To tell a mother that her child is dying?' Fogarty asked. 'A priest has to do that too, remember. Not to tell her that her child is damned.'

But the very word that Fogarty knew had impressed Carmody made the parish priest uncomfortable. 'Fortunately, father, that is in better hands than yours or mine,' he said curtly. And at once his manner changed. It was as though he was a little bit tired of them both. 'Dr Carmody,' he said, 'I think I hear Mr Fitzgerald. You'd better make up your mind quick. If you're not prepared to sign the death certificate, I'll soon find another doctor who will. That is my simple duty, and I'm going to do it. But as an elderly man who knows a little more about this town than you or Father Fogarty here, I'd advise you not to compel me to bring in another doctor. If word got round that I was forced to do such a thing, it might have very serious effects on your career.'

There was no mistaking the threat, and there was something almost admirable about the way it was made. At the same time, it roused the sleeping rebel in Fogarty. Bluff, he thought angrily. Damn bluff! If Carmody walked out on them at that moment, there was very little the parish priest or anyone else could do to him. Of course, any of the other doctors would sign the certificate, but it wouldn't do them any good either. When people really felt the need for a doctor, they didn't necessarily want the doctor the parish priest approved of. But as he looked at Carmody's sullen, resentful face, he realised that Carmody didn't know his own strength in the way that Maginnis knew his. After all, what had he behind him but a few years in a London hospital, while behind Maginnis was that whole vast historic organisation that he was rightly so proud of.

'I can't sign a certificate that death was due to natural causes,' Carmody said stubbornly. 'Accident, maybe – I don't know. I wasn't here. I'll agree to accident.'

'Accident?' Maginnis said contemptuously, and this time he did not even trouble to use Carmody's title. It was as though he were stripping him of any little dignity he had. 'Young man, accidents with shotguns do not happen to priests at three o'clock in the morning. Try to talk sense!'

And just as Fogarty realised that the doctor had allowed himself to be crushed, they heard Mary let Fitzgerald in. He came briskly up the stairs. He was a small, spare man built like a jockey. The parish priest nodded in the direction of the bed and Fitzgerald's brows went up mechanically. He was a man who said little, but he had a face and figure too expressive for his character. It was as though all the opinions he suppressed in life found relief in violent physical movements.

'Naturally, we don't want it talked about, Mr Fitzgerald,' said Maginnis. 'Do you think you could handle it yourself?'

The undertaker's eyes popped again, and he glanced swiftly from Maginnis to Carmody and then to Fogarty. He was a great man for efficiency, though; if you had asked him to supply the corpse as well as the coffin, he might have responded automatically, 'Male or female?'

'Dr Carmody will give the certificate, of course?' he asked shrewdly. He hadn't missed much of what was going on.

'It seems I don't have much choice,' Carmody replied bitterly.

'Oh, purely as an act of charity, of course,' Fitz said hastily. 'We all have to do this sort of thing from time to time. The poor relatives have enough to worry them without inquests and things like that. What was the age, Father Maginnis, do you know?' he added, taking out a notebook. A clever little man, thought Fogarty. He had put it all at once upon a normal, businesslike footing.

'Twenty-eight,' said Maginnis.

'God help us!' Fitz said perfunctorily, and made a note. After that he took out a rule.

'I'd better get ready and go to see the Bishop myself,' Maginnis said. 'We'll need his permission, of course, but I haven't much doubt about that. I know he has the reputation for being on the strict side, but I always found him very considerate. I'll send Nora over to help your housekeeper, father. In the meantime, maybe you'd be good enough to get in touch with the family.'

'I'll see to that, father,' Fogarty said. He and Carmody followed Maginnis downstairs. He said goodbye and left, and Fogarty's manner changed abruptly. 'Come in and have a drink, Jim,' he said.

'I'd rather not, Jerry,' Carmody said gloomily.

'Come on! Come on! You need one, man! I need one myself and I can't have it.' He shut the door of the living room behind him. 'Great God, Jim, who could have suspected it?'

'I suppose I should have,' said Carmody. 'I got hints enough if only I might have understood them.'

'But you couldn't, Jim,' Fogarty said excitedly, taking the whiskey from the big cupboard. 'Nobody could. Do you think I ever expected it, and I lived closer to him than you did.'

The front door opened and they heard the slippers of Nora, Maginnis's housekeeper, in the hall. There was a low mumble of talk outside the door, and then the clank of a bucket as the women went up the stairs. Fitzgerald was coming down at the same time, and Fogarty opened the door a little.

'Well, Jack?'

'Well, father. I'll do the best I can.'

'You wouldn't join us for a – ?'

'No, father. I'll have my hands full for the next couple of hours.'

'Good night, Jack. And I'm sorry for the disturbance.'

'Ah, 'twas none of your doing. Good night, father.'

The doctor finished his whiskey in a gulp, and his long, battered face had a bitter smile. 'And so this is how it's done!' he said.

'This is how it's done, Jim, and believe me, it's the best way for everybody in the long run,' Fogarty replied with real gravity.

But, looking at Carmody's face, he knew the doctor did not

believe it, and he wondered then if he really believed it himself.

When the doctor had gone, Fogarty got on the telephone to a provincial town fifty miles away. The exchange was closed down, so he had to give his message to the police. In ten minutes or so a guard would set out along the sleeping streets to the house where the Galvins lived. That was one responsibility he was glad to evade.

While he was speaking, he heard the parish priest's car set off and knew he was on his way to the Bishop's palace. Then he shaved, and, about eight, Fitzgerald drove up with the coffin in his van. Silently they carried it between them up the stairs. The body was lying decently composed with a simple bandage about the head. Between them they lifted it into the coffin. Fitzgerald looked questioningly at Fogarty and went on his knees. As he said the brief prayer, Fogarty found his voice unsteady and his eyes full of tears. Fitzgerald gave him a pitying look and then rose and dusted his knees.

'All the same there'll be talk, father,' he said.

'Maybe not as much as there should be, Jack,' Fogarty said moodily.

'We'll take him to the chapel, of course?' Fitzgerald went on.

'Everything in order, Jack. Father Maginnis is gone to see the Bishop.'

'He couldn't trust the telephone, of course,' Fitzgerald said, stroking his unshaven chin. 'No fear the Bishop will interfere, though. Father Maginnis is a smart man. You saw him?'

'I saw him.'

'No nerves, no hysterics. I saw other people in the same situation. "Oh, Mr Fitzgerald, what am I going to do?" His mind on essential things the whole time. He's an object lesson to us all, father.'

'You're right, Jack, he is,' Fogarty said despondently.

Suddenly the undertaker's hand shot out and caught him

by the upper arm. 'Forget about it, boy! Forget about it! What else can you do? Why the hell should you break your heart over it?'

Fogarty still had to meet the family. Later that morning, they drove up to the curates' house. The mother was an actressy type and wept a good deal. She wanted somebody to give her a last message, which Fogarty couldn't think up. The sister, a pretty, intense girl, wept a little too, but quietly, with her back turned, while the brother, a young man with a great resemblance to Galvin, said little. Mother and brother accepted without protest the ruling that the coffin was not to be opened, but the sister looked at Fogarty and asked, 'You don't think I could see him? Alone? I wouldn't be afraid.' When he said the doctor had forbidden it, she turned her back again, and he had an impression that there was a closer link between her and Galvin than between the others and him.

That evening, they brought the body to lie before the altar of the church, and Maginnis received it and said the prayers. The church was crowded, and Fogarty knew with a strange mixture of rejoicing and mortification that the worst was over. Maginnis's master stroke was the new curate, Rowlands, who had arrived within a couple of hours after his own return. He was a tall, thin, ascetic-looking young man, slow-moving and slow-speaking, and Fogarty knew that all eyes were on him.

Everything went with perfect propriety at the Requiem Mass next morning, and after the funeral Fogarty attended the lunch given by Maginnis to the visiting clergy. He almost laughed out loud when he heard Maginnis ask in a low voice, 'Father Healy, did I ever tell you the story of Canon Murphy and the Pope?' All that would follow would be the mourning card with the picture of Galvin and the Gothic lettering that said 'Ecce Sacerdos Magnus.' There was no danger of a scandal any longer. Carmody would not talk. Fitzgerald would not talk either. None of the five people involved would. Father Galvin might have spared himself the trouble.

As they returned from the church together, Fogarty tried to talk to the new curate about what had happened, but he soon realised that the whole significance of it had escaped Rowlands, and that Rowlands thought he was only over-dramatising it all. Anybody would think he was overdramatising it, except Carmody. After his supper he would go to the doctor's house, and they would talk about it. Only Carmody would really understand what it was they had done between them. No one else would.

What lonely lives we live, he thought unhappily.

THE MASS ISLAND

WHEN FATHER JACKSON DROVE UP to the curates' house, it was already drawing on to dusk, the early dusk of late December. The curates' house was a red-brick building on a terrace at one side of the ugly church in Asragh. Father Hamilton seemed to have been waiting for him and opened the front door himself, looking white and strained. He was a tall young man with a long melancholy face that you would have taken for weak till you noticed the cut of the jaw.

'Oh, come in, Jim,' he said with his mournful smile. ''Tisn't much of a welcome we have for you, God knows. I suppose you'd like to see poor Jerry before the undertaker comes.'

'I might as well,' Father Jackson replied briskly. There was nothing melancholy about Jackson, but he affected an air of surprise and shock. ''Twas very sudden, wasn't it?'

'Well, it was and it wasn't, Jim,' Father Hamilton said, closing the front door behind him. 'He was going downhill since he got the first heart attack, and he wouldn't look after himself. Sure, you know yourself what he was like.'

Jackson knew. Father Fogarty and himself had been friends of a sort, for years. An impractical man, excitable and vehement, Fogarty could have lived for twenty years with his ailment, but instead of that, he allowed himself to become depressed and indifferent. If he couldn't live as he had always lived, he would prefer not to live at all.

They went upstairs and into the bedroom where he was. The character was still plain on the stern, dead face, though, drained of vitality, it had the look of a studio portrait. That bone structure was something you'd have picked out of a thousand faces as Irish, with its odd impression of bluntness and asymmetry, its jutting brows and craggy chin, and the snub nose that looked as though it had probably been broken twenty years before in a public-house row.

When they came downstairs again, Father Hamilton produced half a bottle of whiskey.

'Not for me, thanks,' Jackson said hastily. 'Unless you have a drop of sherry there?'

'Well, there is some Burgundy,' Father Hamilton said. 'I don't know is it any good, though.'

"Twill do me fine,' Jackson replied cheerfully, reflecting that Ireland was the country where nobody knew whether Burgundy was good or not. 'You're coming with us tomorrow, I suppose?'

'Well, the way it is, Jim,' Father Hamilton replied, 'I'm afraid neither of us is going. You see, they're burying poor Jerry here.'

'They're what?' Jackson asked incredulously.

'Now, I didn't know for sure when I rang you, Jim, but that's what the brother decided, and that's what Father Hanafey decided as well.'

'But he told you he wanted to be buried on the Mass Island, didn't he?'

'He told everybody, Jim,' Father Hamilton replied with growing excitement and emotion. 'That was the sort he was. If he told one, he told five hundred. Only half an hour ago I had a girl on the telephone from the island asking when they could expect us. You see, the old parish priest of the place let Jerry mark out the grave for himself, and they want to know should they open it. But now the old parish priest is dead as well, and of course Jerry left nothing in writing.'

'Didn't he leave a will, even?' Jackson asked in surprise.

'Well, he did and he didn't, Jim,' Father Hamilton said, looking as if he were on the point of tears. 'Actually, he did make a will about five or six years ago, and he gave it to Clancy, the other curate, but Clancy went off on the Foreign Mission and God alone knows where he is now. After that, Jerry never bothered his head about it. I mean, you have to admit the man had nothing to leave. Every damn thing he had he gave away – even the old car – after he got the first attack. If there was any loose cash around, I suppose the brother has that.'

Jackson sipped his Burgundy, which was even more Australian than he had feared, and wondered at his own irritation. He had been irritated enough before that, with the prospect of two days' motoring in the middle of winter, and a night in a godforsaken pub in the mountains, a hundred and fifty miles away at the other side of Ireland. There, in one of the lakes, was an island where in Cromwell's time, before the causeway and the little oratory were built, Mass was said in secret, and it was here that Father Fogarty had wanted to be buried. It struck Jackson as sheer sentimentality; it wasn't even as if it was Fogarty's native place. Jackson had once allowed Fogarty to lure him there, and had hated every moment of it. It wasn't only the discomfort of the public-house, where meals erupted at any hour of the day or night as the spirit took the proprietor, or the rain that kept them confined to the cold dining-and-sitting room that looked out on the gloomy mountainside, with its couple of whitewashed cabins on the shore of the lake. It was the overintimacy of it all, and this was the thing that Father Fogarty apparently loved. He liked to stand in his shirtsleeves behind the bar, taking turns with the proprietor, who was one of his many friends, serving big pints of porter to rough mountainy men, or to sit in their cottages, shaking in all his fat whenever they told broad stories or sang risky folk songs. 'God, Jim, isn't it grand?' he would say in his deep voice, and Jackson would look at him over his spectacles with what Fogarty called his 'Jesuitical' look, and say, 'Well, I suppose it all depends on what you really like, Jerry.' He wasn't even certain that the locals cared for Father Fogarty's intimacy; on the contrary, he had a strong impression that they much preferred their own reserved old parish priest, whom they never saw except twice a year, when he came up the valley to collect his dues. That had made Jackson twice as stiff. And yet now when he found out that the plans that had meant so much inconvenience to him had fallen through, he was as disappointed as though they had been his own.

'Oh, well,' he said with a shrug that was intended to conceal his perturbation, 'I suppose it doesn't make much difference where they chuck us when our time comes.'

'The point is, it mattered to Jerry, Jim,' Father Hamilton said with his curious, shy obstinacy. 'God knows, it's not anything that will ever worry me, but it haunted him, and somehow, you know, I don't feel it's right to flout a dead man's wishes.'

'Oh, I know, I know,' Jackson said lightly. 'I suppose I'd better talk to old Hanafey about it. Knowing I'm a friend of the Bishop's, he might pay more attention to me.'

'He might, Jim,' Father Hamilton replied sadly, looking away over Jackson's head. 'As you say, knowing you're a friend of the Bishop's, he might. But I wouldn't depend too much on it. I talked to him till I was black in the face, and all I got out of him was the law and the rubrics. It's the brother Hanafey is afraid of. You'll see him this evening, and between ourselves, he's a tough customer. Of course, himself and Jerry never had much to say to one another, and he'd be the last man in the world that Jerry would talk to about his funeral, so now he doesn't want the expense and inconvenience. You wouldn't blame him, of course. I'd probably be the same myself. By the way,' Father Hamilton added, lowering his voice, 'before he does come, I'd like you to take a look round Jerry's room and see is there any little memento you'd care to have – a photo or a book or anything.'

They went into Father Fogarty's sitting room, and Jackson looked at it with a new interest. He knew of old the rather handsome library – Fogarty had been a man of many enthusiasms, though none of long duration – the picture of the Virgin and Child in Irish country costume over the mantelpiece, which some of his colleagues had thought irreverent, and the couple of fine old prints. There was a newer picture that Jackson had not seen – a charcoal drawing of the Crucifixion from a fifteenth-century Irish tomb, which was brutal but impressive.

'Good Lord!' Jackson exclaimed with a sudden feeling of loss. 'He really had taste, hadn't he?'

'He had, Jim,' Father Hamilton said, sticking his long nose into the picture. 'This goes to a young couple called Keneally, outside the town, that he was fond of. I think they were very kind to him. Since he had the attack, he was pretty lonely, I'd say.'

'Oh, aren't we all, attack or no attack,' Jackson said almost irritably.

Father Hanafey, the parish priest of Asragh, was a round, red, cherubic-looking old man with a bald head and big round glasses. His house was on the same terrace as the curates'. He, too, insisted on producing the whiskey Jackson so heartily detested when the two priests came in to consult him, but Jackson had decided that this time diplomacy required he should show proper appreciation of the dreadful stuff. He felt sure he was going to be very sick next day. He affected great astonishment at the quality of Father Hanafey's whiskey, and. first the old parish priest grew shy, like a schoolgirl whose good looks are being praised, then he looked self-satisfied, and finally he became almost emotional. It was a great pleasure, he said, to meet a young priest with a proper understanding of whiskey. Priests no longer seemed to have the same taste, and as far as most of them were concerned, they might as well be drinking poteen. It was only when it was seven years old that Irish began to be interesting, and that was when you had to catch it and store it in sherry casks to draw off what remained of crude alcohol in it, and give it that beautiful roundness that Father Jackson had spotted. But it shouldn't be kept too long, for somewhere along the line the spirit of a whiskey was broken. At ten, or maybe twelve, years old it was just right. But people were losing their palates. He solemnly assured the two priests that of every dozen clerics who came to his house not more than one would realise what he was drinking. Poor Hamilton grew red and began to stutter, but the parish priest's reproofs were not directed at him.

'It isn't you I'm talking about, Father Hamilton, but elderly priests, parish priests, and even canons, that you would think would know better, and I give you my word, I put the two whiskeys side by side in front of them, the shop stuff and my own, and they could not tell the difference.'

But though the priest was mollified by Father Jackson's maturity of judgment, he was not prepared to interfere in the arrangements for the funeral of his curate. 'It is the wish of the next of kin, father,' he said stubbornly, 'and that is something I have no control over. Now that you tell me the same thing as Father Hamilton, I accept it that this was Father Fogarty's wish, and a man's wishes regarding his own interment are always to be respected. I assure you, if I had even one line in Father Fogarty's writing to go on, I would wait for no man's advice. I would take the responsibility on myself. Something on paper, father, is all I want.'

'On the other hand, father,' Jackson said mildly, drawing on his pipe, 'if Father Fogarty was the sort to leave written instructions, he'd hardly be the sort to leave such unusual ones. I mean, after all, it isn't even the family burying ground, is it?'

'Well, now, that is true, father,' replied the parish priest, and it was clear that he had been deeply impressed by this rather doubtful logic. 'You have a very good point there, and it is one I did not think of myself, and I have given the matter a great deal of thought. You might mention it to his brother. Father Fogarty, God rest him, was *not* a usual type of man. I think you might even go so far as to say that he was a rather *unusual* type of man, and not orderly, as you say – not by any means orderly. I would certainly mention that to the brother and see what he says.'

But the brother was not at all impressed by Father Jackson's argument when he turned up at the church in Asragh that evening. He was a good-looking man with a weak and pleasant face and a cold shrewdness in his eyes that had been lacking in his brother's.

'But why, father?' he asked, turning to Father Hanafey. 'I'm a busy man, and I'm being asked to leave my business for a couple of days in the middle of winter, and for what? That is all I ask. What use is it?'

'It is only out of respect for the wishes of the deceased, Mr Fogarty,' said Father Hanafey, who clearly was a little bit afraid of him.

'And where did he express those wishes?' the brother asked. 'I'm his only living relative, and it is queer he would not mention a thing like that to me.'

'He mentioned it to Father Jackson and Father Hamilton.'

'But when, father?' Mr Fogarty asked. 'You knew Father Jerry, and he was always expressing wishes about something. He was an excitable sort of man, God rest him, and the thing he'd say today might not be the thing he'd say tomorrow. After all, after close on forty years, I think I have the right to say I knew him,' he added with a triumphant air that left the two young priests without a leg to stand on.

Over bacon and eggs in the curates' house, Father Hamilton was very despondent. 'Well, I suppose we did what we could, Jim,' he said.

'I'm not too sure of that,' Jackson said with his 'Jesuitical' air, looking at Father Hamilton sidewise over his spectacles. 'I'm wondering if we couldn't do something with that family you say he intended the drawing for.'

'The Keneallys,' said Father Hamilton in a worried voice. 'Actually, I saw the wife in the church this evening. You might have noticed her crying.'

'Don't you think we should see if they have anything in writing?'

'Well, if they have, it would be about the picture,' said Father Hamilton. 'How I know about it is she came to me at the time to ask if I couldn't do something for him. Poor man, he was crying himself that day, according to what she told me.'

'Oh dear!' Jackson said politely, but his mind was elsewhere. 'I'm not really interested in knowing what would be in a letter like that. It's none of my business. But I would like to make sure that they haven't something in writing. What did Hanafey call it – "something on paper"?'

'I dare say we should inquire, anyway,' said Father Hamilton, and after supper they drove out to the Keneallys', a typical small red-brick villa with a decent garden in front. The family also was eating bacon and eggs, and Jackson shuddered when they asked him to join them. Keneally himself, a tall, gaunt, cadaverous man, poured out more whiskey for them, and again Jackson felt he must make a formal attempt to drink it. At the same time, he thought he saw what attraction the house had for Father Fogarty. Keneally was tough and with no suggestion of lay servility towards the priesthood, and his wife was beautiful and scatterbrained, and talked to herself, the cat, and the children simultaneously. 'Rosaleen!' she cried determinedly. 'Out! Out I say! I told you if you didn't stop meowing you'd have to go out . . . Angela Keneally, the stick! . . . You do not want to go to the bathroom, Angela. It's only five minutes since you were there before. I will not let Father Hamilton come up to you at all unless you go to bed at once.'

In the children's bedroom, Jackson gave a finger to a stolid-looking infant, who instantly stuffed it into his mouth and began to chew it, apparently under the impression that he would be bound to reach sugar at last.

Later, they sat over their drinks in the sitting room, only interrupted by Angela Keneally, in a fever of curiosity, dropping in every five minutes to ask for a biscuit or a glass of water.

'You see, Father Fogarty left no will,' Jackson explained to Keneally. 'Consequently, he'll be buried here tomorrow unless something turns up. I suppose he told you where he wanted to be buried?'

'On the island? Twenty times, if he told us once. I thought he took it too far. Didn't you, father?'

'And me not to be able to go!' Mrs Keneally said, beginning to cry. 'Isn't it awful, father?'

'He didn't leave anything in writing with you?' He saw in Keneally's eyes that the letter was really only about the picture, and raised a warning hand. 'Mind, if he did, I don't want to know what's in it! In fact, it would be highly improper for anyone to be told before the parish priest and the next of kin were consulted. All I do want to know is whether' – he waited a moment to see that Keneally was following him – 'he did leave any written instructions, of any kind, with you.'

Mrs Keneally, drying her tears, suddenly broke into rapid speech. 'Sure, that was the day poor Father Jerry was so down in himself because we were his friends and he had nothing to leave us, and –'

'Shut up, woman!' her husband shouted with a glare at her, and then Jackson saw him purse his lips in quiet amusement. He was a man after Jackson's heart. 'As you say, father, we have a letter from him.'

'Addressed to anybody in particular?'

'Yes, to the parish priest, to be delivered after his death.'

'Did he use those words?' Jackson asked, touched in spite of himself.

'Those very words.'

'God help us!' said Father Hamilton.

'But you had not time to deliver it?'

'I only heard of Father Fogarty's death when I got in. Esther was at the church, of course.'

'And you're a bit tired, so you wouldn't want to walk all the way over to the presbytery with it. I take it that, in the normal way, you'd post it.'

'But the post would be gone,' Keneally said with a secret smile. 'So that Father Hanafey wouldn't get it until maybe the day after tomorrow. That's what you were afraid of, father, isn't it?'

'I see we understand one another, Mr Keneally,' Jackson said politely.

'You wouldn't, of course, wish to say anything that wasn't strictly true,' said Keneally, who was clearly enjoying himself enormously, though his wife had not the faintest idea of what was afoot. 'So perhaps it would be better if the letter was posted now, and not after you leave the house.'

'Fine!' said Jackson, and Keneally nodded and went out. When he returned, a few minutes later, the priests rose to go.

'I'll see you at the Mass tomorrow,' Keneally said. 'Good luck, now.'

Jackson felt they'd probably need it. But when Father Hanafey met them in the hall, with the wet snow falling outside, and they explained about the letter, his mood had clearly changed. Jackson's logic might have worked some sort of spell on him, or perhaps it was just that he felt they were three clergymen opposed to a layman.

'It was very unforeseen of Mr Keneally not to have brought that letter to me at once,' he grumbled, 'but I must say I was expecting something of the sort. It would have been very peculiar if Father Fogarty had left no instructions at all for me, and I see that we can't just sit round and wait to find out what they were, since the burial is tomorrow. Under the circumstances, father, I think we'd be justified in arranging for the funeral according to Father Fogarty's known wishes.'

'Thanks be to God,' Father Hamilton murmured as he and Father Jackson returned to the curates' house. 'I never thought we'd get away with that.'

'We haven't got away with it yet,' said Jackson. 'And even if we do get away with it, the real trouble will be later.'

All the arrangements had still to be made. When Mr Fogarty was informed, he slammed down the receiver without comment. Then a phone call had to be made to a police station twelve miles from the island, and the police sergeant promised to send a man out on a bicycle to have the grave opened. Then the local parish priest and several old friends had to be informed, and a notice inserted in the nearest daily. As Jackson said wearily, romantic men always left their more worldly friends to carry out their romantic intentions.

The scene at the curates' house next morning after Mass

scared even Jackson. While the hearse and the funeral car waited in front of the door, Mr Fogarty sat, white with anger, and let the priests talk. To Jackson's surprise, Father Hanafey put up a stern fight for Father Fogarty's wishes.

'You have to realise, Mr Fogarty, that to a priest like your brother the Mass is a very solemn thing indeed, and a place where the poor people had to fly in the Penal Days to hear Mass would be one of particular sanctity.'

'Father Hanafey,' said Mr Fogarty in a cold, even tone, 'I am a simple businessman, and I have no time for sentiment.'

'I would not go so far as to call the veneration for sanctified ground mere sentiment, Mr Fogarty,' the old priest said severely. 'At any rate, it is now clear that Father Fogarty left instructions to be delivered to me after his death, and if those instructions are what we think them, I would have a serious responsibility for not having paid attention to them.'

'I do not think that letter is anything of the kind, Father Hanafey,' said Mr Fogarty. 'That's a matter I'm going to inquire into when I get back, and if it turns out to be a hoax, I am going to take it further.'

'Oh, Mr Fogarty, I'm sure it's not a hoax,' said the parish priest, with a shocked air, but Mr Fogarty was not convinced.

'For everybody's sake, we'll hope not,' he said grimly.

The funeral procession set off. Mr Fogarty sat in the front of the car by the driver, sulking. Jackson and Hamilton sat behind and opened their breviaries. When they stopped at a hotel for lunch, Mr Fogarty said he was not hungry, and stayed outside in the cold. And when he did get hungry and came into the dining room, the priests drifted into the lounge to wait for him. They both realised that he might prove a dangerous enemy.

Then, as they drove on in the dusk, they saw the mountain country ahead of them in a cold, watery light, a light that seemed to fall dead from the ragged edge of a cloud. The towns and villages they passed through were dirtier and more derelict. They drew up at a crossroads, behind the hearse, and heard someone talking to the driver of the hearse. Then a car fell into line behind them. 'Someone joining us,' Father Hamilton said, but Mr Fogarty, lost in his own dream of martyrdom did not reply. Half a dozen times within the next twenty minutes, the same thing happened, though sometimes the cars were waiting in lanes and byroads with their lights on, and each time Jackson saw a heavily coated figure standing in the roadway shouting to the hearse driver: 'Is it Father Fogarty ye have there?' At last they came to a village where the local parish priest's car was waiting outside the church, with a little group about it. Their headlights caught a public-house, isolated at the other side of the street, glaring with whitewash, while about it was the vague space of a distant mountainside.

Suddenly Mr Fogarty spoke. 'He seems to have been fairly well known,' he said with something approaching politeness.

The road went on, with a noisy stream at the right-hand side of it falling from group to group of rocks. They left it for a byroad, which bent to the right, heading towards the stream, and then began to mount, broken by ledges of naked rock, over which hearse and cars seemed to heave themselves like animals. On the left-hand side of the road was a little whitewashed cottage, all lit up, with a big turf fire burning in the open hearth and an oil-lamp with an orange glow on the wall above it. There was a man standing by the door, and as they approached he began to pick his way over the rocks towards them, carrying a lantern. Only then did Jackson notice the other lanterns and flashlights, coming down the mountain or crossing the stream, and realised that they represented people, young men and girls and an occasional sturdy old man, all moving in the direction of the Mass Island. Suddenly it hit him, almost like a blow. He told himself not to be a fool, that this was no more than the desire for novelty one should expect to find in out-of-the-way places, mixed perhaps with vanity. It was all that, of course, and he knew it, but he knew, too, it was something more. He had thought when he was here with Fogarty that those people had not respected Fogarty as they respected him and the local parish priest, but he knew that for him, or even for their own parish priest, they would never turn out in midwinter, across the treacherous mountain bogs and wicked rocks. He and the parish priest would never earn more from the people of the mountains than respect; what they gave to the fat, unclerical young man who had served them with pints in the bar and egged them on to tell their old stories and bullied and ragged and even fought them was something infinitely greater.

The funeral procession stopped in a lane that ran along the edge of a lake. The surface of the lake was rough, and they could hear the splash of the water upon the stones. The two priests got out of the car and began to vest themselves, and then Mr Fogarty got out, too. He was very nervous and hesitant.

'It's very inconvenient, and all the rest of it,' he said, 'but I don't want you gentlemen to think that I didn't know you were acting from the best motives.'

'That's very kind of you, Mr Fogarty,' Jackson said. 'Maybe we made mistakes as well.'

'Thank you, Father Jackson,' Mr Fogarty said, and held out his hand. The two priests shook hands with him and he went off, raising his hat.

'Well, that's one trouble over,' Father Hamilton said wryly as an old man plunged through the mud towards the car.

'Lights is what we're looking for!' he shouted. 'Let ye turn her sidewise and throw the headlights on the causeway the way we'll see what we're doing.'

Their driver swore, but he reversed and turned the front of the car till it almost faced the lake. Then he turned on his headlights. Somewhere farther up the road the parish priest's car did the same. One by one, the ranked headlights blazed up, and at every moment the scene before them grew more vivid – the gateway and the stile, and beyond it the causeway that ran towards the little brown stone oratory with its mock Romanesque doorway. As the lights strengthened and steadied, the whole island became like a vast piece of theatre scenery cut out against the gloomy wall of the mountain with the tiny whitewashed cottages at its base. Far above, caught in a stray flash of moonlight, Jackson saw the snow on its summit. 'I'll be after you,' he said to Father Hamilton, and watched him, a little perturbed and looking behind him, join the parish priest by the gate. Jackson resented being seen by them because he was weeping, and he was a man who despised tears – his own and others'. It was like a miracle, and Father Jackson didn't really believe in miracles. Standing back by the fence to let the last of the mourners pass, he saw the coffin, like gold in the brilliant light, and heard the steadying voices of the four huge mountainy men who carried it. He saw it sway above the heads, shawled and bare, glittering between the little stunted holly bushes and hazels.

ACKNOWLEDGEMENTS

Grateful acknowledgement is made to: Hamish Hamilton for permission to reprint 'Uprooted', 'News for the Church', 'Peasants' and 'Song without Words' from *Stories of Frank O'Connor* (1953); Macmillan London for permission to reprint 'The Sentry', 'The Old Faith', 'The Miracle', 'Achilles' Heel', 'The Shepherds', 'The Frying-pan' and 'The Wreath' from *Collection Two* (1964); and Harriet Sheehy for permission to reprint 'Lost Fatherlands', 'A Mother's Warning', 'The Teacher's Mass', 'An Act of Charity' and 'The Mass Island' from *Collection Three* (Macmillan, 1969).

DETAILS OF FIRST PUBLICATION

'Uprooted' (*Criterion*, 1937); 'News for the Church' (*New Yorker*, 1945); 'The Sentry' (*Harper's Bazaar*, 1950); 'The Old Faith' (*More Stories of Frank O'Connor*, Knopf, 1954); 'The Miracle' (*The Common Chord*, Macmillan, 1947); 'Achilles' Heel' (*New Yorker*, 1958); 'The Shepherds' (*Harper's Bazaar*, 1946); 'Peasants' (*An Long*, 1922); 'Song without Words' (*Harper's Bazaar*, 1944); 'Lost Fatherlands' (*New Yorker*, 1954); 'A Mother's Warning' (*Saturday Evening Post*, 1967); 'The Frying-pan' (*The Common Chord*, Macmillan, 1947); 'The Teacher's Mass' (*New Yorker*, 1955); 'The Wreath' (*Atlantic Monthly*, 1955); 'An Act of Charity' (*New Yorker*, 1967); and 'The Mass Island' (*New Yorker*, 1959).